The Unfortunate Life & Death of William Tell

by James P Gavin

Published in Great Britain by

L.R. Price Publications Ltd, 2022

27 Old Gloucester Street, London, WC1N 3AX
www.lrpricepublications.com

Cover artwork by Matthew Gledhil

ISBN-: 9781915330161

Chapter One

Friday 1st July 2016 12:40p.m.
Duns Town Market Square

It was a beautiful summer day. The hot sun beat down relentlessly from a cloudless sky and shone brightly onto the busy Duns Town market square.

The bar staff of the nearby ancient pub, the Red Lion, had set out tables and chairs ready for the many peckish and thirsty workers who would soon fill those weather-beaten plastic seats.

The interior of the, now modernised air-conditioned, pub was soon bursting at the seams with lunchtime drinkers. They were pushing and shoving, trying to get the attention of the bar staff to place their order. They had short lunch breaks that ranged between thirty minutes and an hour. Deduct the travelling time getting to the pub, waiting for service and then returning to their place of work… time was really of the essence.

Opposite the pub was the impressive, newly built, Crown Court building. Even, at its young age, it had conducted a few impressive court cases, attracting media coverage from around the world.

It had been suggested, many times, that the market square had been modernised purely to show off the classy Crown Court exterior, with its larger than life plaque of the Royal coat of arms.

There was plenty of room for media of all sorts. Thus, the usual hustling and jostling of reporters was unnecessary and favourable pictures of the exterior of the building could be taken.

The Red Lion had invested a sizable amount of money to get their share of the media customers and also the people who tried to get themselves on the 'telly.'
But today was Friday and the younger customers, were all buzzing, looking forward to a weekend of fun and laughter. They were exuding excitement and couldn't stop talking about it.

No one had taken any notice of the solitary figure who stood to the left of the Crown Court building, directly below the Royal plaque. He wore a well-fitting dark suit, a crisp white shirt and a bright red tie. He was perspiring profusely in the midday heat. This was evident from the visible damp patches under his arms, that stood out, despite the darkness of his suit.
He never once moved from his sentry-like position. Occasionally, he glanced at the customers of the pub, as oblivious, they knocked back various ice-cold liquids. The man was in obvious discomfort. But he stood there, bolt upright, motionless, as if standing to attention like a guard outside Buckingham Palace.
He looked to be in his early fifties. He had dark hair, that was greying at the temples and his face was tanned. There was an almost Mediterranean look about him. He stood there, still. The only movement was his eyes as he glanced repeatedly at the drinkers.

Two barristers, still wearing their black robes and wigs, came out of the main entrance of the building and into the market square. They appeared to be in a hurry. They rushed to get out into the fresh, open air and then they stopped suddenly. Each lit up a cigarette.

They had both observed the man, who was standing under the coat of arms, and nodded to him. Purely, because he was staring at them for a reason known only to him and because he was a stranger to them both. Probably an ex client?

The barristers were laughing and talking about the case that they were on. Some official documents had been mislaid by the court and were now being hunted down by the court officials. So, the judge called a fifteen-minute recess.

They finished their cigarettes and looked at their watches and then at each other. They laughed and lit up another cigarette each.

They were halfway through their cigarettes when they were summoned back into the court by an over-excited court usher. One of them made a move first. The other took a few extra seconds, a few extra puffs of his cigarette, a little extra time away from the courtroom.

The barrister, who was the first to move back towards the court, drew level with the man who had been waiting under the Royal coat of arms. The man put his arm out to stop the barrister and spoke to him. Then suddenly, a rather large hole appeared in the side of the barrister's head. The centre of the man's face, who had stopped him and spoken to him, disappeared in a bloody explosion of flesh, blood, and bone.

They both collapsed into a heap. The Barrister had fallen face down onto the hot pavement and what was left of his face, scrunched up and splattered more blood and internal facial contents as it did so. The man who had been standing to attention under the coat of arms lay on top of him. His eyeballs, or what remained of them, were sitting either side of his head, on the floor. Prevented from rolling

away by the thinnest sliver of flesh. They formed an almost perfect cross.
Blood poured freely from their bodies, like a mini red river but came to a stop when the victim's hearts finally stopped beating.
The wall of the crown court looked like a pop art painting from the sixties. The blood and brains dripped down, slowly changing the length of the picture.

The remaining barrister saw his colleague collapse and the fountain of blood splashing onto the pavement. He collapsed onto his knees, vomiting and making strange bodily sounds. His arms covered his head but if the shooter had a mind to, he could still have shot the snivelling barrister, as his oversized and shaking backside was stuck high into the air.
Court security guards bravely ran out onto the blood-soaked pavement and dragged him back into the protection of the court. They appeared unconcerned that they too may have been shot at.
Someone inside the court reception had called the emergency services. They kept peeping through the window blinds, hoping that they turned up before someone else fell.

The customers, who were sitting drinking and happily chatting to their friends a few minutes ago, were now laying prostrate on the ground. They lay amid vomit, spilt drink, and hollandaise sauce, whimpering and afraid to move.
Some of the stronger minded people had whispered amongst themselves. Some had acknowledged that the victims had been shot. There was no other way such

injuries could have been sustained, they said as expertly as their knowledge allowed them.
Women and men covered their ears, squeezed their eyes and arse cheeks tightly shut, not wanting to hear or see any more.
But the whispers gradually got louder and then turned to chatter. Now their curiosity was piqued. A natural human reaction. Their growing curiosity pushed them further and further. Gradually, they stood up one by one as if they had all just awoken from an afternoon slumber.
They stared at the blood and the remains of the two dead men's faces. There was now more to see. They bravely nudged out of the way, the persons who were obscuring their view so they would have something, in their old age, to blame for not being able to sleep at night.
They observed that the security guards had not been shot at. Once they were all standing up, they decided that they wanted a reminder of the life-changing experience and started taking selfies, making sure that the prostrate bodies lying in their sticky, congealed blood were included in the shot.

The ambulance arrived first, followed a few minutes later by the police; despite them being only five minutes, walking distance, away. The paramedics looked at the two victims and knew that they were past any medical help. They were declared dead. They took pictures and then reported their findings which were sent directly to the Coroner's office.
Very soon after, more police officers turned up and attempted to clear the crime scene.
There were more blood-hungry onlookers than police available to stop them. Some were now physically

struggling with the police, still trying to get the best selfie standing next to the bodies, that were still in situ, for all and sundry to see.

The bodies were now almost fully exsanguinated. Their once life-giving blood was a warm, sticky river of gloop that was drying fast under the relentless hot sun. The flies had suddenly appeared, as if by magic, sitting in the blood and doing whatever flies sitting in blood did.
The SOCO team arrived and set up a white tent. They erected 'Police Do Not Cross' signage, that they busily unrolled and tied to anything that took their pleasure; especially shop doorways, irrespective of people trying to go about their everyday business or trying to ignore the upsetting scene. A scene that they would carry with them for the rest of their lives and unfortunately would never be able to unsee.
The crime scene had been well and truly compromised by the selfie patrol and also by the police who had attempted to stop them.

Everyone, who remained at the scene, was questioned. But there was not one 'witness' who had seen the crime as it happened. There had been no sounds of a gunshot heard by any of the lunchtime pub customers. They all agreed that they had observed the two victims when they had already fallen or were in the process of falling to the ground.
All trials at the Crown Court were suspended. Everyone, with the exception of the vomiting barrister, the two court security guards, who had selflessly dragged him back into the building, and essential staff had been sent home. They

were currently of no use to the investigation but their details were taken for the records.

Detective Inspector, Claire Callison and her sidekick, Detective Sergeant Leanne Gavin, were handed the job. It was barely five minutes after finally clearing up their previous case, which they had been on for the last six months.
The murderer, of two homeless young girls, had finally been charged and convicted and was now completing the third hour of his whole life sentence. They and their team were about to book an early night off to go and celebrate, at their local Indian restaurant when they were handed this case, totally out of the blue.
They arrived at the scene to find hundreds of bloody footprints all over the place.

"For fucks sake Leanne, it looks like some sort of dancing lesson, without the numbers." She laughed, as they both took pictures of the compromised crime scene.
They were approached by SOCO technicians Michael Chivers, James Mitchell, and Chief Medical Officer Jack Samms.
"So, what do we got? as they say on the TV Jack." Claire asked, with a false American accent.
"Well, firstly the defence barrister, William Tell, aged thirty. Yes, that was his real name. He was hit by a high-powered bullet, which appears to have exploded when it hit him. It killed the man who he had just drawn level with, on his way back into the court. I am only assuming that's what happened because an ordinary bullet would not have done that sort of damage unless it was close-up. But don't hold me to that at the moment. That man had no ID

or anything at all on his person. We will take his prints when we get him into the lab."

"Can you take the victim's prints now Jack? The sooner we know who he is the sooner we can start finding out who the bullet was intended for. At the moment we have two possible intended victims. One of those we know or will know something about. The other we know Jack shit about so now would be a good time please mate" said Claire "and would you have any idea where this shot came from, which direction?" she added.

"Firstly, I haven't got the fingerprint machine with me and secondly, I haven't got a scooby which direction it came from Claire, you will need the big boys to work that out. I will give you the victim's heights when I get them back to the lab and anything else that you require. There doesn't appear to be anything left of the bullet that killed them but there is a very faint indentation in the wall where the second man was, we believe, standing. Sergeant Janine Pratt is keeping the records log here so don't forget to tell her that you are here and what time you arrived." He laughed. "The closest you have as a witness is another barrister, Duncan Lee-Winton. He only saw the men fall. There was no sound of a shot, he swears that and the other witnesses, that I spoke to, said the same thing. One minute they were alive, next minute brown bread.
He is a bit delicate and by the way, he was the prosecutor on the case that they were both working on. So, if you have no objection, I want to take the bodies away. It's getting warmer here and the flies have started to settle."

"Ok, no problems with that, as long as you have got enough photographic and video evidence. Thank you, Jack. I'll be seeing you again no doubt before the day is out."

They reported to Sergeant Janine Pratt and then allowed SOCO to do what they did best.

"I've had a good look around Guv," Leanne said. "I can't see any obvious vantage point that the shot might have come from. We don't know how near or how far away it was."

"The big shots…pardon the pun, forensic ballistic boys are on their way to sort all that out as soon as the scene has been released. We can get the info from Jack. They will soon find out where the shot came from. It looks like we have a shitload of questions that need answering and the first question possibly concerns the case that the barristers were working on. It's a good place to start Leanne. Always start at the beginning, wherever the fuck that is. Let's go and see the prosecution barrister, our star witness. He has a double-barrelled name and I tend to get uneasy with those people."

The two detectives were led into a small side room, near the reception area of the Court. It resembled a basic first aid room.
"This was probably set up for the criminals who would hopefully, suffer a shock when they received their sentence," Callison said aloud.
Mr Duncan Lee-Winton was lying prostrate on the examination bed in the room. He had a damp cloth on his

forehead and was being tended to by a first aider. She smiled when she saw the two detectives and their warrant cards then excused herself and promptly left the room.

"Good afternoon Mr Lee-Winton. My name is Detective Inspector Callison and with me is Detective Sergeant Gavin. I trust that you are feeling well enough to speak to us Sir? I believe that you were uninjured in the shooting and that you witnessed exactly what happened to your colleague, Mr William Tell? Would that be correct Sir?"
Lee-Winton, did not respond. He just lay there and whimpered, holding the back of his right hand over his forehead.
"Sir, I understand that you were not injured, would you like me to call an ambulance for you?" Sergeant Gavin said. She was pretty sure that the man was milking the situation. He could see out of the window and knew that the growing numbers of reporters and TV cameras were looking for a story. She assumed that he wanted to be a part of that story.
She went over and pulled down the black roller blind and switched on the light. He then whimpered slightly, sat up and looked at the two police officers, who were staring at him with blank but expectant expressions. They saw his red, teary eyes but were not convinced that they were the result of tears that he had just shed.

"I'm afraid that your information has somehow been misconstrued detectives. I never witnessed the actual shooting. I looked down to tread on my cigarette butt. When I… when I looked up… Wil…"
He started crying and struggled to get his friend William's name to come out. Callison gave him a drink of water. She

looked at Sergeant. Gavin and rolled her eyes. He cleared his throat.
"William and the other chappie, who I don't know, were in the process of falling to the ground when I looked up. All I could see… and it will haunt me for the rest of my life, was the… the hole in the side of his head and the blood pumping out. I… I erm… was then violently sick; I am sorry detectives I am of no help to you whatsoever I'm afraid."

"Well Sir, let us be the judge of that. I'm sure that somewhere in your vast memory banks there hides the smallest piece of evidence that will eventually help us with our enquiries.
Now is there anything that you can tell me about William? Is he married, single, in a relationship? We will need to inform next of kin."

"No, William is… was single. He lives next…I'm sorry… He lived next door to me in the Blue House apartments. I believe that his father, who is his only living relative, is suffering from some sort of advanced dementia and is in a care home somewhere. Although, I have no idea where."

"Mr Winton, was William a very good friend of yours, were you close?"
"It's Lee-Winton officer. It may be hyphenated but it's all one word. I trust that you will make a note of that for future reference," he gave her a sneer. "We were friends, officer. Very often we worked together on the same cases but in different corners, if you know what I mean? We sometimes hung out together when the mood took us. We shared secrets as mates do. We played squash and

sometimes we played tennis but not very often; usually as guests of slightly better off colleagues, and that is about it, officer."

"And did William have many secrets to share with you Mr Lee-Winton and vice versa?"

"Nothing that would interest you I'm afraid."

"You would be surprised at what interests me Sir." Claire said. She couldn't help sneering back at him.
"Now, I would like to know what the case was, that you and Mr Tell were working on. I don't need the full details, for now. I just want the outline so that I can start forming a picture, Sir."

"Yes of course… err… Detective…?"

"Detective Inspector Callison, Sir, and Detective Sergeant Gavin."

"Thank you, Detective. The case that we were fighting over, that's metaphorically speaking you understand Detective, was just an insurance fraud. Well, not just any old fraud actually. It concerned several millions of pounds but I am not at liberty to discuss those details. I'm afraid that you must go through the Crown Prosecution Service for additional help in that matter."

"Forgive me Mr Lee-Winton. I don't understand the workings of barristers, prosecution and defence. I assume that you work directly for the CPS. Did Mr Tell work with you or is there some professional body that differs from you and the CPS?"

"He was self-employed and still a tenant in chambers, for the Travis and London professional Law company. It's based in Duns Town, Manchester street."

"Was he not a fully-fledged barrister then?"

"Yes, of course he was a fully-fledged barrister. He has all the certificates, insurances and much more than even I have managed to obtain. He was saving up as much as he could, to get his own piece of property and then form a company. I believe that he mentioned, once or twice in passing, that he would inherit a small sum when his father passes away. But the money was being eaten away by medical costs. I doubt very much if there would have been any money at all left."

"Do you know where his mother is or what happened to her?"

"According to William, she was a whore. She died of some STD or Aids-related disease, something like that. He only spoke of her when he was pi… sorry on an emotional downer, as he called it."
"And his father. Would you know where he could be located?"

"I have no idea I'm afraid. But there is no use looking for him, he is on a one-way journey to Alzheimer's land. Forgive me, that sounds so ignorant and insensitive of me. But from what I understand, he had done nothing at all for

his son. William had even hand-dug shit, to earn enough money to pay the high cost of being educated to the high level that is required to become a barrister. He worked extremely hard for every penny that was involved in that education.
I was lucky that I had parents who cared. They too are lawyers and had offered many times to assist William. But he had politely refused every time. All except, that is, for the many parties that my parents threw. He knew that he would meet contacts and get the odd bone to defend that no one else wanted.
William was a great defence barrister and believe me he was getting better at what he was doing. His name was getting attention… I… I am going to miss him."

"Ok, thank you Sir. So, could I ask you hypothetically, depending on the outcome of the court case that you are working on; would killing a barrister, either a defence or prosecution barrister, by the winner or loser of this hypothetical case, feel justified in killing either barrister?"
He laughed and shook his head and suddenly he felt better. Well enough to speak to the Detectives in his role as a prosecution Barrister and attempted using long words and talking down to them. He held onto his stained robes as if he were delivering a speech to the jury.
"No, I'm afraid you have got hold of the wrong end of the stick ladies." He instantly regretted mentioning the word 'ladies.' His sixth sense warned him to tread lightly with these women. He suddenly felt the ice-cold friction in the room. These were not criminals who he could forcibly intimidate. "Forgive me, I meant to say 'Detectives.' I'm afraid that was a professional slip. The hypothetical case that we may have been arguing would in no way prove a

danger to either side because it would be dealt with hypothetically by the insurance companies involved. They are themselves insured and it goes on and on. Eventually, a pre-agreed result from the clients will reach a happy medium and so I hope that answers your question officers?"

"No, not really Sir. The way you explain it makes it sound like a complete waste of money. If it was nothing to do with your profession then it must be personal. Would there be any reason that someone had a grudge against Mr Tell or even you Sir? We have to assume that because there are now three people involved, that's the two victims, Sir, and a potential victim, being you! You could have been the target yourself Sir and because you were both wearing your wigs and robes, it may well have been confusing to the assassin. Forgive me, Sir, I use that word in the absence of a more fitting word under the circumstances."

"No officer, definitely not. Neither of us were gamblers or whatever it takes to be a victim. We are… sorry were still climbing up the ladder and we have a long way to go before we could ever get close to being in a position where we would be threatened."

"Ahh, Mr Lee-Winton, it could have been a case that you or Mr Tell had, have, or are still working on. Maybe someone that you have unmercifully pulled to pieces in the witness box Sir and they took it personally? I know that you have to be good to get where you are. They don't let just anybody stand there, point the finger and demean either party's story or alibi, in such a way that could be mistaken as a personal attack Sir."

"I can assure you Detective, that if you were to go through the proper channels, you will find that neither myself or William have done anything to merit being shot at and murdered. Now, if you forgive me officers, I am not feeling my best, as you may or may not understand. I am going home, where I can rest and try and get my head around this whole business. I want to grieve for my friend William in the privacy of my own home."

"Very well Sir. I would ask that you do not talk about this enquiry to any outsiders, especially the media. It may damage our investigation. You may go now there is no problem but I would like a written statement as soon as possible if you wouldn't mind Sir? I can send an officer to your home, if that is satisfactory, or you can come down to the station. Just one more thing Sir, did you and Mr Tell have an early lunch or maybe a heavy breakfast?"

"I hardly see the relevance of that question officer but yes, it was a rather large breakfast. We had it at the Red Lion pub next door. Thank you, I will drop off a written statement as soon as I can. Now if you will excuse me."

"I will need you to sign that statement in front of a witness Sir and that witness must sign and date the paperwork. Forgive me yet again Sir, just another quick question before you go. Did Mr Tell… William, have any marks, tattoos, scars, or anything of that nature on his body, would you know?"

“No, Williams body was per…’ He stalled and looked at Callison with an arched eyebrow. May I know the relevance of that question officer, and how would you expect me to know if he had any blemishes… scars or what have you?”

“I’m sorry to ask and appreciate that it is very personal but it is just procedure Sir. You must have seen his body if you played squash and showered together.”

“Showered together! Exactly what is it that you are implying? I’m afraid we are not in the habit of cavorting naked in the showers, displaying one’s anatomy and body parts and showing off any imperfections or scars that one might have through sport or other means. I’m afraid I really must go; your questions are making me feel rather ill.”

“I apologise Sir but I thought that questions were your forte. There is just one more question Sir, before you go, may I ask how old you are Sir?”

“You may officer.” He said nothing more but smiled at her sardonically. As he exited the room, they could both smell the stale vomit and other bodily secretions that lingered about his person and on his trouser legs.”

“He must have had a bloody gut-buster of breakfast to make that kind of mess Claire. Probably a gut full of oysters. So, what do you think about him Guv?”

Callison lifted the blinds and watched Mr Lee-Winton; in the middle of the media and enjoying every second of it. She hoped they would go for a leg shot.

"Like anyone in his job Leanne. They are confident, sometimes overconfident and bloody pompous. But our Mr Lee-Winton, I believe was more than just a work colleague to William. That doesn't mean anything at the moment but I would have thought that it was worth a mention from him. So, Leanne, in answer to your question. Not a lot, not a lot at all."

The two Detectives questioned the security guards but, as helpful as they were, they had seen even less than Mr Lee-Winton.

They returned outside to find that the bodies had now been removed and in their places were the familiar white chalk outlines in the rough shape of a cross, underneath the white tent. SOCO were digging microscopic bits of brain, blood and anything else they could find from the wall, directly below the coat of arms.

Crime scene protective fencing was being erected around the whole site in an attempt to keep it private. It was a bit late for that considering the crime scene had been compromised within seconds of the murder.

Callison had ordered that the media be sent away. That was another waste of time because they had soon dispersed themselves to more suitable vantage points looking down onto the bloody scene; as did the many ghouls who were there, for whatever reason drives them to these blood and gut strewn sites?

She looked around the site. It was just a mess. She saw Lee-Winton's mountain of vomit that had created a frenzy of feeding flies. It was enclosed by road cones and police tape. She shook her head, wondering how so much food came out of his gut. He had now disappeared from the scene.
He probably raced off home to shower and feed himself. He must have been starving, she thought to herself.
It had certainly put her off the Indian meal, that was now cancelled. Well, it was for her and Leanne. She believed that most of her colleagues were still going.

Leanne bought her a coffee; they found a place to sit and said nothing. They took the murder scene deep into their minds and slowly re-enacted that murder as they believed it to have happened.
They put the three victims into different positions, asking themselves the many 'what if?' questions, as only a detective can do. They would then have discussed their different theories about it to see which one was the nearest to a logical assumption.
But this was a different homicide. It seemed likely that an assassin was employed and that the bullet he used exploded on contact; that probably meant military involvement or something connected to people wearing black clothing or carrying violin cases. She laughed at that thought but the sky was the limit in this particular case.

The forensic firearms team had arrived on site. They were inspecting the faint bullet indent left in the wall of the Crown Court building, directly below the coat of arms.

Chief Medical Officer, Jack Samms, had sent the height of the two victims. Claire passed on the details to DCS Denver Copperstone, who was now the S.I.O in charge of the case.
The unknown victim was 69 inches (177.2 cm) tall including shoe height.
William Tell was 71inches (180.5 cm), which was only a rough estimation of the bodies now in the prone position but as close as possible.
The centre of the wound, or as near as, in the first victim was 67 inches (170.2 cm).
The centre of the wound, or as near as, in the second victim was 69¼ inches (175.5 cm).
The forensic team measured the approximate height of the small indentation, on the blood-spattered wall, from the centre to the ground. The resulting distance was 65 ¾ inches (167.1 cm).
The team punched their measurements into the computer and then used their lasers to work out a suitable distance and trajectory.

Callison and Gavin were still interviewing the lunchtime witnesses, which was a complete waste of time. But at least they managed to get copies of the selfies, after threatening them with official charges of withholding information. It was just a bluff but it worked.

Copperstone called over to her. She noticed a group of armed police talking to him. As she neared, he walked towards her but then stopped dead when his phone rang. He held up his hand whilst he took the call.

"Ok, it's happening now." was all that he said. He closed and replaced the phone to his pocket.
"We have the possible position of the shooter; it is the balcony of the town hall. The armed police are going to see if he has left any incriminating evidence. I wouldn't have thought that he is still there but we can't take a chance. I have a team ready to enter the site and another team is evacuating the rest of the building.
There was garbled communication on the handheld radios.
"Ok, Claire you, Sergeant Gavin and I will wait here while they go and take a look."

"No bloody way Copperstone… err… Denver… Sir. This is my case I am going with them. There are more than enough coppers here and I don't want them to compromise any more evidence. I need to make sure that everything is covered and evidence protected. Not like this shit heap."

"May I remind you that I am the SIO here. It hasn't got anything to do with me Claire it comes from upstairs. Only the armed boys are to go in. They know their job and they know all about protecting evidence. So just sit tight. They are about to enter the room and hopefully we will be lucky."
There was shouting coming through on the radios, and every other word was 'Clear!'
Finally, the message came through that all was safe.
The procession of police officers entered the meeting room. The doors that led to the balcony were wide open they were waiting for SOCO now, to search the balcony for any signs that the killer may have left.

Callison looked out over the large balcony. She could see the view across the town to the Crown Court, although there were a couple of small branches that were moving about and blocking the actual killing scene.
"Jesus, that is some distance Denver. The killer must be a professional to hit something that far away. There is so much that has to be quantified to even get close. Why would someone go to this much trouble to kill someone? We haven't got a clue as to who the victim was."

"The distance between here and the Crown Court is 1,064.5 feet exactly," said Copperstone. "I have just been passed the details and depending on the type of bullet used we are talking about roughly 0.30-0.35 seconds for the bullet to hit its target. Whatever target it was."

"Half a second... So, am I then assuming that William Tell wasn't the victim? It must have been John Doe, who was standing at that exact point. William Tell was…collateral damage! Now it's all becoming a bit easier. All we have to do is find out who the fuck this John Doe is."

"We have CCTV video Guv," said Sergeant Gavin. "I have just called up the Fixed Assets Department, where there are nine officers constantly watching the one hundred and thirty-nine, CCTV cameras throughout Duns Town. They have everything ready and are waiting for us Guv."

"Bloody hell Leanne! How the hell did they get all that information? It usually takes ages for them to move their arses."

"A cousin of mine, Guv. Cherise Day. She is the manager of the department. I called her earlier and told her what we wanted. She said that she would sort it all out and call me as soon as it was ready. Now it's ready!"
Copperstone said he wanted a copy of all the evidence that was collected from any CCTV and he would call Claire if he found anything else. But it didn't look promising.

The two detectives walked to the Assets Department, which was only a few hundred yards behind the town hall. Cherise Day was waiting for them. Leanne introduced them and followed her into a small office that resembled a recording studio. The three women sat down at a table with a large screen in front of them.

"Ok, before I start this show. I have used all our resources and we have about thirty minutes of video footage. I have tracked it back to your John Doe getting off a bus near the Library square. Unfortunately, his face is a bit grainy but he's your man." Cherise said, confidently, as she passed a remote control to Claire. "Just press play," she said.

10:40 a.m. - they observed a man getting off a bus. He was circled in a mauve colour, obviously by Cherise. He stopped and waited until the other passengers went past him. When he was on his own, he emptied the contents of his pockets into a nearby litter bin and stood with his arms in the air. He lifted his jacket up and turned full circle twice. He then sat on a bench and stared up at the large, town hall clock.
When the clock struck eleven the man stood up, wiped his eyes and then, slowly, walked through the town. Claire stopped the video.

"We need to see what he dropped into the bin."

"It's on its way Claire. I called to get the whole bin picked up. It should be here any minute." Claire looked at Leanne, who smiled and mouthed the word 'family.' She switched the video back on.

The man walked through the town centre towards the Crown Court, stopped directly under the coat of arms and never moved. Many people stared at him but no-one spoke to him.
They watched, as the shooting unfolded and saw the bodies fall. They observed the people, who were at first scared and then were brave enough to walk through the men's blood. The video then cut away to the town hall. They saw a movement, the outlines of a man; they noticed a muzzle sticking out of the lower part of the balcony. Then, at precisely 12:45 the clock bells rang and the fatal shot was fired. The gun disappeared. Claire stopped the video and looked at Cherise.

"Is there CCTV in that building Cherise and if so, who is responsible for it?"

"There is CCTV there and we are responsible for it but we don't have Jack shit I'm afraid. The power to the cameras was switched off, from the town hall itself, at 11:30 a.m. It could have been done by anyone and because there were different lunchbreaks it wasn't noticed. We will be investigating it along with your department."

"And what about before and after Cherise? Someone must have entered and left the building carrying a case with the weapon in. Could you check for that?" Leanne asked.

"I have already done so. There is nobody that looks suspicious or carrying a case big enough to hold a rifle. The closest that I found was three people with mobility scooters who were driving around town, which I have saved on another hard drive. If you give me a minute. I will pull it out."

There was a knock on the door and a PCSO came in carrying a waste bin metal insert.

Claire stood up and looked into the insert. She put on a pair of clinical gloves and started going through the contents. She picked up a wallet and looked through it. There was cash, credit cards and… a driving licence with a photo of their John Doe!

The man's name was Dermot Dolan and he was fifty-five years of age. His address was 22, Queens Road, Duns Town.

Leanne looked again, through the bin insert and picked up loose change, a photo of a young girl and a sheet of paper with written instructions telling Mr Dolan to do exactly what he had done in the video. She passed it over to Claire, who looked at it, placed it into a plastic bag and returned it, along with the licence, which was also bagged.

Within a couple of minutes, Cherise came back and switched on another monitor. The detectives watched the three mobility scooters driving around the town. Two of the scooter drivers returned their loan scooters and were collected by family. They were followed to the main car park and were seen being driven away. They were old and

infirm, not a logical choice for a sniper, but the details of their cars were recorded.
The third Scooter went into a fast-food restaurant and never came out again.

“We need to go to that restaurant to see their CCTV.” said Claire.

“There is no need Claire,” said Cherise. “I will get them to send me over what they have and then we can see where the scooter driver went.” Once again, Cherise left the room but she was only gone a few minutes when she returned red-faced and breathing fast.
“It appears that the scooter was left in the disabled toilet. It was reported to police who have determined that it was stolen earlier from… the town hall. There was no weapon found, just the scooter. They are sending over the video from the time that the scooter entered the building. They have looked at it but they say that there is nothing in there that can help us. Excuse me whilst I prepare it for you.”

Cherise again left the room. Claire looked at Leanne and shook her head.
“Fuck my old boots Leanne. It’s all ending up like some James bloody Bond film. As soon as we have looked at the video, we will have to go and see if there is a Mrs Dolan and break the bad news to her. We can hardly ask her to go and identify the poor man. No, forget that. We will go and see Kearney and fill her in before she starts squawking about not keeping her informed.”

Cherise returned and switched on the monitor.

"This contains a short video from the restaurant and a couple of our CCTV cameras following him."
They watched as the scooter drove into the large disabled toilet and then after a few minutes, a scruffy dishevelled old man with a walking stick walked out and left the restaurant. He went into the mall and temporarily disappeared. The monitor flashed a couple of times and then they saw the old man scuffling along towards the main exit. He stopped, looked around and then went into another toilet. He never came out again.

"The bastard is playing games with us." Claire shouted.

"There is no CCTV in those toilets for the sake of privacy Claire. I'm afraid that we will have to watch that area and try and match up with whoever comes out but as you can see it is very busy. We just don't have the manpower to spend on it. You are welcome to send a couple of people to watch it and then maybe we can follow anyone of interest."

"Thank you, Cherise. I would be grateful if you could do that. I have to go and see my boss and see if she will allow a couple of guys to watch and report but I feel that, whoever this guy is, he is very clever and knows that we were watching his every move. I know that he came out of there but he had obviously changed his appearance. Thank you again. I will mention to my boss just how helpful you have been. I'll see you soon."

The two detectives walked back up to the crime scene to pick up their car. They met the crime scene manager. DCI Frances Kearney.

"Hiya Frances. I would like to share with you what we have found out so far. Firstly, our John Doe is now Dermot Dolan. I need to go to his address and find out if there is a Mrs Dolan. I was going back to the depot but maybe I can pass you the evidence that we have collected so far and see what else that I can find out about the victim. Have you found out anything else?" Claire asked with a smile.

"Well funny you should say that Claire. I had no idea where you had all disappeared to and what information you were able to get. I have spoken to Jack Samms and he has filled me in as far as they are both dead. Where is DCS Copperstone? He is not answering his phone. You and he left a crime scene with no senior officer in charge. So what the hell happened Callison?"

"Sorry Frances. We left Copperstone at the town hall balcony. He knew where we were going. The way things unfolded it was like something out of a James Bond movie. I need a couple of officers to work with the Assets Department. Cherise Day has bent over backwards in trying to find the shooter but she hasn't got anyone spare to sit and scroll through all the videos. Our man is in there somewhere."

"I'll get a couple of officers over there in the morning because it's getting late; the town is packing up. Go and see where this victim lives. I want you to report to me and DCS Copperstone first thing in the morning. We need to collate all this information with you and Sergeant Janine Pratt.

While we are at it who is responsible for fucking this crime scene up? It's an embarrassing mess."
"It was like it when we turned up. I made sure that there were pictures taken and we have the details of most of the, she held her hands up. 'witnesses' quote-unquote. The crime scene being compromised, was the fault of the officer in charge at the station. The ambulances turned up before we did. I suggest, Frances, that you start there."

"Yeh… well, I'll definitely be looking into it. It appears that we now have all the information that we can glean from this crime scene. The council boys will be cleaning up all this blood. The CCTV that you obtained was a gift. I have also collected the CCTV from the businesses between here and the town hall. Hopefully, the forensics can see more than we can. So off you pop and don't be late in the morning. It's going to get a bit crowded in there and I will make sure of that." She pointed to her foot.

Callison and Gavin jumped into the car. Gavin was driving. She looked at her partner, laughed and shook her head.

"Sorry Claire. It's just that this has been so far away from being a textbook homicide case, it was fucked up when we got there and it still seems to be fucked up… 'scuse my French. Then you were getting it in the ear from Frances."

"Yeh you're right Leanne. I think that we have been spoilt as far, as the previous murder cases that we have been on were almost too easy. But I think that this one is going to be far from straight forward. The murderer has it seems, gone to a lot of trouble to prepare this assassination, including the getaway. I believe that the old man that we saw still had the weapon on him, disguised as a walking stick."

Leanne stopped the car and ran into a fast-food shop and got tea, bacon sandwiches, and a handful of energy bars. They were both starving but hadn't noticed.
She returned to the car and was just about to bite into the sandwich when Callison put her hand on hers.

"We haven't got time to stop and eat Sergeant Gavin, carry on driving."

"With respect Guv, no bloody way." They both laughed for a micro-second before stuffing the sandwiches into their mouths. They finished their snack and brushed away the crumbs.

"We would have been slapping on the make-up about now Leanne. God I could murder a curry. I was alright until I tasted that sandwich. Now I'm bloody starving.' They both giggled.

The detectives pulled up at the address of Mr Dermot Dolan. The house was in darkness. There was a Range Rover parked on the driveway. Leanne got out of the car and went to the front of the parked car and put her hands on the bonnet.

"What are you doing that for Leanne?"

"I've seen them do it in the movies, to see if the engine is warm. Believe it or not it is!"

Claire knocked loudly on the door with her fist and then noticed a doorbell at the side; she pressed it a couple of times but there was no answer. Leanne signalled that she would go around the back way. Claire peered through the windows but could see nothing. She rapped on the window with her knuckles, just in case, then she saw a movement inside the room. She looked again but there was nothing. She was then joined by Leanne.

"I think that we have a problem Claire. That was me that you saw inside the house. I think that we have a suicide in there; some old bloke is sitting in the back room, with a rifle between his knees and some of his brains decorating the ceiling. There is blood and all sorts still dripping down."

"I'll go and have a look. Call it in Leanne, see if you can get hold of Kearney and Copperstone."
Claire reappeared after a few minutes, her face was a deathly pale colour, she looked at her partner and shook her head.
"Fuck me Leanne. I'm not really sure, I couldn't get a good look at the guy's face because I didn't want to touch anything. But that looks like the old man who was playing games with us from the mall this afternoon. This is either going to be a very easy case or one mother fucker of a job."

Chapter Two

Friday 1st July 22:25
22, Queens Road, Duns Town

The Duty Medical Officer, Andi Qureshi, confirmed that the man was dead and also confirmed that the time of death was between one and two hours ago; the body was still warm. He had taken as many pictures as he thought necessary to aid the investigation.

"Was it suicide Andi, or is that asking for too much too soon?" Claire asked.

"To be honest Claire there is no way of telling at the moment. It looks, to all intents and purposes, that it is indeed suicide. But unfortunately, we cannot take anything at face value and we can't move the body until we get the firearm made safe."

"Did you get a good picture of his face? because I believe that was the guy, we were searching for earlier today?" Andi scrolled through his digital camera and stopped when the victim's face came up. He showed the two detectives the face of the victim.
"Fuck! I'm not sure that it is the same guy although we never got a good likeness on the CCTV… Thank you Andi."
Copperstone turned up without using his blues and twos for a change. He sauntered over to the two detectives and the medical officer.
"Hi Andi, can I go and have a look at the victim?"

"If you are quick Denver, I have handed it over to SOCO and they are waiting to have the firearm made safe so that it can be examined. Everything is still in situ or you can look at the pictures on my camera, if you want. I can't say whether it was a suicide yet but its early days."

"I thought at first, Denver, that it was the old man from the mall this afternoon," Claire said. But now I am not so sure. I have found out that the car, which was still warm when we first arrived here, is registered to Dermot Dolan; the deceased victim from the Crown Court shooting. He is now, obviously, well past the driving stage. So, could that mean that the suicide victim in there is the shooter? I'm hoping ballistics will confirm that the rifle between his legs is the same rifle that he used this morning. It doesn't look like a shotgun. It looks like some sort of high-powered rifle, that he blew his brains out with."

"It's hard to say at the moment Claire," said Andi. "But we will soon know. Ballistics are on their way to make sure that it is safe to move and take it away. Hopefully, there will be no more weapons found in there and we can close this case up."

"So, I'm afraid Denver, that William Tell's death was purely accidental. But I won't dot the Is and cross the Ts just yet." Claire said with a smile.
Just as she finished speaking DCI Kearney turned up. She climbed out of her car, walked over to the growing crowd of detectives and went straight to Claire.

“Ok Callison, what have you found? You should be tucked up in bed, not earning yourself a fortune in overtime, that we can ill afford.” she laughed.
Claire filled her in and everyone around added their bit. Then they were interrupted by yet another visitor, John Moody, from forensic ballistics. Copperstone introduced him to Andi and the three men disappeared into the house, that now seemed to light up the whole street.
Gradually, one by one, all of the neighbours had turned up to find out what was happening. Claire and Leanne introduced themselves to the onlookers and started asking questions about Mr Dolan.

They found out that he was married to Cara and had a daughter, Maria, who lived with them; she was twenty-three years old. The family were described as very sociable, they would always speak and pass the time of day. But they hadn’t been seen for the last few days, except for Dermot, who had left his house earlier that day, and stood at a bus stop. This was unusual for him as he would always drive to work or to the town in his beloved Range Rover.
He had been offered lifts from neighbours that knew him but he had just ignored them and turned his back to them. Claire returned back to DCI Kearney.

“Mr Dolan, has a wife and daughter somewhere Frances. They haven’t been seen for a few days, and it’s been noticed by the neighbours because they are a sociable family. So, where are they? There is no one in the house apart from the killer or victim’s body, whoever he might be?”

"I'm afraid that we can do nothing until SOCO has finished. We have to sit and wait. I still want you in early in the morning Claire so I think that you and Leanne should go and get some sleep. I will be going as soon as I am relieved."

"Sorry Frances, I just can't go home until I find out about the wife and daughter. I won't sleep so there is no point. Don't even think about ordering me home. What about you Leanne, how do you feel?"

"Same as you do. As far as we're concerned, we have two missing persons and we haven't got a bloody clue where to start. I'm with you Claire."
Before Frances could think of a reply the neighbours bought over a table and chairs. Tea, coffee and biscuits seemed to rain from the sky. The officers stared open-mouthed, not knowing whether it was a gesture of kindness or a ploy to get information.
They sat there for just under fifteen minutes until one of the SOCO technicians, Michael Chivers, came out and spoke to Frances. She was busy trying to persuade the neighbours to go home. He pulled her to one side and whispered in her ear. Kearney called her detectives over and gave them the news about the firearm.

"The firearm is not a high-powered rifle. It's just an ordinary single barrel shotgun. There were a few cartridges found under the chair that the victim was sitting on. It is being tested for prints as we speak. But when Andi and his team moved the body for a better look, on the seat, directly under him, was a piece of paper. It was covered in a plastic document sleeve, with an address on it

that appeared to be written in blood." She showed the picture, that Andi had just sent to her, to Claire and Leanne. Claire looked at the address and screwed her face up.
"That address is in Stundon, which is a village not far from here. I'm not sure what it means but I think that we need to get there. I have a sinking feeling that this is not going to be an easy case, far from it. So, any thoughts from anyone?"

"Ok Claire," said Copperstone. "Go and have a look but don't go kicking any doors in. Let me know if you need back-up."

Claire and Leanne jumped into their car and wheel spun it, much to the annoyance of Kearney. They put on their blues and twos and floored it the five miles to the village of Stundon. As they neared the address, they switched off the flashing lights and then their headlights. They parked a hundred yards away from the house in question and switched off the engine. They sat there for a few minutes allowing their eyes to adjust to the darkness. They each picked up a torch, then exited the vehicle and walked slowly towards the large, detached house. There were no lights on in the house. They both looked to see if any curtains twitched or for any movements at all.
The night was dark and now that their eyes were fully adjusted to the darkness they split up. Leanne went to the front of the house and looked through the windows for any movement. There was none.
Claire was standing on tiptoe trying to look inside the window at the rear of the house. She saw nothing. She told Leanne, who had just joined her, to go and knock on the

front door as loudly as she could. She would wait here just in case.
She heard Leanne rapping at the front door and then she heard someone moaning from an open upstairs bedroom window. She was unsure as to her next move but that was decided for her. The voice got louder, and they heard a distressed woman's voice.

"Help me… Help me." and then sobbing. "Please help me…please…"
Claire tried the door. To her surprise it was unlocked. She opened it a fraction and then she caught the smell; that unmistakable smell of death.
She left the door ajar, went to fetch Leanne and told her to make as much noise on the front door as she could. Then, she would go in through the back way.
As soon as Leanne started knocking and banging on the door, Claire went in through the back door as silently as she could. The smell that hit her was overpowering. She covered her mouth as best as she could.
There was no sound other than Leanne. She looked for and found a light switch then turned it on; it fizzed, flashed, and popped. She saw Leanne peeking through the letterbox and indicated for her to stay where she was. She took a deep breath.

"Armed police" she lied, "make yourselves known… armed police, you are surrounded."
There was no movement, no sound except the whimpering of the female voice upstairs. Claire changed her mind and let Leanne into the house. She instantly covered her face to stop herself gagging. They both searched downstairs but there was nothing. Leanne was going to put the

landing light on but was stopped from doing so by the strong arm of Claire.
"Use your torch Leanne," she whispered. "Until we know what's up there and keep watching behind us."
They furtively climbed the stairs. The smell, along with the whimpering increased.
"Hello, armed police, you are surrounded!"

"Praise be to God," a woman's voice weakly said. "Help me we are in here."
They reached the top of the stairs. There were four doors, two open and two shut. Claire indicated that she would open the first door and when she did, to switch on the landing light, which was close by, and to be prepared for anything.
She took hold of the doorknob and turned it slowly. It was unlocked. She pushed it open and jumped inside the room, not unlike some American detective from the 1960s. Leanne switched on the landing light. The room was empty. It was safe. Claire switched the light on in that room and left the door open. Then she went to the next door. It was open but she again jumped into the room flashing her torch about like a loaded gun. It was the bathroom. It was safe. She switched on the light and left the door open.
The third door was open. She repeated her manoeuvre and stopped dead in her tracks. She tried hard to stop herself from gagging then she switched the light on.
Her eyes stared wide open at what she saw in front of her; the remains of a woman's body had been left spread-eagled against a wall, the same side as the door. The woman was still wearing underwear but going by the smell, had been long dead. She had been gagged and there

were, as far as she could see, ligature marks on her neck. She thought that she saw the body moving but then noticed that it was maggots. They were freely gorging on the victim's mouth, her eyes and nether regions. She came out of the room and gently closed the door behind her. Then suddenly she returned to the bathroom and spewed her guts up.
Leanne looked inside the room and saw the underwear-clad body; she quickly closed the door. Claire had almost recovered. She went to the last door, slowly turned the handle and pushed it open. She switched on the light and saw two fully clothed women, tied up on a bed, directly in front of her.
"Get the ambulance, a Duty Medical Officer and SOCO Leanne. Get Kearny and Copperstone."
Claire went over to the whimpering woman. The other woman, beside her, was unable to speak because her gag was still in place. "Are you all right, are you the Dolan Family?" Both women nodded frantically and Claire released them. The younger woman, once her gag was removed, thanked her and turned to the older woman.

"We are safe now mum. Dad will be here soon to take us home." They both cried with joy. The young woman looked at Claire's face, and somehow, she knew… She sobbed, screamed out and held onto her mother.

"I'm sorry but we are going to have to ask you some questions, do you know who the person is in the other bedroom?"

"We don't know but we were forced to look at her by the bastard who put us here. He said that's what would happen to us both if my father let him down. We have been here for two or three days I think and no one else has come in that we know of. He left us here tied up with no food, no water, and that foul stinking dead body filling our nostrils. God rest her soul, whoever she was."

"Could you give us a description of the man who brought you here and can you remember how it happened? I'm sorry but I have to know as much as you can remember while it is still fresh in your mind."

"We never saw anyone. We were eating dinner and then we were here. We never saw his face. We only heard his deep posh English voice. It was a man, if you can call him that. That's all we know. My father… what has happened to him? Is he dead? Please don't hide it. We have to know because he wasn't here with us. Please tell me… please… please," she sobbed. The flashing blue lights signalled the arrival of the ambulance.

"I'm sorry Miss. We are still investigating and it is through our investigations that we managed to find you. I'm sorry, the ambulance is here and they need to take you to hospital to clean you up, and to make sure that you are safe. We need the clothes that you are wearing for evidence."

"We don't want a fucking ambulance; we want to see my father please, where is he?"
Claire sat down beside the women, and they saw the real tears in her eyes. They both knew that the tears meant that they would never see their husband and father again.

"It will be better for you both if you can just concentrate on each other at the moment. I will come and see you at the hospital tomorrow, talk to you more and hopefully get a statement from you."
The paramedics took the sobbing women away. They used great care, compassion and understanding. Two female constables followed the ambulance and would stay close to the two women.

Copperstone and Kearney turned up. Copperstone pushed past everyone to get a look at the body. He re-joined them, shaking his head. Claire described the dead woman and the ordeal of the other two women. Kearney ordered Claire and Leanne home despite them pleading otherwise. But they accepted that they were tired and they needed rest. There was a long day or days ahead of them. The two detectives relented and went home.
They wouldn't and couldn't sleep. If they did, those bodies and other bodies from past enquiries would haunt them, every time they attempted to close their eyes.

Claire sat on the edge of her bed looking at photographs of her parents Kevin and Katie. They had both succumbed to the big C, ten years ago. Both heavy lifelong smokers. Katie went first and was followed shortly after by Kevin. Claire, who was now thirty-one, had never smoked. But she often thought that growing up in a house constantly filled with smoke, may one day affect her. She never dwelled on the subject. Once her parents had passed, she was on her own. There were no other living relatives. They had all succumbed to different forms of Cancer. They had all been taken early in their fifties when they should have been enjoying life and looking forward to their retirement. But their lifelong investment paying Income Tax and National Insurance would go to other people. None of them, including her parents, had taken out life insurance and so it was a costly experience for the remaining relatives. She had paid for her parent's funerals out of her life savings because she could afford it. She had never been a great spender and would never waste money on clothing or other accessories simply because her friends had done so.

Claire had a skill that was passed down from her mother and that was dressmaking. Her mother could have made a name for herself designing one-off pieces of clothing but she had decided to do it purely as a hobby; supplying friends and family especially for parties, weddings and in most cases, in their family, funerals!
There was a spare bedroom in her mother's house that contained many rolls of materials. They had been collected over the years, along with three sewing machines, and a knitting machine; the only things that brought her mother close to her after her death.
Her parents left her the large house and a few debts but she gladly settled their estate. The house was a family home and she sometimes felt lost and lonely. She hoped that one day it would be filled with her own family but as yet there was no time for any long-term romance in her life.
She looked tearfully at all the pictures on the wall. Pictures that were given to her, when she left her previous employment, by the many students who begged her to stay. But her mind had been made up.

Claire was a secondary school teacher at the time. Something that she had wanted to be from her early school days. But gradually, since her parents passing, she had started to lose faith in the education system. She had noticed that the students were showing less and less respect for their teachers. She had got on well with all her students but other teachers had different opinions on how to pass on their knowledge.
Claire had seen a gradual decline in the overall behaviour of the younger students and their constant brushes with the law, mostly associated with drug abuse. She wanted to reach out to them but she felt that she was on her own and never had the backing of her colleagues, despite her pleading with them and trying to get them on board. Frustrated with her career, she spoke to one of her oldest friends who had joined the police force after leaving school. She persuaded Claire that she could help youngsters more by becoming a police officer.
Claire changed her career and returned to university to take a degree in law and sociology. But on joining the police force she was fast-tracked to detective status and soon progressed to the bloodier side of investigations in which she had excelled. Her quick mind, asking the correct questions and providing the correct answers, impressed her potential bosses. She never forgot the reason that she joined the force in the first place and whenever possible she would volunteer herself and sometimes with Leanne. They would go to schools, talk to the students and hold a 'surgery' as she called it. They listened to the student's troubles and tried to point them in the right direction. At these times she missed being a teacher but enjoyed the rapport that she had with the majority of young people. Some of those young people

were now colleagues of hers and would still come to her when all was not well.

Saturday 2nd July 07:30
Duns Town Police Station

DCS Copperstone and DCI Kearney walked into the operations room together. They were both surprised to see that the detectives had all got there long before them and were already discussing the suspicious deaths. Especially the double killing by the ‘assassin.’ They were already drawing a sweep to work out a suitable nickname for him. Kearney called for attention.
“Right you lot. It appears that we have four dead bodies in our manor. I assume you all know about them but nevertheless I will bore you with the details.
At approximately 12:45 yesterday lunchtime, a person or persons unknown, shot and killed two individuals; a defence barrister by the name of William Tell and a Mr Dermot Dolan. Both died instantly at the same time from, we believe, a single bullet. DI Callison and Sergeant Gavin went to Mr Dolan’s address and found, an as yet unidentified, IC1 male body. We believe, at the moment, that the person died as a result of a fatal shotgun wound. At first, we thought that he was the ‘assassin’ who killed Tell and Dolan but I have just been informed by ballistics that the weapon found last night was not the weapon used at that scene.
When the weapon was taken away by ballistics, SOCO moved the body. There was a sheet of paper underneath him with an address on it, written in blood. Callison and Gavin went to that address and found Mrs Dolan and her daughter tied up in a bedroom.

There was also a naked body at the premises. A woman who, at the moment, remains unidentified. SOCO have been there all night doing what they do best." Claire interrupted her.

"Excuse me Ma'am but I think you have made a mistake; she wasn't naked she had her underwear on." She looked at Leanne who nodded in agreement.

"Well I admit that I too thought that she was wearing underwear but she was in fact, covered from head to foot in tattoos of underwear. Very delicate tattoos I may add. I would have thought it would have taken maybe a year or so to complete but yes, tattoos. I'm afraid Claire and DCS Copperstone have seen the body in situ."

"Bloody hell that must have made her eyes water," shouted out one of the other officers followed by giggles.

"Thank you for that needless and childish input Sergeant Watts. I would have expected a little more compassion from someone in your position. This is somebody that has been murdered. She has had her life taken away from her and she deserves some respect. Anyone else who sees fit to make wisecracks, will cease to be working in this station, do I make myself clear? That requires an answer from everyone here."
Everyone in the room acknowledged the question.
"Right, ok, let's get back to the grown-up world. We have since found out that the residence is owned by a Miss Petra Tancred but that is all we have at the moment. Now Claire, can you tell me what you and Leanne have planned for today?"

"Our first port of call this morning is to take a statement from Mrs Dolan and her daughter. We need to find out exactly how they got to where we found them and why they seemed so frantic about Mr Dolan. We need to find out more about the shotgun victim. I have a gut feeling that it was more than a suicide."

"What makes you think that, apart from your gut Claire?" said Kearney.

"The address was written in blood. He was sitting on it and if it were a suicide that address would more likely to have been in a more visible position. The odd man out at the moment is the woman, Miss erm… Tancred, and… I had at first wondered how do ballistics know for sure that it wasn't the same gun? But I now know that. There is something else that |I have been thinking seriously about and that is the first shooting. Now I am not an expert in firearms but for someone to take a shot like that puts him or indeed her way up into the professional bracket. And… this is the question that is without a doubt bugging me. The shot and the distance involved, from what I have been told, took about half a second to reach the victims. Now… if the assassin was a pro' he would have seen the barrister getting closer to his target and would have waited until he had passed before he pulled the trigger, knowing that it was just a half-second away. But he didn't wait and he… and I'm bloody sure of this, he would have seen the barrister so why did he shoot? Why did he pull the trigger knowing that he would hit the barrister as well? So, could I ask you Frances, what are your thoughts at the moment?"

"Well Claire, I was going to say that my thoughts were pretty much the same as yours but I am way behind your forward-thinking. Yes, it would answer a whole host of questions and we could be looking at either Tell, Dolan, or even Lee-Winton as the victim? But as you say it looks more like Dolan. We are waiting for the, shall we say at the moment 'suicide victim's' prints to come through. Hopefully, he is on record. He had no identification on him. The woman that you discovered had been there for at least three days. As for the weapon concerned it has been identified. It is an old single barrel shotgun and would not be capable of hitting the target from the distance quoted; which I believe was somewhere in the region of 1064.5 feet. But it would have been very easy to use it to commit suicide. It had a barrel length of twenty-seven inches. Obviously, tests are being carried out as we speak…"
She was interrupted by one of the detectives, Chris Marlow, who stood up and asked from the information that they had, what was the connection?
"That's a very good question Detective Marlow and I would like you to know that you will be responsible for giving me the answer to that excellent question as soon as possible, thank you for volunteering. Come and see me afterwards. We know that Dolan and the suicide victim are somehow connected and the wife and daughter being taken to the house is a big question mark. But I assume, for that reason, that they too are connected. So, I want you all to go and detect, detectives. Show me what you are made of. Now are there any more questions, because I wish to assign you to your duties? I have a list here compiled by DCS Copperstone and myself assigning you to specific jobs that cater to your skillset. I want you all share your information. You don't get brownie points if

you are not a team player. On the contrary officers, you are more than likely to lose those precious brownie points if I see anyone playing solitaire.
Detectives Claire and Leanne are the go-to girls at the moment. I will see you all at the same time tomorrow. These empty whiteboards behind me are sadly lacking information at the moment but I know that you will all be busting your balls to decorate them for me. Ok, let's get detecting.
I need to speak to you Claire and Leanne before you leave to go up to the hospital. Grab a coffee and I will be with you in a few minutes, Marlow follow me."

Twenty minutes later Kearney caught up with them and the three sat down.
"Ok, I am hoping that this was going to be a quick investigation but your thoughts Claire, have put the kibosh on that. We may have to involve other departments in finding the assassin if it isn't the suicide guy. I have to report upstairs and I want to keep them happy. I was hoping that the shotgun victim was the end of the trail and he was responsible for the whole shebang. We desperately need to find the weapon that kicked off this case. I have uniform searching every inch of the Town Hall, the shopping mall and everywhere in between in the hope that they find it. I've got SOCO using some facial recognition tech' against the man, that you saw in the mall.
Then we have to link him to the killing of Mr Tell. We thought at first that he was in the wrong place at the wrong time. But I have a team that will be checking him and his colleague Lee-Winton's court cases, on Monday, just to be on the safe side. They will be in direct touch with the CPS, who will supply all the necessary information.

I know that I don't have to tell you how important this is to get a quick result. The tight-wads upstairs are constantly cutting back and want to see some good reports. At first it looked like an easy one but I have this nagging fear, thanks to you two that it is gonna be a mother of a job.
Can you let me have the statement from Mrs Dolan and her daughter as soon as you have it? Hopefully, by then I will know for sure if the female body is Miss Petra Tancred. We may have it all sewn up by this time tomorrow," she said not quite believing what had just come out of her own mouth. She was aware that Callison, with her copper's gut instinct, knew that there was more to this case than either of them had at first thought.

Chapter Three

Saturday 2nd July 10:30
Duns Town Hospital

Detectives Callison and Gavin met with the hospital supervisor, Mrs Mary Pratt. Coincidentally, she was the mother of a colleague of theirs, Sergeant Janine Pratt; she was involved in the case at the moment as a collator of evidence.
They followed her to her office.
"I'm afraid officers that we had to sedate Mrs Cara Dolan and her daughter Maria, just after they were brought in. They, as you know, were both in a bad physical and mental state. They were asking the whereabouts of Mr Dolan, saying that they thought he was dead and we, of course, had no answers to their questions.
They both became disruptive and because of their condition, we thought it best to calm them down with medication. We inserted drips to hydrate them and they are both under supervision. I don't believe that they are in any condition at the moment to answer your questions officer but I will go and check for you.
Mrs Pratt left the office and they heard her walk down the hallway. After a few minutes she returned to the office with a smile on her face.
"Well, I'm pleased to say that the patients are awake. I will allow you to question them Detective Callison but only under supervision. I will not let you subject them to questions that will upset them in any way, shape or form. Do we agree?

“Yes, of course, Mrs Pratt. Although, I have to try and break the news to them that Mr Dolan is dead. There is no way that they can identify his remains because of the severity of his injuries and that, I know, is going to upset them. But I must try and find out how they came to be where they were and how they had an idea that Mr Dolan was dead?”

“Ok, under those circumstances, I will send a senior nurse to accompany you Detective. But please try to be as tactful as you possibly can.”

“Trust me Mrs Pratt, I have done this, many times. I can, through my professional experience, try and relay the news as gently as possible. I am grateful that you will have a nurse nearby because they have both suffered so much.”

Claire and Leanne followed the senior nurse, Shannon Hunt, to the ward where Mrs and Miss Dolan were. They were awake and both sat up when they recognised the two detectives from the previous night. Marie, the daughter looked at them with a tear-filled face.
“We both know that my father is dead. We want to see him and hold him and say goodbye. Can you take us to him Detective?”

“I am so sorry for your loss Miss Dolan. I’m afraid that your father was killed yesterday and because of his injuries, I am afraid that we cannot possibly allow you to see him. I’m sorry.”

"We don't care what he looks like, we need to say goodbye. He knew that it would end badly, he told us as much."

"Please, I know that you are hurting but can you explain how all this came about? We have nothing to go on except what you said last night about being drugged" Mrs Dolan put her hand on her daughter's shoulder.

"My husband told us both that a few years ago he had done something bad, something very bad. But he wouldn't actually say what it was. He just asked us to trust him. He also said that someone had found out where he was living and that person was going to blackmail him into doing something bad but he didn't know what that was. He said that if he didn't do what was asked of him, we would both be killed and he would be forced to watch us die. He never said who this person was and what he was capable of. He never told us anything except that we were in danger. So, we had decided that we would go and stay with my sister for a few weeks but we never made it. All I remember is someone, a man, injecting me and…Oh… God no… please tell me that I am wrong… no God no!"

"What is it Mrs Dolan? What have you just remembered?"

"I… I… it was… no. That can't be right… He… he wouldn't do that to us."

"Who did it to you Mrs Dolan? Please tell me."

"It was my father," Maria said. "It was him that did this to us. I couldn't see his face but I can remember his aftershave. I can remember being pinned down, by the weight of his body, on my bed. His hand covered my mouth as he injected me in my backside. My own father why would he do such a thing… why would he?"

Maria burst into tears and jumped out of the bed and held onto her mother. She pulled the drip from her arm in her haste. The nurse rushed towards the women and asked the detectives to wait outside whilst she administered to their needs and attempted to pacify them.

"Jesus Claire. What the fuck? Dolan took his wife and daughter and dumped them in that hell hole. What sort of sick man would do that?"

"Leanne, we can't just assume that it was anything like that. There is no evidence to say that it was Dolan who took them to that house. There is more to this part of the story. We have to wait a little while and question them more. If we are allowed to under the circumstances."

"I know that Claire, and I apologise. I let my emotions get the better of me. This is a murder enquiry and we need to ask questions of the only witnesses that we have. But do you think that they are telling us everything?"

"They could well be confused by the drugs, their emotional state and of course the circumstances of their imprisonment. But hopefully, we will find out in a little while. They have both remembered something. Let's hope that it has jogged their memories and they can tell us more."

They sat outside the side-ward and listened to the grief and sobbing from the two women. It was a painful experience. They both wanted to shut out the women's suffering but they had a job to do.
After about twenty minutes, nurse Shannon came out and told them that both of the women wanted to talk to them. She advised them to play it by ear but she would stop them if they upset the women unduly. She added that they were now a lot calmer.

Claire walked in first, followed by Leanne and then the nurse.
"Please forgive me for upsetting you and accept our sincere condolences for your loss. We don't, of course have any real understanding of how you must feel but it is important that you try and remember as much as you possibly can."

"I think that we were both mistaken officers," Maria said through the tears. "I don't think that it was my father but I believe that he was there with us, close by somewhere. We were all at home on Wednesday evening; sitting around the table eating dinner, which my father had just prepared. Suddenly, there was a loud knock on the door. After a few seconds there was more knocking but it was much faster and louder. Whoever it was never pressed the doorbell. My father raced to the door and opened it. His face was red with rage at whoever was trying to cause damage to the door and disturb the neighbours. He opened the door and the next thing I knew was that my father was hurtling backwards He went into the wall, opposite the front door and collapsed…"

She stopped talking and put her arms around her mother, who was sobbing loudly. Claire said nothing. She watched and felt the suffering of the two women. After a short time, the mother looked at Claire and spoke to her, after reassuring her daughter that she was ok.

“It happened just the way my daughter said but neither of us are really sure what happened next. From that time until the injections, everything seems like it’s lost in a fog. I see things that don’t make sense to me.”

“If you can tell us anything at all that you saw or even think that you saw, we might be able to decipher it. Whatever it is Mrs Dolan, the smallest piece of information may end up being the most important.”

“Well, when you were outside, I told my daughter what I thought that I saw after my husband opened the door and was sent flying. After I told her she laughed at me and then suddenly her smile disappeared. She said nothing for a minute but then she started nodding and said that she remembered the same thing. It just doesn’t make any sense to either of us.”

“And what exactly did you see… or thought that you saw Mrs Dolan?”

“It was… it was like erm… like he was wearing a…a… a wig like you see in the old-fashioned days. It was a white wig with curls all over it… and… and there was something else that I remember. He had a black cloak!”

"Yes," her daughter interrupted. "I can see him now he was dressed like something that you see on the telly; he was dressed like a judge… yes a judge with a big white wig…and…I can't remember anything else." Her mother agreed with her.

"I know that this is very hard for you both but is there the slightest chance you saw his face at all? If he had a wig on then maybe his face was visible"

"All I can see is blackness officer. There was no face, just blackness. Maybe it was the Devil himself come to punish us for whatever it was that my husband had done in the past?" Both women started crying again. Nurse Shannon told them point-blank that the interview was over.

"Thank you both for helping us with our enquiry. If you remember anything at all please get in touch with us. I'm sorry but there is just one more question. What was your husband's employment Mrs Dolan?"

"He was a chauffeur. He worked for Lobson Investment Bankers, in the town and would drive special clients wherever they wanted to go. It was a good job and he was happy there."

"Thank you, Mrs Dolan, please keep in touch."
They left the private ward and returned to their car, still trying to comprehend what they had just heard. They said nothing but their minds were racing and searching for an answer.

Claire's phone rang, she looked at the caller ID and saw that it was Kearney.
"Yes Frances, we have just left Mrs Dolan and her daughter. Neither of them made a great deal of sense and we are none the wiser; except that the attacker was dressed as a 'Judge' they called it. I don't really believe in coincidences but…" she laughed, "I was hoping that it was going to finish with the phantom suicide. But something tells me that isn't going to happen, unless we find the murder weapon and now a Judge's outfit. So that means that we have to check William Tell's robes for DNA and get a warrant to search his boyfriend, Mr Duncan Lee-Winton's robes as well."

"Unfortunately, I think we are on the same page Claire. Ok leave that with me and I will get someone to follow it up. I need you two to get over to see Andi Qureshi, at the morgue. He said that he has more information for you regarding Miss Petra Tancred. He wasn't forthcoming with anything on the phone but he said by the time you get there he would have something, 'enlightening' was the word he used. So, can you see him and then get back here to me so that we can dot the Is?"

Kearney hung up without saying anything else. Claire called her back.
"Yes, Claire, what is it, did I forget something?"

"Yes, Frances. If you can get the warrant then I will serve it to Lee-Winton."

"But of course, Claire but it will have to wait until Monday I'm afraid. I have tried calling Mr Lee-Winton about his statement but he is not answering his phone. He is back in court on Monday so it can wait till then. I can't afford to pay overtime as you well know."

"Frances I will do it for free!"

"Claire you will do it on Monday. There will be no time today anyway. The day will soon be over. When you have finished at the morgue, report to me directly after. Keep your obvious dislike of that man to yourself. You are a professional remember that."

She hung up again, Claire stared at the phone and shook her head.
"It looks like we have to go and see Miss Tancred, Leanne. I'll stop at a chemist and get some Vick. We will be prepared this time. We'll also get a chance to take a proper look at these 'tats' of hers."

Saturday 2nd July 13:50
Morgue

The two detectives arrived at the medical examination laboratory, which was in the depths of the underground, under the main hospital. There were, it seemed hundreds of different alleyways and multi-coloured signs to find each different department. The two detectives had been there many times in the course of their careers. They were met at the doorway by Andi Qureshi. He always had a smile on his face, showing off his perfectly white and even teeth. They followed Dr Qureshi through other alleyways and rooms until he finally stopped.

He pointed to a closed door and told them that was where the two shooting victims, from outside the Crown Court were. They were being examined by forensic specialists from the Met' along with one of their own medical examiners, Jack Samms.

He who took them into the examination room but not before they had each stuffed a large dollop of Vick around their nostrils.

He introduced them both to Professor Cradle He was the Coroner but he was only observing.

They saw that the victim, Miss Tancred, was covered in a white sheet up to her neck. They both looked at Qureshi and nodded. Qureshi pulled the sheet completely off the body and both detectives gasped when they saw it.

The victim had tattoos from her neck to her toes. It was the most intricate tattooing that either of them had ever seen or would ever dream of seeing. The body was, apart from the obvious signs of decomposition and being dead, in perfect physical condition. This woman worked out big time. The v-shaped scars on her chest were stitched heavily and spoiled the, once perfect, specimen of physical perfection.

"It is pure artistry Detectives," said Professor Cradle. "Whoever has taken the time to draw such intricate and detailed work on a human body was surely a master of his or her trade. Even I had to look twice at her. It looked to me as if she were wearing a bra, panties, suspender belt and stockings but there is more." He pointed to the victim's breasts and indicated her pierced nipples and then to her vaginal area, where there was evidence of more piercings.

"We had to remove all her piercing when we x-rayed her. There was historical evidence that she had, at one time, a perineum piercing. Forgive me if you know already but I will tell you anyway; that is the area of skin between the genitals and anus, it is a dangerous place to have a piercing for obvious reasons that is why she probably had it removed."

"I would say that she must have been a very popular person professor. She was, from what I can tell, very attractive. We know very little about her at the moment." Claire said.

"Well, autopsies throw up all sorts of surprises Detective and if you are ready, we have for another one. She was in fact, intact, as we say. She was still a virgin so she wasn't raped at least. We are pretty sure that we can rule out any anal activity at any stage of her life too. We believe that the female is between forty-five and fifty-five. We do know that she died from asphyxiation. Her hyoid bone and larynx have been severely damaged and we can plainly see the trauma around her neck. There are finger marks, which is a very personal way to kill. There was substantial pressure used by whoever took her life. I'm not a detective, Detectives but I would safely hazard a guess that Miss Tancred knew her assailant. Unfortunately, I can only give an approximate time of death and I would say that she has been dead for about five days. It is just as well that the windows of the house in which she was found were all closed, except for the bedroom window which the other two women were being held. Otherwise, her body would have been far more decomposed. So yes, about Monday…"

"Sorry for interrupting again Sir," said Claire. But when I saw the victim, she had maggots all around her vaginal area. Yet her hymen was still intact?"

"My compliments Detective. The hymen had been nibbled on, if you pardon the expression. But yes, it was still intact." He was interrupted by an assistant who told him that DCI Frances Kearney had more information regarding the victim, which she was faxing over. Could Detectives Callison and Gavin return to base ASAP?
He passed on the message to the two detectives and promised that he would send a detailed report and photographs before, during and after the autopsy.

"Can I just ask Sir, if you have made any headway with the supposed suicide victim? I know that you have dropped everything to do Miss Tancred but I'm hoping that you have something." Claire asked with a pretty please look on her face.

"I'm afraid that I have not had a chance to look at the victim yet. But as soon as we are finished here, I will personally make a start, along with Chief Medical Officer Jack Samms, who is also up to his neck with work. You are gathering quite a collection of bodies," he laughed. "Forensics have already done a few tests on the victim but we have a steep hill to climb with that one Detective. I would say it would be at least a week."

"Wow, that's longer than I thought. Ok thank you Sir, and thank you Andi."

The two detectives left the morgue, deep in thought; not speaking until they were almost at the police station where Kearney was waiting for them. The silence was broken by Leanne.
"Would you have tattoos and piercings like that Claire? All over your body and showing off everything to whoever had personal access to your most intimate places?"

"Tattoos or piercings have never interested me Leanne. My parents had my ears done when I was a kid and I occasionally wear earrings. Less chance of losing them, if you were in a bit of rough and tumble," she laughed.

"And she was a virgin too? That is hard to believe but if they examined her, they don't make that sort of mistake. There are so many questions going through my head as to why someone would go to all that trouble and not get a leg over. Why did she do it?"

"Maybe she was saving herself for Mr or Miss Right and giving them one hell of a surprise on their wedding night," Claire said, laughing and shaking her head.

Kearney was sitting at her desk. There was no one else about. They were probably all at home with their family watching the sports results or just playing mummies and daddies. These days nobody works unless it is an absolute emergency. All cost-cutting by the 'big knobs' upstairs; keeping the purse strings tightly closed. Kearney waved them into her office without even looking up to see if they saw her.

She looked over her glasses and waited for the two detectives to make their report; starting with the Dolans. "Hmm, so they think it was someone dressed up as a judge. If that doesn't beat all Claire. I have some news of my own and it concerns both Miss Petra Tancred and the suicide. There is a connection. Detective Chris Marlow has worked his butt off finding out about Miss Tancred. She is a forty-nine-year-old defence barrister. A partner in a top-end law firm. She has a flat in Paddington, she is single and at the moment we are trying to locate friends and acquaintances to find out a little bit more about her. Her house in Stundon contained very little paperwork. All that we found were a few bits of underwear and very little else."

"So, Frances, it appears that everything is indeed connected and barrister related. All we have to do is find out about the suicide. Maybe, he is something to do with the law courts?"

"Funny you should say that Claire," Frances said with a smile.

"Go on then! I know you can't wait to tell me. What is he a fucking judge or what?"

"Nothing as glamorous I'm afraid. He was a court usher by the name of … you ain't gonna believe this… Robin Hood. His name is Robin Hood," she said with a big smile on her face. Claire and Leanne stared at her open-mouthed.

"Robin Hood… William Tell… I can see the funny side and I'm glad that there is a connection. But how exactly are they both connected, apart from the obvious?" Leanne asked.

"That is all I know at the moment. Apart from him being sixty-five years old. I'm hoping you will find out a lot more when you interview your friend Lee-Winton. I have arranged a warrant for you to take possession of his, and Tell's robes or silks or whatever they are and wigs for DNA testing. I think he definitely knows something. I have another team who will be checking the court files to see how these people may be connected.
The Met will be assisting us with the first two bodies and chasing up any information about Miss Tancred. I am arranging for Detective Marlow to liaise with them and staff at the Old Bailey, where she has worked many times apparently. Of course, there will be a search of her flat in Paddington; in the hope that it may be of some help in our investigation."

"And what about our Mister Robin Hood? How the hell did Marlow find out about him in such a short time?"

"Detective work Claire. He ran the fingerprints and it came up with him being a court official, with all his details. Marlow and forensics are on their way to his address as we speak. Hopefully, they will find the murder weapon, then it's downhill from there… I hope. As I said, I have arranged that your warrant be ready, first thing Monday morning. Now remember it is only to collect his robes and wigs. The warrant covers nothing else. Can we be clear on that point Claire?"

"But of course, Frances. Perfectly clear."

Saturday 2nd July 2016 16:57
Duns Town Police Station

DCI Kearney was alone in the office as usual. She was busy typing out a report for the big boss upstairs, who was probably playing towards the nineteenth hole by now, she thought. She looked up at the clock on the wall and decided to take the work home and finish it over a few glasses of Southern Comfort.
She hadn't realised just how tired she was until she thought of her bed. It seemed that lately, she was doing more and more paperwork than ever before. She heard distant echoes in her mind saying that 'As soon as they had got used to computers, paperwork as we know it would cease to exist.' How wrong they were. She believed that it had actually doubled, if not trebled because everything had to be done in triplicate. It was probably easier for the people above her to sit on the loo whilst reading them. She laughed to herself at the thought of it and then tried to unsee the vision that she had just created.

Her phone rang. She picked it up before the second ring and started yawning, which prevented her from hearing what was being said on the phone.
"Oh, excuse me. It's been a long day, who is this?"

"It's DC Chris Marlow Ma'am. The forensic team and I are at Mr Hood's premises. We have found a woman's body here inside a bedroom. There are all sorts of medicines and everything there, Ma'am and quite a bit of …err… shi…err, human waste Ma'am. I've called for a medical examiner to be here Ma'am, but we need a senior officer."

"Can you tell if the woman was attacked or is it natural causes Marlow?"

"Well, she has a cut on the head but the forensic guys here believe that she fell or slipped in the shi… err waste Ma'am. But we are waiting for an official verdict before we can continue in that room."

"Is the mess contained in that one room Marlow?"

"Yes Ma'am, forensics have taken precautions and photos of the scene."

"Ok, Marlow I will be there in a few minutes. Start looking in the other rooms for as much information as possible. As we discussed earlier, I need you to find a sniper rifle or evidence that it at least exists."
Kearney's shoulders slumped as the thought of Southern Comfort disappeared from her thoughts. She knew that it was going to be a long night.

Kearney arrived at Hood's house just as the body, of the woman found in the house, was taken away in the ambulance. Andi Qureshi was standing by the entrance gate to the property.
"Ok. Andi. How did the poor woman die, is it suspicious?"

“I don’t think so Frances. You could see where she had actually slipped on the spilt waste and banged her head. She has been dead approximately twenty-four hours. I am pretty certain that we can say it was accidental and from the medication that she was taking it looks like she was terminally ill. There are morphine drip bags in the fridge, which is in the room. But I can’t find any signs of palliative care or anyone who has kept a record of medication. The medicine was well beyond her reach.”

“So, I imagine that it would have been Mr Hood, her husband, who was looking after her. Caring for her and administrating her medication. Unknown to her he was dead”

“Well I will check up on her medical records back at the lab’. It should give me all the answers to that little conundrum Frances. At least they will be together again.”

“Well we have to find out if there are any relatives but I somehow doubt that. Even so, they probably left a will of some description. Anyway, thank you for your help, we really must stop meeting like this.” They both laughed. “I’m hoping. Andi that this will be the last body in this case. Now I had better help search through this house and find some answers.”

“Oh, by the way, Frances, I found a diary. No…no… far more than a diary. It was more of a journal really; an unabridged life story of two people in love. It was underneath the woman’s pillow and it was quite heavy. She must have struggled to make her entries in it. I took pictures of it and then I gave it to Detective Marlow, who

seemed more than just a little excited at the thought of reading it.
The poor woman had made many entries over the years. I had a brief glance at it and it's very strange. When she first started writing it, her writing was strong and bold but as the years progressed, it slowly appears weaker, fainter, and leaning to one side. As if it's wasting away with the body. I have never noticed that before."

"I'm afraid that I have seen it Andi, many times and it shows how some murderers change over the years; from schoolwork to writing their confessions. I used to think that it was so interesting but now I have no time unless I'm hunting for a murderer. Thank you again Andi. Can you let me have the results as soon as possible please?"
She went inside the house. Apart from the smell she knew that there was a military presence facing her; she recognised that much from her own childhood.

Her father was an ex-army Major and never realised his obsession of measuring equal distances between any object. He was meticulous in everything that he touched. But her mother had tried to ignore his obsession with a compassionate mix of love and understanding.
He suffered from PTSD. A result of his years in the middle of so many battle zones. He constantly apologised when it was brought to his attention and sometimes purposely made a mess and laughed about it. He was a kind-hearted man and was loved very much by the two women in his life. When he died suddenly, they found that they had inherited his meticulosity. Not because it was contagious but it was done as a matter of love and it seemed to help them through their grief process. Her

father moulded her, without attempting to do so. She had learnt so much from that man just by watching and talking to him. He never once shouted at her, even though she was so argumentative in her teenage years. He seemed to want her to argue for what she thought was either right or wrong and then encourage her to explain why. She had never found a man or woman that could give her that freedom. To allow her to safely argue that black was white when she wanted to. She, of course, knew that it wasn't, but that was the fun. Whoever disagreed with her would have to prove that she was wrong but they could never keep pace with her. When her mother died, she was on her own but the life of a copper called to her. So, she went back to university and became just that.

Kearney's heart felt a little heavy when she saw the neatness of the Hood's living room but it soon passed. She had a job to do and her grieving process had been dealt with long ago or so she kept telling herself.
She found Marlow standing near a cupboard. He, not through any fault of his own, made the room look scruffy and untidy. She was sure that Mr Hood would not have been impressed. But Marlow was there to find answers that would hopefully find his killer.
She saw that he was looking through the journal, flicking through the pages as if he were looking for something specific. He tipped the journal upside down so that the pages fanned out like an accordion. He then placed both books in a sports bag that he had with him. He lifted the bag and was about to go. He didn't hear her come into the room but he suddenly felt her presence standing behind him.

“Would you like a piece of cake and a cup of tea Detective?” she asked haughtily.
He didn’t jump, but he turned around slowly and smiled.

“I’m just inspecting the evidence as you asked me to do Ma’am. This book explains a lot about Mr Hood’s life from very long ago, it’s very interesting.”

“Does it say in there where he hid the rifle by any chance Marlow? Then we can go home to bed and get some of that err... what’s it called… oh yes, sleep!”

“No sign of any rifle I’m afraid Ma’am but I have found a… well it looks like a professional C.V. belonging to Mr Hood. It goes right back to when he left school and joined the army as a boy soldier, and continues until the present day; with names of everyone he has worked for since he left the army. It almost corresponds with everything, as far as I can tell, that his wife wrote in her diary. I was going to take them back to the station Ma’am.”

“Very interesting Marlow. Leave them there and I will take charge of them. Have you found any official documents or anything regarding next of kin?”

“I have his and his wife’s, birth certificates, marriage certificate, and passports. There is also a name and address of his solicitors, Tell, Gail and Tancred, that rings a bell Ma’am.”

“Just a little bit Marlow, just a little bit.” She stood there shaking her head.

Ok time was getting on; she called the forensic lads together and made a note of anything that they had found. She herself had found a stash of official-looking papers in the kitchen cupboard. The time was 22:15 so she told everyone to go home. She called the local nick and arranged for a uniformed copper to stay there overnight. Then she carried the paperwork and the diaries to her car and went back to the office to correlate her findings.

Kearney made herself a cup of tea and started looking through the 'journal' and the CV belonging to Mr Hood. They both made for some very interesting reading. She started making notes as she went, although she was more than tired. Questions were being answered and associations were between made. She worked relentlessly throughout the night, constantly getting up, checking other papers and reports that the other detectives had on their desks. She pulled out blank whiteboards and wrote snippets of information on them. Four dead bodies were joined by a red line and each line had writing attached to it. Not satisfied with what she had already done she pulled out another white-board and added bullet points with different names. At the top of that board, the name that was underlined and stood out was; 'William Ascot Vladimir Tell.'

Kearney looked at the clock, 05:39 and made the conscious decision to go home, have a bath and something to eat. Under the circumstances her Southern Comfort would have to stay in the bottle as she would be returning straight back to the office.
Although it had only been two days since the first two killings, she didn't want the investigations to be slowed

down by complacency. She was leading this operation, and that is exactly what she was going to show to her detectives first thing Monday morning.

Chapter Four

Sunday 3rd July 2016
The Home of Claire Callison

Claire had a Sunday lay in, which made a change for her. She never slept much but she enjoyed watching the sunrise snuggled up in her duvet. Then she realised that there was housework to be done.
It never took her long to get on top of the chores. Once she had completed her housework and caught up on a few more domestic jobs that seemed to always get put off for the flimsiest of excuses. She hung her laundry out on the line, knowing that it would soon dry in the heat of the morning sun and the slight breeze.
She sat down, had a coffee and did a bit of surfing the net; mostly to catch up on any news that might concern her about the case. But there was nothing.
She called Leanne and arranged to meet for a late lunch at their local restaurant.
As she waited for the washing machine to finish its cycle, she Googled Miss Petra Tancred, her life and all her academic qualifications.

It seemed that from a very early age Miss Tancred's thirst for education was a never-ending journey. Starting with her perfect results in her GCSEs in science, English language and literature. She qualified for a place at the University of Cambridge, studying law, sociology, and history. Miss Tancred was a very intelligent woman by all accounts, with an IQ of 169.
After she graduated, she was only one of the very few candidates to take the Watson Glaser test and passed with

a hundred per cent. She applied to a top law firm: Tell, Ashridge and Gail. She was asked to do the test again in front of the pupillage intake manager.
She had beat her previous best time by twenty-five seconds. It may not seem a lot but it was more than enough to guarantee her a placement in the pupillage system which lasted a year; two six-month sections.
The Chairman was a William Ascot Vladimir Tell.
Mr Tell was amazed at her intelligence; the speed at which she could analyse and evaluate any given argument and draw the best possible conclusion every time. Her mentor certified her at the end of each six-month section. So, after the twelve months, she was offered a tenancy in chambers. Within a very short time, she had taken on and won cases of her own.
Miss Petra Tancred had become a partner in the firm when George Ashridge retired. He passed on very soon after his retirement and because he had no children, he left everything in his will to Miss Tancred.

The information didn't come easily. Claire had to use a variety of search engines to get as far as she did but as is usually the case, she knew that there was far more to know about Miss Tancred. She looked at the clock and was surprised at the time. She barely had enough time to shower and dress before meeting Leanne. Claire walked into the restaurant carrying her laptop and saw that Leanne was already sitting at a table; her head stuck into her laptop, she only paused momentarily to look up when Claire sat down in front of her.
"I hope that I'm not disturbing you Leanne, should we cancel lunch?"

"No, I'm sorry Claire. I've actually been working 'Pro Bono' so to speak, digging up some fantastic information but I can pause it for a while." She laughed. "So, what have you been up to then? I know that you haven't been sitting on your arse?"

"Well, Leanne this time you are wrong. Apart from my domestic slavery I searched for any info' on Miss Tancred and I found out what an intelligent person that she actually was. You wouldn't believe it."

"Wouldn't believe that she had an IQ of 169 and that she excelled in everything she touched? I'm sure I would believe that Claire," she laughed.

"Ok Leanne, clever bitch! I can tell that you know far more than that, so spill the beans but let us order first cos I'm bloody starving."
The meal was ordered, they knew that they would have a bit of privacy for a short while; the food was cooked fresh the only reason that it was their and their colleague's favourite restaurant.
"Right I have spent all night and this morning searching for information on Miss Tancred. I know why she was tattooed the way that she was so are you sitting comfortably Detective?" She giggled like a little girl who knew the answer to a riddle that no one else knew. She saw the intensity of her boss's concentrated look.
"Ok, there is a club in the West End of London called 'Tastefully Naturally' and it caters for very special people. I mean *elite* special. After much surfing and some phone-calls to my friends in the Met' I found out some little bits and pieces. Each piece led me to a further search and I

have only just… I think I have got everything so eyes down. This Club started off in the sixties, as did everything that was bad for us," she laughed. "This club started life as a nudist club but gradually the clientele started to get more hedonistic and certain moralistic values seemed to have been lost. So, in or about 1969, the rather shady old clientele were kicked out. They apparently started up somewhere else but a new dress code was drawn up by the four original founders, Walter Gail, George Ashridge, William Ascot Vladimir Tell, and Mrs Gladys Catherine Tell.
The membership was for life and the dress code was simple. We know what the women wore; as in the tattooed Miss Tancred. The men had speedo shorts tattooed. The men and the women had compulsory genital tattooing. Failure to comply with the dress code would mean failure to become a member of the elite club. Many applications by the Royals, the rich and the famous were turned down because of their flamboyant lifestyle. Most memberships were by invitation or recommendation only, with photographic proof of the required dress code required. After which, an interview would be arranged and the subjects would be tested to make sure that the tattoos were real and not made by artificial means in an attempt to gain false admission to the club. Are you still with me Claire?"

"Yes, course I am but slightly confused. When is a nudist club not a nudist club?"

"Well from reading between the lines I believe that it was a sense of decency that prevailed and maybe a bit of sex involved. It was erotically hiding what was in plain sight.

I must admit it does sound rather intriguing, to say the least," Leanne said with a girlish giggle.

"Well I get that and it may lead to a certain itch that needs scratching. But she was a virgin, so sex wasn't a part of it or it was but she wasn't interested in it. I would like to be a fly on the wall of this club to find out the reason for its existence."

"Hmm, I think the jury is out on that one Claire. So, this William Ascot Vladimir Tell, would he be related to our Mr William Tell I wonder?"

"Well it's a very strong possibility and our Mister Tell's father is in a care home somewhere. We know that much according to Mr Lee-Winton, who also said William is free of tattoos. But we can ask him that again tomorrow or check it out with the Coroner."

"I don't suppose you found out anything more about the mother? According to Lee-Winton, she was a whore who died from Aids. Did you not come across anything that referenced her? It seems awfully strange to me. Something isn't adding up and it certainly doesn't sound like Mrs Gladys Tell."

"I know that it's early in the investigation and it isn't gonna be over any time soon but I think that tomorrow Mr Winton… Oh, I'm sorry Mr Lee-Winton may help us more than he wants to."
She was interrupted by the waitress with their order, they both decided to have a glass or two of Rosé.

Halfway through her second glass of wine, Claire's phone rang, she looked at it and then mouthed the words 'Kearney.'
"Good afternoon Frances and to what do I owe the pleasure of your attention?"

"Just a bit of a heads up really, Claire. I have been at Mr Robin Hood's house most of last night and have made a few notes that you will all see tomorrow, on your return from speaking to Winton. Detective Marlow and the forensic team found a body at his premises. It appears that it was Hood's wife. From the information that we have gathered it looked like she was terminally ill. It looked as though she had tried to get out of bed because her urethral indwelling catheter bag, along with her colostomy bag, were full up.
The poor woman must have slipped over in the ensuing mess and banged her head. It appears that she died a long lingering death, waiting for her husband.
As I have said we have found some interesting paperwork, but I will fill you in tomorrow. Sorry to disturb your afternoon."
She hung up; Claire passed on the information to Leanne.

<u>Monday 4th July 10:00</u>
<u>Duns Town Crown Court</u>

Lee-Winton was discussing a court case and was interrupted by a court official telling him that two detectives wished to speak to him. He excused himself, joined the detectives and invited them into his office.
"Good morning Detectives. How may I be of service to you?"

He had a smarmy cocky attitude about him and there was nothing that showed that he was grieving for his friend and playmate. Claire showed him the warrant requesting his robe and wig and the whereabouts of William's locker so that they could take his spare robes and wigs.
"Oh my God! You are taking the piss Detective. This robe is the only one that I possess and I have just had the robe dry-cleaned. William was wearing his only robe and you have that already I assume? You have a misunderstanding somehow of how we operate. As far as the garb goes, even the most successful barrister has maybe only two gowns or silks. They are not going out clothes, we only wear them for a few hours a week. Have you any idea how much a wig costs?"

"I am sorry Sir. I am here to take your robe and wig for DNA testing and to gain access to Mr Tell's locker to take any evidence that I see fit. So, if you would remove it Sir and put it into this bag. I will return it as soon as possible."

"I have court appearances throughout the week, I'm afraid that is out of the question, Detective."

"I'm sorry Sir but if you do not hand over the robe and wig, I will have you arrested."

"All you had to do officer, was to just ask me for it. I would have given it gladly but I am now going to seek legal advice because according to this warrant it concerns a case that I know nothing about and it has nothing to do with William."

"It has everything to do with William Sir and all we want to do is rule you out of the equation. I thought that you would only be too pleased to assist in the capture of your…err your friend William's murder. I know you have nothing to hide but we have to get it on paper that we have checked every avenue. My boss has asked for your assistance. I apologise for the way I've handled it and you still in grief. Forgive me Sir."
Lee-Winton looked at her and her fellow detective. He believed he felt their contempt for him but he wanted to get rid of them to avoid embarrassment to himself and the court. He took off his robe and placed it in the evidence bag along with his wig. He opened the cupboard in the corner of his office and showed them his jacket. Nothing else. He walked over to the corner and picked up a bag and handed it to them.

"That is William's bag. It contains toiletries and a change of clothing," he said with a tear running down his face. He sat down at the desk and invited the detectives to join him. He looked at Claire.
"I'm sure that you have somehow guessed that we were lovers. That seems such an out of date saying but we were in love. It's surprising but in this day and age there is still a stigma about people like us. We have had the same hopes and aspirations as any couple. We are not that different. I was going to go in with William as an equal partner as soon as we had found a suitable property. As strange as it may seem, William had the lion's share of investment money. He was such a hard worker. I wish that I were like him but I still rely on my parents. How sick is that?

He knew me. He knew what I was before I did. I have no idea how to grieve. I'm not supposed to be like this… like a… I don't have a clue… I… I…"
Lee Winton broke down and cried like a baby. The two detectives couldn't help themselves; they both put their arms around him and comforted him. He cried harder and they felt their own tears falling. It seemed like an age before he stopped crying. The two detectives moved away and wiped their faces, allowing him to compose himself. He apologised to them for the attitude that he had shown them but he had no idea how to control his emotions.

"What you have just done Sir is the start of grieving," Claire said. "You must take a few days off and grieve properly. I'm afraid that it isn't a five-minute job but you must allow the tears to fall. Fuck everyone else Mr Lee-Winton, excuse my French. You are not anything but you. People try to put labels on everyone but that shows their weakness and lack of understanding. You two had a goal in life and some bastard moved the goalposts and left you to carry the burden and the grief. I was wrong about you Sir and I apologise for that. I had a bee in my bonnet and perhaps deep down I missed something that I had forgotten about. Go home Sir. Be who you are for you and no one else.
I'm afraid that there is a search team at Williams flat as we speak. If there is anything that you want please tell me and I will arrange it." She gave him her card. "Please keep in touch. I will let you know when they release Williams remains and we can help with the funeral arrangements. But please go home Sir. She held her hand out for him to shake. He took it and squeezed it tenderly then did the same with Leanne.

“Did you know Detective, that barristers don’t shake hands?” he said tearfully.

“No, I didn’t know. Why is that?”

“It’s just a stupid manly thing that goes back hundreds of years. A load of old bollocks Detective, if you will excuse my French.” They all smiled nervously.

Chapter Five.

Monday 4th July 13:38
Duns Town Police Station

The drive back to the station was full of silence and noisy thoughts for Claire and Leanne. Claire, who was driving, pulled over and stopped at the side of the road, she looked at Leanne tearfully.
"Fuck me Leanne, I've made some real fuck-ups in my time but that was the 'mother lode.' How was I so wrong? How did I mistake his grief for a cocky attitude? How?"

"Don't be so hard on yourself Claire. I was the same. I felt that he was hiding something. Well, he was but not what we thought unless he is playing us both?
How come that someone, who is still being virtually spoon-fed by his parents, has absolutely no idea how to grieve? Maybe that's why he is a prosecutor. Some of those bastards are really nasty, as we know. But where the hell does that leave us? We have to start doing the detective thing and detect."

"Seems that way Leanne. I was expecting so much from Lee-Winton but I too have this nagging feeling at the back of my mind that we have missed something. Something that is staring us in the face. Maybe you are right and he did play us. I think we have to find out about his father and his mother come to that. There doesn't appear to be too many friends floating about either. I hope they find something at William's flat that would point us in the right direction; like a birth certificate, or death certificate even. Or maybe we should get our arses tattooed and join that club?" They both laughed in the hope that it would chase away the tears that were still close by.

"So, ladies," said DCI Kearney, "I never had you down as emotional blubbers. You have certainly enlightened me as far as that goes. You obviously believed Mr Lee-Winton in his moment of apparent weakness? I must reserve my own thoughts on that issue because I have seen prosecution council pull tears to order, with conviction, to gain a conviction. I'll say no more on that point. But watch this space ladies."

"I find it hard to believe that anyone could have pulled that off if it weren't true Frances. I actually felt his grief, felt his sadness, as did Leanne. But saying that there is still that 'copper's gut' telling us both that we may have missed something."

"I suppose he even had a snotty nose to help his story. Some men are getting so much better at that crocodile tears thing. But anyway, enough of the dramatics today what is your next step? I hope that it is real detective work Detectives. Right, I want us all outside I have been putting in a bit of free overtime."

They followed Kearney as she headed towards the white boards, where there was a group of other detectives and uniform looking over the boards and making notes. Kearney stood loud and proud as she called for quiet. "Right, myself and Detective Constable Marlow have both worked hard to find you some carrots to keep your minds on the investigation.

At this moment Marlow is at the premises of Mr William Tell, our shooting victim. But I am expecting him to present me with even more clues in this strange case. Now I want your full, undivided attention to what I am going to tell you. There are a few twists and turns in this story, so listen up. I hope that you have a pen and paper at the ready because I am not going to repeat myself. You see, before you, a list of names, starting with Mr Tell senior. Then…" she stopped when she heard whispering.

"Excuse me," she stood on tiptoes cupping her ears. "Is there someone out there who wishes to take my place here and knows more than I do? I would like that; it would prove that you have been working harder than me so please feel free to stand in my place… No offers? Well, in that case, please have the decency to let me finish talking. I know that you can all read but I want to try and explain why these people are on this board… Thank you.

The second person on the board is William Tell, junior, son of senior. I have proof that they are father and son.

The next person is Petra Tancred, a business partner of William Tell senior. You will notice that there is a question mark next to her name and Tell senior, I will come back to that in a minute or two.

Next, we have Mr Robin Hood, who has worked directly for Tell senior since 1975 as a security consultant. In the nineties, he became a court bailiff at Duns Town Crown Court. But he still worked for Tell and I guess Miss Tancred too.

Next is Mr Dermot Dolan; taxi driver and part-time security consultant for Tell senior and company. He was eighteen or nineteen when he first worked for Tell senior and was still employed, up until his death, alongside William Tell Junior. Mrs Dolan believed that he worked for Lobson Investment Bank but they were only casual customers of his.

Now as you know these people are dead except for, we think, Mr Tell senior. He is probably in his eighties or nineties and we believe that he is in a care home somewhere. I think that we could safely hazard a guess that he is not the sniper or has anything to do with any of the murders but he is of interest to our enquiries.

On the bottom of the board, as you can see, there is a faceless face and a question mark. I believe that face will turn out to be another Tell. A Mr Bernard Barton Tell. Disowned son of Mr William Tell senior. We have absolutely no information about this person. He disappeared in 1982 after his father's accountants caught him embezzling funds from the client's accounts; along with rumours of sexual deviation, and perversion.

From the evidence that I have, Mr Hood and Mr Dolan, persuaded him to vacate the premises but they were a little over-enthusiastic about it. He spent several months in intensive care then subsequently disappeared. We also believe that his girlfriend, at the time, overdosed but that's as far as the evidence goes. He was born in 10-11-57, so he would be about fifty-nine now; young enough to be a murderer because of the secrets that have just come to light.

So, I want a team dedicated to finding him and another team looking for Mr Tell senior. I will supply you with a copy of the evidence that will assist you in that search. DCS Copperstone will allocate the teams. William Tell junior was self-employed and worked for the Travis & London Professional Law Company. It's based in Duns Town, Manchester Street. DCS Copperstone has spoken to them and he is going there to interview Tell's boss."

"Ok back to Miss Petra Tancred. We have heard that she was an intact virgin and that was discovered during her autopsy. Hard to believe in this day and age but it's true. But there is also something else about the late virginal Miss Tancred… She had her audience exactly where she wanted them. They were eager for every word that came out of her mouth. So, what more was there to know about the deceased victim?"
She continued to hold her secret, like a politician, an actor or even a comedian holding her audience, waiting for the punchline.
"Miss Petra Tancred, gave birth to a baby boy, exactly thirty years ago. Yet she had still remained a virgin."
Her audience was gobsmacked at her revelation.

"How the hell was that possible unless her name was Mary?" Claire shouted out followed by everyone else in the room. Kearney held up her hands to silence everyone and waited patiently until the room was once again silent.

"Miss Tancred received artificial insemination from the sperm of Mr William Tell senior under laboratory conditions. She gave birth, via C-section, again under laboratory conditions. She was then under the care of a plastic surgeon, flown in from New York. The resulting scar of the C-section was virtually invisible, especially under the tattoos and that was probably why the coroner had missed it.
But I have asked him to have another look at her abdomen for proof that this happened and of course to double-check that her hymen was truly intact and not a result of the American's plastic surgery."

She waited for more questions but there weren't any. She was about to start speaking again when she saw Claire with her hand up and she acknowledged her.

"Why would anyone go through that pain? What was the reason for it?"

"Good question Claire and here comes the answer to that. It was a wish of the father, William Tell senior that she would have his child. He wanted an heir to leave his vast fortune to but there were also conditions from both parties. Miss Tancred was promised sixty-five million pounds, on her 50th birthday, if she remained a virgin. She would be checked every twelve months. When the child was thirty years old, he or she would inherit the 'kingdom' so to speak. Miss Tancred's contract condition was that she would never have to be a mother to the child and that he or she would never know her identity. The contract was signed by both parties. A third signee was Mrs Gladys Catherine Tell.

When the child was born, he received Mrs Tell's name on his birth certificate but she died a few years later.

The child was bought up by a relative of Mrs Tell in strict secrecy and the child saw very little of his father. He kept him fed and paid for his basic education but he wanted him to find his own way in the world. When he reached thirty everything would come to him.

Miss Tancred was just a couple of months away from receiving her millions. So, I'm hearing you ask, why did she have to remain a virgin? Well that is logical, if she had got pregnant through some another man the deal would be off because the child would be related to the Tell baby and all sorts of court cases would ensue. I'm sure that Miss

Tancred got her jollies some other way. So, I'm sorry that I am going to ask this but are there any questions?"

"So, William Tell deceased is Miss Tancred's son and they are both dead. That points to the disinherited son being the killer" Leanne called out.

"It certainly seems that way, Leanne but we know Jack about this guy."

"But he must have a birth certificate so that we can trace him," Leanne added.

"If he is the killer, chances are he has changed his name; changed everything about himself. If he can't have the money then the pretender to his throne was certainly not getting it. I imagine all this killing is as a result of jealousy?" Claire said.

"Again, I'm afraid it looks that way. Ok people, we all have jobs to do so let's get detecting. But don't forget one of the main facts of this case, we do not know who the intended victim was outside the Crown court; was it William Tell or Dermot Dolan? Keep that question close to your lips guys?"

The other detectives and uniformed officers were once again taking notes and discussing the wanted man. Kearney indicated to Claire and Leanne to follow her to her office. Claire came straight out with the first question.

"I want to know if they have found any paperwork at William's flat. I want to know where the father is being cared for and what happened to the mother. Hopefully, there is a birth or death certificate or we will have to go the hard way and that is time-consuming and costly Frances."

"Funny you should say that Claire. Chris Marlow who, bless his little cotton socks, has been doing some real detecting. He is on his way in with a shedload of paper and a locked laptop, which he is dropping off at Cyber forensics. He said the paperwork is of some interest to the case. I am waiting for confirmation from the Met' for him and another officer to meet at Miss Tancred's flat tomorrow."

No sooner had she said that, when they heard Marlow making his cocksure entrance. He put an armful of paperwork on an empty table and offered his cheesiest smile to Frances. He headed to the office and walked in uninvited, still with his cheesy smile. Frances said nothing but gave him a look that spoke volumes.

"Excuse me Ma'am, sorry to disturb you and for not knocking but I have some papers I think that we should all go through as a matter of urgency."

Thank you, Marlow. Be a sweetie and get me a fresh coffee while I finish my debrief."

"Yes of course Ma'am. I believe that its two sugars and black?"

"No, I keep telling you, Marlow. It's strong, white and no sugar."

"Damn it, so it is, no problem it's on its way Ma'am."

He left the office and trundled to the kitchen humming some tune or other. Claire looked at her with a raised eyebrow.
"I thought you didn't like coffee Frances?"

"Sometimes I do and sometimes I don't. But he should have knocked and waited. No one is too big to forget their manners. Even the people upstairs knock on the door. Right, he is on his way back. Let's go and see what he found and I hope that it's relevant."

Marlow headed back to the table and offered the coffee to Frances. She looked at it and turned her nose up. He put it down on another desk, his feelings well and truly hurt.
"Ok, Marlow lets go through with your evidence. What have you found?" She was interrupted by her office phone ringing. "Carry on without me. I'll have to take that. Tell them what you have Marlow."

"I have; a birth certificate, a death certificate of, I think, his mother and some bank and insurance documents. There was a cross shredder filled to the brim. I poured it into a waste bin and I dropped that off at forensics along with the laptop, but they weren't very convinced that they could use the shreds. They started working on the laptop straight away. So, I'm hoping there is enough information to help us crack the case."
Claire picked out the birth and death certificate from the pile of papers. The birth certificate belonged to William Tell. born 01-07- 86. It had both his parent's names on it. William Ascot Vladimir Tell and Gladys Catherine Tell.

The death certificate was of Gladys Catherine Tell, born 09-09-1937, deceased 07-10-1992; death by misadventure. Callison stared once more at the birth certificate.

"How the fuck…" she shouted out. "It was his birthday the day he died. Exactly thirty years old and no one said a fucking word! Lee fucking Winton said fuck all about his, supposedly best friend's, birthday.
William senior was born 02-03-36. William's mother died aged fifty-five when he was six years old, yet… so… something is so not right here. These dates what am I missing here?"

Kearney rejoined them looking rather pleased with herself. "I have just spoken with the lawyer of Miss Tancred. He wishes to meet me, at her apartment in London, at lunchtime tomorrow. DCS Copperstone and I will travel up to speak to him and take the opportunity to search through her property along with officers of the Met'. Apparently, there are papers of a rather delicate nature that she had been working on from home. Right, so what have I missed?"

"Look at these two certificates Frances. Check out the dates, am I missing something? It was his birthday when he died. How strange is that?"
Kearney looked at the documents and shook her head, then handed them to Leanne.

"I can't see anything wrong there Claire, it all seems Kosher to me. A pure coincidence that he died on his birthday. It happens and it's pretty much verified by the evidence we have. Maybe we can check out the death by misadventure call. It's been a long time Claire. It's all paperwork that gets chewed up by worms but we will follow it up."

"Apparently, according to Lee-Witney, Tell's mother was a whore. Death by misadventure when she had a six-year-old kid, why would he even say that? Why didn't he just say that she died when his friend was just a child? Are there any more official documents in those papers Chris, legal or otherwise?"

"Only his legal barrister documents, driving licence ID, for the courts and utility bills. There are no bank cards or any banking documents. They must be in his wallet at the morgue or on his laptop."

"If there was a wallet, we would have had it passed over to us and I don't believe that a wallet has been produced as evidence. There is nothing else in that paperwork that a normal 30-year-old would have, cluttering up his flat. Especially a barrister who is saving up to buy a business"

She was interrupted by Kearney's office phone ringing again. Kearney excused herself. Whilst she went to answer the phone, Claire sifted through the paperwork again and again.

"I thought that you had more evidence than that Chris. There is, in fact, very little here that would make any difference to this case. Are you sure you searched everywhere in his flat?"

"Honestly Claire, the flat is so small. it's too small to call a flat. There is no cupboard space or any hidey-hole. There are no carpets to look under; it's all Ikea furniture, if you can call a table, two chairs and a recliner chair, furniture? And, before you ask, we searched every inch of the recliner. In fact, anywhere else that would hide even a USB flash drive. We covered everything. I thought that the certificates would help but I'm sure that everything is on the laptop."

"I'm sorry Chris it's just…"

She was again interrupted by Kearney heading towards them and not too happy.
"That was the 'cyber-men.' They opened the laptop and found that it had been erased but they managed to find out the day and the time that it was erased; Friday the 1st of July at 17:45. William had been long dead by that time. Six hours to be precise. Whoever erased it has done a proper job. They doubt that, even with their skills and technology, they can rescue it. But if it comes to it, we may have to ask the spooks to help us."

Claire looked at Leanne and they both looked at Kearney.
"I've got a very sneaky suspicion that Lee-fucking Wilton has more to tell us… a lot more. Can we get a warrant to search his flat, which by all accounts is very close to Williams flat?"

"What evidence have you got Claire? Nothing, I can't get a warrant just because your guts are tingling. All you can do is arrange to speak to him again but watch out for his snotty nose." She laughed. Chris Marlow was waiting for someone to tell him the joke but Kearney was on her way back to the office and Claire and Leanne left the exit door swinging behind them.

“Bastard… bastard… fucking slimy-faced bastard” Claire said as she headed towards Lee-Winton’s flat, her blues and twos flashing. She was banging the steering wheel with her fist and cursing herself for falling for the tears. “Leanne, if you are ever with me again and a man cries in front of me… if I don’t hit him first, just fucking Taser me.”

“Listen Claire, just chill. Don’t let him get to you. The mood you are in could lose you your job and no tosser is worth that. He caught both of us. He knew which buttons to press. If he knows that he can make you like this, he will be harder to break. Don’t give him the ammunition to hurt you, please.”
Claire looked over at her best mate and knew that she was right. She slowed down, turned off the blues and twos and started to breathe normally.
“Kearney knew it, Leanne. Somehow, she knew that we were well and truly fucked by that bastard. How the fuck did she know?”

“Experience Claire. That’s why she is where she is and also the fact that she doesn’t trust anyone. She is good and so are we. It won’t happen again, that’s for sure.” They both laughed as they got nearer to Lee-Winton’s flat. She stopped the car and phoned Lee-Winton but he didn’t answer. She phoned the Crown Court. They said that he had gone home, after they had left him, and that he was visibly upset.

“He isn’t at work. So, he must be at home patting himself on the back.”

“We could insinuate that we had a search warrant, Claire.”

“No, the wanker is too smart for that. He knows that we have fuck all on him. He will call our bluff straight away. No, I’ll try and talk to him normally. He doesn’t know what we know about the laptop.”

“Sorry Claire, I have to disagree with you there. If he is guilty, he will know that we know about the laptop.”

“Oops, good point partner. You are getting better at this job. I will have to watch my step or you will start ordering me about... more than usual.”

Monday 4th July 16:45
Blue House Apartments

They parked the car in the ‘emergency vehicles only’ box and went and rang the entrance bell to Lee-Witney’s block. There was no answer so they rang all nine bells. The buzzer buzzed and the door unlocked.
They stood outside Lee-Winton’s flat and knocked heavily on the door but there was no answer. Leanne opened the letterbox and was about to shout when she noticed blood in the hallway. She couldn’t see anything else so she called it in asking for ambulance and supervisor. Claire tried shouldering the door open but found it too painful. They had to wait for emergency services to gain access to the flat.

"I think he topped himself Leanne. It all got too much for him. He knew that we had caught him out and he bottled it. He didn't want mummy and daddy embarrassed in front of their friends."
The caretaker had turned up, opened the door and was about to go in but he was stopped by both detectives. Claire took the master key from him and sent him on his way. They looked through the open door. There was certainly a lot of blood that had not yet congealed. They decided not to go any further until the supervisor had turned up. Whoever that might be?"

DCS Denver Copperstone arrived with Jack Samms and the SOCO team; who put stepping blocks on the floor and followed the blood into the living room/kitchen. They went into the bathroom and then returned to the waiting detectives with the news that there was no body in the building but there was sufficient blood loss to cause death from exsanguination. They declared it a crime scene and returned inside the flat with their kit, taking samples and fingerprints.
"As it's a crime scene Sir I want to see every bit of evidence that comes out of that flat and I require a search warrant for his office in the Crown Court."

"You don't need a warrant Claire but the place is closed so you will have to wait until the morning. There are no blood marks anywhere else in or around the exterior of the building, so it's another dead end."

"I think that we should look inside William's flat. I just have a feeling that we may find something in there. Whoever it is, knew that we had searched his flat and left with virtually nothing. So where would you hide a body?" She held up the master key.

"Ok Claire but give the key to SOCO, just in case there is something in there. I hope not. I think we have had more than our share of deaths so far. Four definite bodies in four days. It's a bloody massacre."

She gave the key to one of the SOCO technicians and they went into William's flat. They came out shortly afterwards with the news that there was no body but there were bloody footprints scattered throughout the flat as if someone were searching for something.
There was very little anyone could do until SOCO had finished and handed the two flats over to them. Copperstone told them to go home and get some rest. They both agreed but nevertheless, took a wasted journey to the Crown Court, just in case. But it was all locked up.

Tuesday 5th July 09:00
Blue House Apartments

Claire and Leanne, turned up at Lee-Winton's residence and found Copperstone already there, talking on his phone. He acknowledged the two detectives; they gave him privacy and distance to finish that call.
He was pacing up and down and waving his arms about. It was obvious that someone had upset him. Finally, he finished the call. With his back to the two women, he wiped his brow he started to calm down and compose himself. He then turned around and smiled at the two detectives.

"Thank you and forgive me for keeping you waiting. I'm afraid that was the Big Chief on the phone asking, how far away we were from cracking the case. It was my fault. I sent him a report of the evidence DCI Kearney had found and now he thinks that the murderer is hiding around the corner within arm's reach; even though we have no idea who he is or what he looks like. I'm afraid he didn't like my answer.
Unfortunately, I can only be here for a short time. DCI Kearney and I are going to see Miss Tancred's flat and speak to her legal advisor. To be perfectly honest I would rather not go but pressure from upstairs deems it so. Anyway, I am curious, as to what we might find here. Before I forget, I went to Tell's law firm yesterday and we searched through his previous clients. There was nothing that stood out, unless he had private clients that he had advised. But it isn't looking good."

"Why doesn't that surprise me? Did SOCO find anything in either of the flats Sir?"

"Well they never found a body but they found some strange goings-on at both flats. Shall we go and see?"

Copperstone opened the door of Lee-Winton's flat and the stale smell of blood hit them full-on. They saw the dried blood on the floor and stepping blocks laid out by SOCO. The two women looked around, not only as detectives but they cast their female eyes over the choice of décor or rather the lack of it. The surfaces had residues of fingerprint dust and on the floor were bloody footprints that looked as if they were made on purpose. Leanne looked in the kitchen cupboards and shook her head at what she saw.

"I've heard of minimalistic but this kitchen makes a normal minimalist look like a hoarder. There are two of everything; exactly half of a dinner service, a set of saucepans and tins of soup. Half a cutlery set, two egg cups, two of everything… is more than weird. Any bets that the freezer is full of microwave meals?"

"Maybe he split the dinner service with William." Claire said as she searched through the empty drawers. "This looks like a flat that has been prepared to put on the market. The cooker is bloody spotless or maybe unused and normal people stuff all sorts of rubbish into a kitchen drawer."

They walked into the living room, which was almost bare. Understandably really because there was very little room. A small armchair sat in the corner facing a small TV that was placed on top of what looked like a bedside cabinet. There was no paperwork or any proof that anyone had ever lived there.

They went into the bedroom which was a fair size. A large double bed sat in the centre of the room with a single bedside cabinet that matched the TV stand in the living room.

The wardrobe was half-full of shirts, suits and trousers, with pleats sharp enough to cut steak. At the bottom of the wardrobe were three pairs of shiny black brogues and one pair of brown slip-on shoes.

The bed looked as if it had been used recently and was left unmade, which was in total contrast to the rest of the flat.

Copperstone pulled back the duvet cover to reveal a bare mattress with red circles all over it.
"It seems that this was the lover's bed. The sheet and mattress protector have been taken away for DNA testing. It would seem that as far as the rest of the flat was immaculately presented, the bed had not seen the laundry service for quite a while."
The two women shivered and pulled faces at the thought. They slowly backed out of the room. They went into the bathroom and it too was immaculate. Apart from the bed and the crazy footprints on the floor it looked as if the flat was seldom used. Claire looked around and then looked at Copperstone.

"It appears to me that these bloody footprints and the fingerprints everywhere were left on purpose. Do you know how many different sets of prints there were here?"

"SOCO are pretty sure that there are four sets of prints. They are searching the database as we speak. I haven't been into Mr Tell's flat but I'm afraid I have to go now. I will leave you two to it."

"Just one more thing Sir. There is all this blood on the floor and plenty of it. But there is no evidence of a fight or altercation; no broken furniture, no scrapes on the floor or walls, in fact, there is nothing at all that says anything happened here. Nothing at all."

"That's exactly what SOCO said. But I think that between the two of you and the two flats, you may come across what SOCO missed. I'm sorry but I really must go."

Copperstone left and the two women went to William Tells' flat. The minute they opened the door, as with Winton's flat, the smell of blood hit them.
They followed the stepping boards and they saw that the flat was identical to Winton's flat, except exactly the opposite. Like a mirrored reflection. The blood was plentiful, all dried and giving off those sickly fumes. Footprints and fingerprint dust were prevalent in every room and they saw, that as in Winton's kitchen, William had two of everything also. They looked in the bathroom, it was immaculately clean. The bedroom was equally sparse in furniture and with a similar amount of clothes in the wardrobe. But the bed and the red circles pointed out that the two men shared everything between them.
"Ok, Leanne. We have seen both flats and saw no sign of any damage that one would expect to be associated with all this blood. So, your thoughts on the matter?"

"I think that someone is taking the piss. All these footprints and fingerprints, someone is purposely playing with us. There is no way that all this blood could even come out of one body. This is just a wild guess Claire, well more of an educated guess; I don't even think that it's human blood. Someone has gone to a lot of trouble to try and either confuse us or is somewhere close by laughing at us. With no disrespect to Copperstone, there is no way that we will find anything that closely resembles evidence in these two flats."

"I think that you have got it all sussed out Leanne and I think that you are absolutely bang on. So, let's go and have a full English and try and work out what, whoever they are, wants us, or expects us to do."

They sat and ate a hearty but late breakfast and looked at the printout that Kearney had given them from Robin Hood's Diary. They both made notes as they read it and then ordered more tea.
"Where has this Bernard Barton Tell been all this time and what has he been doing? He studied law but never finished his education. He found it easier stealing Daddies clients' money. If he was a crook maybe he knew where he could get a false ID and maybe false papers that would allow him to maybe practice law; or just turned into a murderer to prevent William and his mother from getting their prize." Leanne said, still making notes.

"It's possible of course that he left the country after he disappeared from the hospital, as he was advised to do by Hood and Dolan. Then he returned as the big payday got nearer. I'm pretty sure that he was close enough to observe everyone and he had plenty of time to plan it but the big question is how does Lee-Winton fit into this? He never shot William and Dolan but I'm sure that he has a partner, as in Bernard Barton Tell."

"So, Claire, a question? What if this Bernard Tell was killed before he could make his escape? Hood and Dolan came pretty close to killing him and got away with it. They could have snatched him from the hospital and finished the job. Hood is not going to confess to that in his diary, C.V or whatever it was."

"Jesus, Leanne. If that happened, we would have absolutely fuck all to go on. I mean even less than we have now. As it is, we are only guessing that Bernard Tell is the suspect, with absolutely no evidence. We have nothing else except Lee-Winton and to be honest, we have nothing at all on him; except keeping a few secrets from us about his boyfriend and having something to do with staging his own disappearance. Now I think the obvious move would be to try and get a warrant to get Winton's details from the CPS and his bank. But as Kearney said, we have nothing on him. We can at least find out who owns the flats that they were both in. I believe that they were rented or leased. We can find out that information back at the station, from the Land Registry. From there we can find out who they rent it from. But first, there is something that I want to check out."

The two detectives returned to the Blue House Apartments, went into both flats and started making notes. Then they went outside and took pictures on their phones. Claire headed back towards the car but was then called back by Leanne who was looking at the pavement. She pointed to something. They both took pictures of it and Leanne found something else that caught her attention. They both took more pictures, had a look around but could not see anything else. They returned to the car; Claire patted Leanne on the shoulder.
"Thank God for your eyesight Sergeant Gavin. Finally, a solid clue. Well done!"

They drove off and disappeared around a corner.
Less than a minute after they had left the area, a small dark grey hatchback car pulled up outside the Blue House Apartments. A middle-aged gentleman alighted from the vehicle, looked around and then started looking at the area on the pavement that the detectives were taking pictures

of. He couldn't see anything and suddenly realised that he had fallen hook line and sinker into a trap. He literally, dived back into his car, floored it and then disappeared just as Claire and Leanne appeared and started chasing him. The driver of the hatchback obviously knew the area better than they did and vanished.
"Please tell me that you got the registration number Leanne"

"Got it, and also the make of car. It's a Nissan Micra. I'm gonna get an address. I got the driver too but it isn't very clear, it was too far away. But what a clever move Claire and what an idiot he was for falling for it."

"I had an idea that he may be close by. The CCTV cameras that were there in the flats were a dead giveaway. He probably heard everything that we and SOCO said. Call it in Leanne and let's go hunting."

Leanne excitedly called in the registration number, only to find out that the car had been stolen from a car park earlier in the day, whilst the owner was at work as a baker, in the supermarket. They took the address of the man who had his car stolen and paid him a visit. The gentleman in question looked nothing like the man who had driven it earlier but they took his details, just in case. They both returned to the car and shrugged their shoulders.
"Shit happens! We were that close Leanne. Let's take your picture and see if we can get it blown up and get the old facial recognition doo dah on to it…"

She was interrupted by her phone ringing, she stopped the car and answered it.

"Ok, that's great news… Oh, I see. Ok, we are on our way back anyway. See you in a minute.
That was Marlow, the footprints from Winton and Tell's flats matched the bloody footprints at Dolan's house, around Hood's body. The fingerprints have pinged up but there is a problem. He said it would be better if he explained exactly what that problem was when we turn up. It looks as though we will soon find out who the killer is."

Claire and Leanne walked into the detective's area and saw Marlow pacing backwards and forwards. He looked far from happy. He was on the phone, he saw Callison and said goodbye to whoever it was that he was talking to.
"Ok, Marlow, your face looks like a slapped arse. What's the problem exactly?"

"Well, SOCO found four sets of fingerprints at Lee-Winton's and William Tell's flats. They pinged up. Two of the sets of prints belong to a Mr Robin Hood and a Mr Dermot Dolan. The other two sets of prints belong to a Gordon Grafton and a Richard Starkey; two petty thieves both with form as long as your legs,"
he said looking at Claire's legs.

"Arms, Marlow. It's as long as your arm, not legs and not my legs," Claire said angrily."

"I'm sorry Guv, just a slip of the tongue. There is a search going on for them as we speak, but how the hell did the other two get their prints there when they are brown fucking bread?"

"Well I wouldn't pay too much attention to those prints. They were either there before their demise or our murderer planned this, took their prints and left them so that we could find them. He is fucking with us but I can't understand the other two leaving their prints? Anyway, we think that we saw him. Leanne has a picture of who we think it is. We set a trap and he fell for it but he was too fast for us. We have his picture. Let's get it printed out."

Chapter Six.

Friday, July 1st 10-30
Duns Town, Town Hall

A man, carrying a briefcase, stood outside a pair of large internal oak doors, on the top floor of the Town Hall. The doors were from another time and had been rescued and reused before the 'recycle' became such a common everyday word. The wood was heavy; held up by three large brass hinges either side.
The handles and the large shiny plates on both doors were made from brass that had ornate rolled and scrolled edging. The ancient Patina on the doors showed a long history of usage. Many secrets had been discussed in the chambers on the other side of the doors, by Mayor's past and the many council leaders and of course their opposition.
He took off a glove and gently touched the wooden door, with a certain adoration and respect for the skill and professionalism of the carpenters, who he knew were now long dead. He t followed the action by pressing an ear against it as if trying to hear the ghostly goings-on of arguments in the chamber from years long gone. He made a fist and was going to knock on the door but he changed his mind and smiled. He knew that the room was empty. He let his hand slide slowly down the wood, savouring the texture, the patina, the history, whilst he had the chance, for he might never get another.
He replaced his glove and withdrew a large shiny but ancient brass key from his pocket and placed it inside the door lock and turned the key slowly, feeling the vibrations

of the lock being moved. He replaced the key in his pocket and turned the handle. He felt the old mechanism of the door handle moving smoothly.

The old door squeaked momentarily as he opened it. He felt the heaviness and the age of the door. He smelt the mustiness of old leather and ancient cigar smoke, that seemed to come from the equally ancient carpet, and modern furniture polish. Not the beeswax smell that he had anticipated.

In the centre of the room was a very large, long, empty oval table with a light film of dust that looked like a sheet of polythene had been placed over it to protect it. He took a small rolled-up cotton sheet out of his pocket and laid it on the table. He then laid his briefcase onto the sheet and undid the zips either side. He walked over to the large bay window that overlooked the town centre, a sight that only the chosen few had seen before. He checked that the window wasn't alarmed and opened it slightly, then closed it again.

He returned to his briefcase and picked up one of twenty-four pieces that were encased in foam within. He began to assemble the pieces, mostly through memory. Every now and again he would glance at his watch and smile at his steady progress.

Less than ten minutes later, he had finished assembling all the pieces. He tightened the occasional screw and finally, he had the finished object in his hand. The rifle was a one-off handmade powerful sniper shot. Made purely from a 3D printer, based on the AK47. It would only ever fire one shot, because of the delicacy of the breach and barrel. The powerful bullet that it would shoot out would distort the whole weapon.

He used a portable laser to check the straightness and aim of the barrel. He had no doubts about the rifle. He had made three previously that were all a hundred percent accurate. He was a professionally trained gunsmith, amongst other things. Killing was another skill that he had learnt first-hand.
He walked over to the window and opened it wide; he took a single bullet from his pocket and kissed it. It was a special bullet that was loaded with a secondary charge that would detonate when the bullet hit its victim.
He looked at his watch and then looked through the telescope and found his target standing there as he was ordered to do. He saw the leaves of the tree between him and the target moving in and out of his sight. He wasn't worried. Once the rifle was 'sighted' he could pull the trigger with his eyes closed.
He looked at his watch again, two minutes before he would have to start steadying his breathing, which was a vital part of the exercise. Everything was arranged, everything was timed and in exactly five minutes the deed would be done.
He put on a pair of gloves that went up to his armpits, covering the sleeves of his jacket. He was finally in position. The barrel rested on the balcony. He would be there for five minutes and there was only one building that overlooked his position, a car park on the roof of the mall but he had paid some junkies to keep the area clear. He was pretty confident that he would go unnoticed.
He steadied his breathing and concentrated on the task in front of him. It was extremely important that he hit exactly what he aimed at. If nothing else it would confuse the police about who was the actual target. He could hear the inbuilt clock in his brain; the seconds ticking down, ten,

nine, eight, he prepared himself, five, four, he touched the trigger, two, one, zero, he gently squeezed the trigger. He looked at his target and smiled to himself. A perfect hit; two birds.

He picked up the spent shell and put it in his jacket pocket it was still hot, he closed the door, and started to disassemble the rifle, and replaced the pieces back into the briefcase.

He rolled up the cotton sheet, put it in his jacket pocket and then he took off the long gloves, put them into the briefcase and closed it up. He put on another pair of gloves, looked around, went back through the large oak doors and locked them behind him. He touched the doors tenderly, one last time, and smiled, knowing that there was yet another secret behind them.

The man carrying a briefcase went down the posh marble stairway and disappeared amongst the many people that were going about their everyday business.

He exited the town hall, via a virtually unknown emergency tunnel, used by the Mayor in case of terrorist attack. It led to a stairway that exited into the centre of the Mall car park. He knew where the CCTV cameras were located and he walked with his head tilted down. He clicked a remote control which unlocked a Range Rover. He climbed into the car and waited.

The man waited patiently. He listened to the local news. After fifteen minutes, he was joined by another man who looked rather scruffy and dishevelled. He sat in the passenger seat and put on his seat belt. Without speaking, the man began to drive and exited the car park.

Friday, July 1st 16:00
Dermot Dolan's House.

The man driving the Range Rover drove through the older part of Duns Town. It still had a large section of detached and semi-detached Victorian houses that were over-expensive and costly to run; with alleyways conveniently placed all around them, like rat runs that made suitable escape routes for burglars, rapists, and ne'er do wells. There was no public CCTV. Only the posher houses had the luxury of being able to record who was burgling them. Duns Town had grown over the centuries from being a rural farming area, into a major industrial town, that imported goods all over the world. Houses, in and around the town, were built to house the many workers who had flocked there in Victorian and Edwardian times, and even into the sixties. It thrived, at the height of industrial growth, until the unions had slowly destroyed all that was good in the town. But still, the ever-expanding town encircled the antique homes. 'Modernisation' knew no bounds.

The Range Rover pulled onto the drive of Mr Dermot Dolan, 22, Queens Road, Duns Town. The drive had started out its life, as a hedged garden at the front of the house. But in line with other householders, they concreted over the once green and pleasant piece of land.
"What are we doing here, Mr Bee. This is not the plan" said his passenger.

"Relax Robin. I need to tie up a couple of bits and pieces before I take you home."

“I’m sorry Mr Bee. It’s just that I have a feeling that something bad is going to happen.”

“Nothing is going to happen. You have paid back what you owed me. We are all square. You can go back to your boring mediocre life and die happily of old age, without having to constantly look over your shoulder; secure in the knowledge that you no longer owe me anything. Your debt is paid in full.”

“Thank you, Sir. I… I really do not know what it is that I err… that I have erm… actually done for you, to warrant you err… cancelling the debt; except to follow your directions to act suspiciously in front of the CCTV camera’s. But if you are happy to accept that as a debt paid then I am glad and I will be able to sleep at night. All that I ask now, is that we hurry and then I can finally return to my dear wife, who, as you know is close to the end.”

“I just need you to give me a hand with something that I need to do. I can’t do it on my own. Just come inside for five minutes and it will be all over.”

Robin followed the man with some trepidation. He just wanted to see the back of this man, who had threatened to take his wife’s life and looked forward to being reunited with her. Bee stepped inside the house and then stopped to put on the light. He gently pushed Robin forward and laughed. Robin felt Mr Bee’s hand on his shoulder and was surprised to feel a sudden sharp pain in his neck. He turned and saw him holding a syringe and smiling fiendishly at him.

"That is just to relax you Robin. You really didn't think that I would let you off as easily as that did you?"
Mr Bee dragged Robin into the centre of the front room of the house and roughly manhandled him into a chair. Robin was paralysed but he could still breathe and move his eyes. He tried as hard as he could but his body ignored his attempts to move.
He watched, helplessly, as Bee took a handful of shotgun shells and dropped them on the floor underneath the chair. He seemed to be nervous as he loaded the shotgun. He slid a plastic sheet with writing on it directly underneath him. Robin tried to read the writing before it was placed there but he couldn't because his eyes were now reacting to the injection. His movement was restricted. He did however, see Mr Bee disappear briefly. He screamed silently as he saw Mr Bee reappear wearing a larger than life overcoat. He carried a shotgun which he placed in between Robin's legs, with the barrel inches from his face.
"Your debt to me is almost paid Robin. You, my father, and that bastard Dolan, caused me to lose so much. You caused me the loss of my mother's love and the future that was my inheritance, my destiny. Yes, I have found out so much and I had to bide my time all these years; protecting someone who you had also tried to kill. You fuelled my father's already sick and perverted mind with your fabricated lies; with your arse licking and all for the Judas purse that he and that other lying, twisted, bastard dangled in front of your greedy faces. He, my father, will be the last one to go. I'm making sure that he will suffer every last second of his hypocritical and perverted life. It gives me great joy to put my father where his mind is now imprisoned. He is, to give him his due, still as sharp as shit. But thanks to some South American Indians, I have

his mind in my pocket. He is aware of every sensation and you can see the tears run down his face when he shits himself. It gives me… well, what it gives me… that's between me and my maker."
He laughed, almost maniacally. His eyes filled with evil and the need to kill.
"But there is yet another that will feel my vengeance. He is responsible for a lot of evil things and he is nervous now. He knows that I am coming. He knows that vengeance will be slow and painful. Dolan has already taken the express road to hell, along with that bastard, my half-brother; the test tube child of the woman who is herself in the darkness and waiting for you. Yes, she has gone before you and you will see her in just a few seconds. It gives me a sense of satisfaction that you will all soon be reunited and where you belong.
Oh, please forgive me Robin, I do tend to ramble on sometimes, a bit of a drama queen, so I have been told. Oh yes… I remember that it was you that told me that, when you dragged me kicking and screaming thirty-four years ago and then kicked the shit out of me. But never mind, I will end it now for you and concentrate on the job in hand. But I must say Robin, after all this time, being silent… it's good to talk!"

"I'm awfully afraid that this is more awkward than I thought, at first. I am going to need a little assistance, a little help with the trigger pulling thingy. Sharing is caring as they say but we will get there. Oh, and by the way your wife… she is alive and well… as long as she doesn't try to get out of bed."
Mr Bee laughed when he saw the tears fill Robin's eyes. They were tears, not for himself but for his wife.

He took off the overcoat and held it up between himself and Robin. He placed Robins thumb on the trigger and held it in place with his own thumb.
"I would like to say this isn't going to hurt Robin but how the fuck would I know that? Are you ready? Ok, say cheese."
Mr Bee threw the blood-covered overcoat on the floor. He purposely stepped in the pool of blood and walked around the chair, leaving a trail of bloody footprints heading out of the back door. Then he disappeared into the labyrinth of alleyways that surrounded the Victorian houses.

Chapter Seven.

Tuesday 5th July 12:45
Paddington, London

Kearney and Copperstone arrived at the Mayfair Towers building, in Paddington, London. It was a large Victorian building that had been reinvented as high-priced homes for the rich, famous and the odd infamous ex-bank robber. They were met outside by two Metropolitan uniformed police officers and a man, in civilian clothing, who rushed forward to introduce himself and the police officers.
"My name is Leonard Gail, and this is Constable Robert Janson and Sergeant Mick Rickman, from the Metropolitan Police. I am the legal representative for Miss Tancred and I would just like to say that there are some very sensitive documents in Miss Tancred's apartment. We would appreciate it if they were not looked at. I understand that you could easily get a warrant to inspect the documents but I assure you that they were not in any way connected to her sad demise."

"Murder, Mr Gail," interrupted Copperstone. She was murdered by someone who used their bare hands… sorry gloved hands to take her life and we are pretty sure that we know who that person was. Just to set matters straight, we foresaw that you would try and prevent us from examining Miss Tancred's possessions. As you now know she is a murder victim and we do not need a warrant but I managed to obtain one, as soon as you called DCI Kearney yesterday Mr Gail.
You will be there to oversee us; we are not interested in anything that does not concern this investigation Sir. But

new evidence has come to light and we have to act on that evidence as I'm sure you will understand?"

Kearney was more than a little annoyed that Copperstone had pulled rank and jumped in when he did. She was all fired up and ready to give Leonard Gail a piece of her mind. As they followed Gail to Tancred's apartment building, Copperstone apologised. He knew that she would not hold back at telling the pompous lawyer where to go. She accepted his apology and smiled, knowing that he was right. He probably saved her from embarrassment and the many fences that Gail would erect to make their job harder than it needed to be.

They followed Gail into the reception area. He nodded to the desk clerk and proceeded to the lift. He pressed on the numbered pad and the lift doors opened. The five entered the lift and the doors closed, within a couple of seconds the lift door opened, they all exited and walked towards apartment number 9a. Gail punched in another set of numbers and the door opened silently on its own.

The party entered the flat and instantly Kearney thought of the Tardis. The entrance hall was big enough inside to build a bungalow and still have enough room to park a car. Being a detective, being a woman and being downright nosey; Kearney asked for a tour of the apartment first so that she knew where everything was. Gail was about to refuse but he saw Copperstone staring at him and then pulling the search warrant out of his pocket. He obliged Kearney's request and gave her a guided tour; satisfying her feminine and enquiring curiosity.

The apartment was big beyond belief. How could someone live in such a large building on her own? The thought that it could house many homeless people struck her as she saw the vastness of each room, the wasted space that meant nothing to people who were beyond rich and beyond caring.

After the tour they ended up in the study, where there were white filing cabinets all along one wall. There were printers and copiers along another wall and a desk and chairs along a third wall. In the centre of the study were four white leather sofas, that faced each other making a square shape. There was a coffee table exactly in the centre. The study looked cold in comparison to the rest of the apartment. Maybe to remind Miss Tancred that when she was in the study, it was purely to work and not for comfort.

"Mr Gail, I wonder if it would be possible to move the desk into the middle where the coffee table is and then we can make a start looking through the documents. I suggest starting with the filing cabinet furthest away from us and then as we get tired, we have less distance to walk. Does that make sense to you Sir and is that a possibility?"

"Might I suggest that if you tell me what you are looking for Detective, then I may be able to help you find whatever it is you are searching for. I am very familiar with Miss Tancred's files and her filing system. I have a good idea where everything is."

"That is very kind of you Sir but the truth is that I have no idea what I am looking for. I will know when I see it. I think that we will start the search at the beginning. That way we will have more chance of finding whatever it is that will help us to reveal the answers, to so many questions that are still formulating in my mind. So, the desk in the middle then Mr Gail?"

Copperstone tried to hide his smile as he assisted the two police officers in moving the very heavy oak desk, into the position required by Kearney. Gail stood and watched, under the pretence that he was writing notes in his little book but soon stopped writing when the job was done. The first filing cabinet was opened and everything that began with 'A' was looked through. The constable sat beside Kearney and the Sergeant beside Copperstone. Gail watched their every movement, with eyes that were as sharp as an eagle.

The search was long and laborious. It took an hour to go through the 'A files' and as is often the case with paper files they released a certain amount of dust.
"I suppose refreshments are not heading this way anytime soon Mr Gail? It's rather dry and dusty here," Kearney said with her usual bluntness.

"I believe there are tea making facilities in the kitchen Detective Kearney but I must point out that we will not be held responsible for any damage that occurs as a result of you entering into the kitchen. Also, any damage to the said kitchen will result in a compensation request by ourselves," Gail replied with a smirky grin.
Kearney stood up, walked over to the window and looked out at the shops across the road. She then walked back, staring Gail to death. She sat down and said to the constable sitting beside her, who himself looked a little thirsty.
"I don't suppose that you would do me a very great favour Constable Janson. Would you mind going across the road and getting us some refreshments, if I make a list for you?"

“There is no need for me to go over to there and waste time, Ma’am. I took the liberty of taking their phone number when we were waiting downstairs. I can order it and they will deliver it, if that is ok with you Ma’am?”

“Upon my soul, it is so refreshing to see a forward-thinking copper these days. I bet that you are as thirsty as I am and had the foresight to be prepared. Thank you, officer Janson. Right, now who wants what? My treat, including you Mr Gail.”

Leonard Gail had got on the wrong side of Kearney, but it never fazed him. It was water off a duck’s back. He was watching the time and he didn’t want to spend longer than was necessary, watching these people looking at paperwork. It grieved him that they had the audacity, to stop and have refreshments delivered. They would be consuming those refreshments in the study and wasting even more time.

He tried to get them to go faster but his attempts seemed to have the opposite effect. The documents, that they were inspecting, seemed to have got thicker in content. As they arrived at the ‘D’ section, he had had enough. He looked at his watch, it was 17:25.

“I am afraid that I must now bring this search to a close. Whether you have found anything or not Detectives, I have to go I’m afraid. I have a family to get home to.”

“Then I suggest that you make arrangements with your family Sir. We are nowhere near finished and we will not leave here until every inch has been searched. It isn’t something that we can walk from once we have started, as it clearly states in the search warrant. May I remind you

Sir, that the owner of this apartment has had her life cruelly taken away from her. We are all, except for you, doing our darndest to find anything that can lead us to her killer, or killers; regardless of how long that takes. Do you understand Sir? I don't want to be here out of choice. I have to be here, it is my job and as I have said, now that we have started, we have to stay until completion.
So, if you wish to leave us here then I suggest that you go home to your family, have a sleep and re-join us in the morning. We intend to work all night if need be. Are we good on that point Sir?" Copperstone said, his face going red at the stupidity of the man.

"I'm afraid that it's more than my job is worth leaving you here alone with such important paperwork and valuables. Incidentally, Miss Tancred is not the owner of this property it belongs to Tell holdings. Miss Tancred was just a guest, while she worked for us."
Kearney, Copperstone and the two uniformed officers stood up at Gail's outburst but Kearney was the first to speak.

"I wish that I had recorded that outburst Sir but I must warn you that I am now recording this. You have just said that the four police officers in this room are not to be trusted. Is that right Sir?"

"I never actually said that I said that. It is more than my job is worth to leave anyone here without my being present."

"And what about when you mentioned and I quote, *Important paperwork and valuables* and that *Miss*

Tancred was only a guest in this apartment while she worked for you. Not that Miss Tancred had a full partnership in the firm."

"I apologise, I did say that but in the heat of the moment. This apartment is owned solely by Mr William Tell and Miss Tancred was a long-time guest. I did not wish to insinuate that you could not be trusted officers. I must just clarify that point."

"I am starting to believe that you may know more than you let on Mr Gail and you are trying to prevent us from accessing vital information for reasons known only to yourself. I am not sure what experience you have of working alongside police officers, Mr Gail but we are here, at your personal invitation.
The Metropolitan Police and the Three Counties police, as a joint task force, are investigating more than just the murder of Miss Tancred. It concerns other individuals who have also lost their lives at the hands of some homicidal maniac. They are all connected Sir, by Mr William Tell and his associates.
There are certain questions that I wish to ask you and I hope that you will make yourself available to answer them in a forthright and truthful manner. Mr Gail, we need you to work alongside us to find the answers, not to keep putting up walls that do nothing but point suspicion your way. So, what say you Mr Gail?"

"I think that you are in the wrong job Detective Kearney. I apologise. I have great respect for the law and I deeply apologise for giving you cause for suspicion. I have worked very closely with Miss Tancred for many years.

She taught me many things. She was my Father's and Mr Tell's light and guided us all. This apartment has so many good personal memories for me. I know that you have a job to do and I just forgot how much you would have to do to search for answers. All I saw were strangers touching Miss Tancred's personal possessions and I am afraid that is totally against my professional teaching. I allowed emotions to take over my thoughts. I also apologise for that weakness. I, of course, trust you and your colleagues and I will give the apartment to you to do as you will. There are enough beds for you if you feel tired. I will return in the morning at around ten and to prove further, that I have nothing to hide, I will draw to your attention that there are personal items in Miss Tancred's bedroom bureau. The key is on top of the wardrobe.
I trust that you will find what you are looking for officers. I was not hiding or preventing you from finding anything that you would eventually find."

Gail turned his back to them and walked out of the apartment leaving the four officers standing there open-mouthed. They stood there for a very short time in silence, which was soon broken by Kearney.

"He was in love with her! Maybe it was one-sided but he could never relinquish that love, in spite of the contract. I am sure that we will be having an interesting conversation tomorrow. But in the meantime, we have much to do and very little time to do it. Constable, could you please call the sandwich bar, and see if they are open late? Ask them for a tray of sandwiches, some cake and drinks for about

21:30. I think by that time a sugar boost would be most welcome."
The team got stuck into the files and for some unknown reason, the search seemed to be going much faster without Mr Gail hovering about, like a mother hen.
They were interrupted by the reception calling up and telling them that their refreshments were on the way up. They washed their hands and their mouths watered when they saw the feast that lay in front of them. Copperstone reached for his wallet but the young couple who delivered it said that it had been already been paid for by a gentleman a few hours ago.

"He said that you would soon be ordering food, and then shortly after, Constable Janson called us and placed the order. We… We err… We know why you are here," the young lady said, "Miss Tancred was a regular customer of ours and we will, of course, miss her. She was a lovely woman and would always take the time to talk to us. She never looked down her nose at us. It is such a sad time; we hope that you find the people responsible."
The team ate the meal in silence. They had so much going through their minds. They were probably the same questions that had as yet no answers. The break was soon over and they went straight back to work. Kearney and Copperstone cleaned up the mess and then, it was straight back to the job in hand.

Whilst Kearney and the constable searched Miss Tancred's bureau, Copperstone called Claire to see if there were any updates or developments that he should be made aware of. She told him about the fingerprints and that they almost caught their probable suspect when they were at

Winton's flat. He laughed but agreed that someone was keeping a close eye on the investigation. Claire also told him that the Blue House Apartments were owned by Tell, Gail, and Tancred's law company. The flats were maintained by a private agent and they took cash payments for the rent and paid it into the company's bank account.
"Have you found anything at Miss Tancred's flat yet?" she asked.

"Nothing at the moment but there may be something happening soon that I am not quite sure of, as daft as that seems. I will fill you in, in the morning.
It, of course, goes without saying, that the owner of the two other sets of prints are the people that need to be caught before anyone else is killed."

"Yes of course, Sir, we are on it as we speak. I don't suppose that the whereabouts of William Tell senior has been discussed yet Sir?"

"I'm afraid not Claire. A situation arose beyond our control and there are many more documents here than we thought at first. We are going to have to go some to try and reach the end but I will call you as soon as we find anything relevant to the case. Can you give me the name of those two suspects, whose fingerprints were found?"

"Yes Sir, we have matched them to a Gordon Grafton and a Richard Starkey. They both have records of petty thieving and B&E, nothing heavy. They do most of that thieving up in London. Have you heard of them at all Sir?"

He wrote the names down, as he was talking to her and read them out.
"No, I'm afraid not, no bells ringing with them but I'll have a word with the two officers from the Met' who are with us for the duration."

"Ok Sir, thank you. I'll speak with you tomorrow."

Copperstone mentioned the names to the two uniformed coppers but they had never heard of them.
Kearney came out of Miss Tancred's bedroom carrying a large wooden box. She huffed and puffed but refused help from the men. She gently placed it on the table and lifted up a lid, music started playing. Copperstone look quizzically at her.
"To save you asking," she said with a grin, "Contained in this box is the history of William Tell Junior and his Father, William senior. This from a woman I believed had no heart. There are diaries going back thirty years. There are photos of him from baby to man and it looks like some of the pictures have tear stains on them. I have read that woman totally wrong.
There is the contract that we know about but I'm not so sure if that contract is as cut and dried as we first thought. I certainly have more than a few questions for Mr Gail when he shows up in the morning. Feel free to have a look gentleman, in case there is something that I might have missed. Please feel free to make a list of any questions that you think need answering from him. Meanwhile, we have a shedload of paperwork to look through and I will not be here another night, even if it is five-star luxury."

Chapter Eight.

Tuesday 5th July 13:10
Violet Woods, Duns Town

Mr Bee sat on a fallen log and watched the Nissan Micra, in the distance. It was pouring out black, poisonous toxic smoke across the clear blue sky.
The fire brigade had got as close as they could, to put out the fire but unfortunately not close enough. The Micra was light and fast and squeezed easily between the many trees, that were now themselves on fire.
He cursed his luck and the two smart-arsed detectives whose trap had almost caught him and ruined half a lifetime of planning.

I should take their lives really. He thought to himself. But they are the good guys, I respect them. They are proper coppers but if they get too close to me and plans, I will have no option. It hurts me to think like that. Even that Marlow copper; a bit of a dipshit arse licker. He is as bent as a nine-bob note, giving police secrets away and certainly not to be trusted. I have him in my sights and that is the worst place he could be but for the moment I need a car. A good killer can't be without a car. He laughed, stood up and then started to walk away from the fire and the gathering band of onlookers; and more to the point, the police helicopter that was hovering above the trees.

Claire and Leanne were sitting in a different car, watching the Blue House Apartments and hoping against hope that their man would show up. They both knew that it wouldn't

happen but some criminals are idiots. If they can make one mistake a second one was sure to follow.
Claire had just been informed that the blood in the flats was pig's blood and the DNA on the sheets from the two flats were from the same two men, on both sets of sheets. But there might be a problem with the results, they would have to undergo more testing.
They had no DNA from Lee-Winton to check against but William Tell's DNA was prevalent on both the sheets, that was an easy match.
The two detectives were more than a little pissed off that the murderer had been fucking with them. Taking the piss after killing his victims for his own sick pleasure.
Gordon Grafton and Richard Starkey, had gone to ground. None of the snitches had seen or heard from them for three or four days. They would normally be buying everyone pints and bragging about the jobs that they had pulled. It was certainly out of character for these blaggers to not be around; unless they had managed to pull off the 'big one' that they had been bragging about recently, whatever that was?

Tuesday 5th July 19:45
Parade Industrial Estate, Duns Town

Mr Bee had managed to steal a small truck; he took it to a commercial lock-up garage and loaded two, bright yellow, forty-five-gallon drums onto it and then covered them up in a tarpaulin that came with the truck. He changed the number plates and hid the original plates in the lock-up, just in case he would ever have need of them.
He drove around Duns Town looking for an ideal spot to park. This was hard enough with a normal-sized vehicle

but a truck was a little more awkward. It had to be in a place that would cause people to complain about, as they usually did.
"Unforgiving bastards that they are," he said aloud.
He remembered that there was a petrol station nearby that had gone bust. He drove the vehicle on to the main forecourt, pulled up his hood and wore a beany hat over it. He knew that the CCTV security camera would pick up his actions and send a security guard to investigate but they would find a sign in the window saying;
'Apologies, but the vehicle has run out of fuel, the driver will return ASAP.' Mr Bee locked the vehicle up and disappeared, making sure that his face was not picked up by the CCTV.
He found a secure place where he could see the truck and be able to watch what happened if and when the security guard turned up.
He waited twenty minutes and then a van that looked like a police vehicle pulled up and a security guard stepped out. He looked at the truck whilst he was talking on his phone. Then he did something that was purely unexpected; he clamped the large vehicle's front wheel and then stuck a notice on the screen. It didn't take Mr Bee much to work out what was on the notice and he was flabbergasted at the cheek of the greedy security company. But he laughed to himself. The longer that truck was there the better it would be. He headed towards the town centre looking for another car. Hopefully, a Micra. He liked that car and the music that was inside was his genre of music. Still *'Shit happens'* he thought to himself.

Wednesday 6th July 10:30
Duns Town Police Station

Claire was sitting at her desk up to her armpits in paperwork, when her office phone rang. It was Andi Qureshi. He asked her if she wanted to see some of the results that they had received about the suicide victim Robin Hood. She grabbed hold of Leanne, on the way out, and was happy to turn her back on her loaded table of paperwork.
They found Andi in his office and he called them in.
"I don't suppose this is going to surprise you but the suicide victim never pulled the trigger. His finger-tip, or rather his thumb, was bruised, which categorically shows that someone had forced him to pull the trigger. The Coroner is still sorting it out but you can definitely rule out suicide.
We have finished with Miss Tancred and found a lot of DNA on the body which we are still waiting on. We will have the report by Friday at the latest.
We rechecked and she was indeed intact. She had the smallest ever c-section scar that my colleagues and I have ever seen. Whoever did that stitching was a master and could make megabucks."

"He was American, Andi and we believe that he was certainly in the 'rich as fuck' bracket. He would charge more over there than he would here. That's a fact. So, what else do you have for me?"

"Nothing, I'm afraid. I was expecting more DNA results when I called you but there is some sort of hold up with it, so I'm afraid that you had a wasted journey. But when I receive them, I will come and find you."

"No worries Andi. It was good to get away from the desk. But we have to return there unfortunately and carry on doing the hardest but important part of being a copper."

"I'm sorry Claire I lied. I have a bit more news for you, sorry I couldn't resist it. But I'm sure that you will be pleased."

"I hope so Andi, it's bad enough the suspect winding us up but go ahead please."

"In that case, I truly am sorry. I intended to put a smile on your face. Apologies. Ok, as I said, we found that pressure was placed on the victim's thumb. We found a fingerprint on the victim's thumbnail, and another partial print on the bottom of the trigger guard. We believe that the partial print was because of the pressure needed to force the victim's thumb down onto the trigger." He smiled at Claire.

"That is the best news I have had for a long time. Have you put it through the database yet? We have an idea of who it might be but a fingerprint on the victim and the rifle would be the bollocks."

"I'm afraid we are still searching it on the database, no hits yet. But we found more prints on the barrel of the rifle. We checked it out and it pinged back as Richard Starkey and there's more. We recovered a serial number on the rifle that had been filed off. Our guys soon found it.

The rifle was stolen from an address in London. A house in the Kensington area had been burgled and two weapons, a handgun and the rifle were taken from a gun safe that was hidden behind a cupboard.
The handgun had been found at an attempted armed robbery, at a shop in Hammersmith. The manager of the shop attacked the robbers with a broom. He knocked the loaded gun out of the robber's hand and sent them running. One of the robbers had been injured and was bleeding. The DNA of that man was found to belong to a Gordon Grafton and his fingerprints were also on the handgun.
While we are on a roll Detective; the cartridges left at Mr Hood's murder scene had three sets of prints; Starkey's, Grafton's and the third man's prints were the same as the thumbprint and the trigger guard prints. So has that put a smile on your faces?"

"Just a bit Andi. These three men are connected all the way through. We have enough to arrest two of them we just need to get lucky with the third. As I said we have an idea who that man is but we have no idea where he is. But thank you Andi."

"As much as I would like to accept all the credit on behalf of my team, I'm afraid Jack Samms had the Met's scientific technicians behind him. They were and still are, at the forefront of this investigation. So, they do indeed deserve the credit. But at least they share their information."

"That's brilliant, Andi pass on to them our gracious thanks. I will inform Copperstone and Kearney as soon as they contact me but now the hunt is definitely on. By the way, was the body of the shooting victim William Tell tattooed?"

"No, his body just had the normal scars associated with a normal man."

Wednesday 6th July 09:45
Mayfair Towers, Paddington

Copperstone had just left the bathroom after a quick freshen up. There was a knock on the front door. He opened it and saw Gail and the young couple from the sandwich shop carrying a tray each of bacon and egg sandwiches and croissants, along with tea, coffee, fresh orange juice and bottles of water. The refreshments were placed on the table and the young couple was about to walk away when they were called back by Copperstone.

"May I enquire as to the cost of this and last night's food please, if you don't mind?"
The couple looked at each other and said that it had all been paid for.
"Yes, I understand. I am aware of that I would just like to know what the total cost was if you wouldn't mind?"
They looked at each other and then looked at Gail, he nodded to them.
"It came to £37.59 in total Sir," said the young man sheepishly. Copperstone took out his wallet and handed the couple £45 and told them to keep the change and to return the money to Mr Gail. Certain people could misconstrue that act of kindness,
"So, we must protect ourselves."

"Thank you, Sir but he paid by card. Should I just give him the cash Sir?"

"I'm afraid not. I am sorry to mess you about and I apologise to Mr Gail but if you could credit it back to his account, I would be most grateful."

"Very well Sir but we need his card to return the money."

Mr Gail handed them the card and told them that he would collect it as soon as he had completed his business "Which, will not be long. Of that I can assure you. Thank you for your service."
The couple left not quite understanding what had just gone on.

"I am sorry Detective Copperstone, I really can't understand the reason why you have just insulted me in front of that young couple."

"I apologise but we have rules that we must adhere to Mr Gail. As I have said, we must protect ourselves at all times. It wasn't intended as an insult to you Sir. I can assure you of that and again I apologise."

"That young couple who have served Miss Tancred and I, for… well for years. They will probably look at me as if I am some sort of villain the next time that I use them."

"I will personally go and explain what just happened Sir. Thank you for your kindness. Now maybe we could get back to work because Detective Kearney and myself have drawn up a few questions, that may assist in bringing these foul murders to an end, and lay to rest the victims whose lives were stolen from them."

Gail never acknowledged him. He just walked around making sure that everything was as it should be in Miss Petra Tancred's apartment. He sat down on the edge of a sofa then stood upright and started wagging his finger at Copperstone.

"I have just realised what this is about Detective Copperstone. It is about what I said last night. I have already apologised profusely for the inconsiderate and unfair words that left my mouth but I think Detective, that what you just did was downright childish and totally unnecessary."

"Well Sir. There are two sides to that argument and I think that we should both put it behind us and get on with the job in hand."

"That of course Detective, is the reason that we are all here. Now may I ask how much progress you have made. Is the end in sight? May I ask Detective Kearney?"

"We are just attacking the last couple of files but I doubt whether I will find anything in there. May we sit at the table Sir and ask you a few questions that need solid answers?"
Mr Gail agreed and then they replaced all the paperwork into the filing cabinets. All that remained in view, was the wooden box that sat on the coffee table.

The four police officers and the lawyer, Mr Gail, sat around the table and waited until that magic moment when they knew that Kearney would be the first to speak.
"Mr Gail, Sir, I was under the impression that Miss Tancred was an uncaring, selfish, money-orientated female. No! 'bitch' was truly the word that I had for her and I know that I wasn't alone in that thought. That was until I saw the contents of that box on the coffee table. It put Miss Tancred into a whole different light. So, can you tell me Sir exactly what sort of woman was she?"
He looked at the people around him then looked at the box on the coffee table.

"Miss Tancred was the kindest, most loving person I ever had the good fortune to meet. Everyone who came into contact with her was moved by her loving, caring attitude. She had the highest I.Q. that I had ever heard of and that far exceeded anyone else in the company but she had never used her intelligence to put anyone lesser than herself down.
My father, Walter Gail, George Ashridge and William Ascot Vladimir Tell, had all fell in love with her as soon as she opened her mouth. Mr George Ashridge left her everything in his will; she was the daughter that he never had and always wanted.
My Father put it before the board that she became a partner, almost before Ashridge had been buried. William Tell agreed and it was he that drew up the contract that gave her the partnership.
I believe that her youthful beauty had opened many doors for her but that wasn't intentional Detective. We were the same age and we were friends, very good friends. She

taught me more than I would ever learn in a university classroom.
We were…err… very good friends as I said. We might have been more if it wasn't for that scumbag of a son of William Tell; fucking hers, mine, and everyone else's life up"

"I assume that is Mr Bernard Barton Tell, that you are referring to Sir?"

"Yes, that is he, one of God's miscreants. A practitioner of thievery and perversion, that included sodomy of young boys that he had bought with the promise of drugs and riches. But he was caught. Wrongs were righted and that 'Devil's spawn' was gone forever but that was only the start of the emotional suffering of Miss Tancred and I."

"What happened to Bernard Tell after he was admitted to the hospital? We know that he was put there by Robin Hood and Dermot Dolan and ended up on a life support system for quite a while. Can you comment on that Sir?"

"Hood and Dolan were supposed to finish him off, if you know what I mean. They dumped him in an old, abandoned lock-up garage and set fire to it but it went out shortly after they had left the scene. A concerned passer-by followed the smoke and found him clinging on to life. The emergency services took him to hospital. The police had put him into protective custody. He never mentioned the truth of what had actually happened to him, making up some story that he had been robbed, blackmailed and tied up because he couldn't give them money that he didn't

have. But the police had found no such corroborating evidence.
Hood and Dolan found out where the police were keeping him and managed to slip him a message. From what I know officer, he left the country with some woman and a child; We believe that chid was as a result of an affair that he had with a young woman who died of a drug overdose aged seventeen.
Mr Tell paid a lot of money for information and wanted to know if the child was his grandson but he never found them. There was no birth registered. We believe the son was called Nathaniel Tell. Maybe they are dead, maybe they all overdosed."

"We believe or should I say that we are fairly certain that it is Bernard Tell who is responsible for the killings but we know that he is not alone. We need to find Mr William Tell senior to do a blood test for familial DNA."

"Huh, I am afraid that I have no idea where he is. He phoned me up and said that he had had enough of the care home and wanted to die somewhere alone. We have people out looking for him and I am worried, even more so, now that you believe that Bernard is back and looking for his inheritance."

"I understand that he is suffering from Alzheimer's how bad is it exactly?"

"Alzheimer's? My God who on earth told you that? There was nothing mentally or physically wrong with him. He decided to go into a private care home because he was fed up with being alone. That is why I have people searching for him."

"I have a feeling Sir, that he and his son have been reunited. I hope that I am wrong. Could we go back to Miss Tancred and why everything changed for you both?"

"Mr and Mrs Tell were heartbroken that there was a chance that they had a grandson out there somewhere. But they decided that needs must; they needed an heir to leave their vast fortune to. Mrs Tell was unable to have any more children, because of complications with Bernard's birth. It was Mrs Tell's idea that Miss Tancred could become a surrogate mother and give them a child that they would leave their fortune to. But it wasn't as easy as that. Mrs Tell absolutely forbade any sexual intercourse taking place, so the action took place via a test tube. Contracts were signed and it was all overseen by Mrs Tell herself. She was from a family of lawyers who, it was rumoured, used to read law books before they could walk.
It was Mrs Tell's idea that Miss Tancred remain a virgin until her fiftieth birthday and be given a pay-out of sixty-five million to ensure that a man would never enter her. There would never be a chance that she would give birth to a child that would try to steal her new child's birth right. Forgive me for saying this and it wouldn't be the first time but it was easy to see where Bernard's genes came from. That woman teased Miss Tancred relentlessly; coming into the office and letting everyone hold the child except for Miss Tancred. The bitch would even pretend to breast-feed it and enjoyed seeing the resulting tears."

"You were in love with Miss Tancred Mr Gail, would that be right?"

"Is it so obvious?" He smiled. "Yes, we were in love and I went on hands and knees many times to try and release Petra from the contract. I would have signed another contract saying that I would have gladly had the snip, as it was called then, to prevent any more children. But the evil bitch had put it into the contract and there was no way it could be broken, without Petra being labelled names which even I cannot utter. Even when the bitch died there was no getting out of it lest William junior and Petra's name and details would be made public. So, Miss Tancred and I became lovers of the sort that I am sure you do not need to graphically know."

"May I ask about the tattoos Mr Gail?"

"Again, that was Mrs Tell's idea. She believed in Naturism but wanted to hide temptation away from her husband's eyes. So, it was she who insisted that everyone got tattooed. But as any man will tell you, it was a much more erotic sight than she had thought. But it was too late, she had co-signed the main contracts and she knew if she changed just one word in that contract it would become null and void; so she had to watch the men walk around, obviously excited."

"I really cannot, for the life of me, see the reason for the tattoos. May I ask Sir and you do not have to answer that question?"

“Thank you, Detective, I would rather leave that to your own imagination, your educated guess.” He looked into her eyes.

“Miss Gladys Catherine Bank, that was her maiden name, had been married before. I do not want to speak ill of the dead but in her case, I will gladly make an exception. She was very popular with the gentlemen.
Mr Tell had a dalliance with her and Bernard was the result of that meeting. Wedding bells were soon to be heard. I don’t know when or how the tattoos came about. But I was happy that Miss Tancred came about. Apart from the sixty-five million-pound, pay out for the contract, which was only weeks away, everything that she owned was to be left to Master William.”

“So, Mr Gail, if you could just bear with me for a second. I know that you are taking care of Miss Tancred’s estate and I assume that you are in some way responsible for Mr Tell senior’s estate. So, what about William Tell juniors estate? Could it be a possibility that he may have left a will of his own, leaving whatever few pennies that he owned to a friend? Does that make sense to you Sir?”
The other police officers sat up in their seats when Kearney mentioned a will.

“Right, ok, Mr Tell junior will be the sole beneficiary of his father’s will when he dies. Technically, if he has left a will, of all that he owns to a friend and his estate receives the inheritance after his death then the will is legal unless it goes before probate. Miss Tancred has, through no fault of her own, failed on her side of the contract and the monies will remain in the Tell’s bank vaults. But that is a valid argument alone and normally I would have taken it further. I would gladly take on that fight but it is now immaterial. Everyone is either dead or missing as is Mister Tell senior."

"But, Mr Gail, there is a possibility of a grandson that may just pop up with his hands open ready to take what is in fact now legally his."

"I believe, for that to happen, a valid birth certificate and a DNA test would be the first avenue. As I said, we found no births registered to any Tell that would have been in the slightest way related to Mr Tell or Bernard Tell. I'm afraid that it would drag slowly through the courts forever and a day and by that time, any financial gain would have been eaten away by legal fees."

"But Mr Gail and this is a big but; could Mr William Tell Senior, draw up another will that supersedes all previous wills and would therefore allow his grandson to clean up the proverbial jackpot?"

"If Mr William Tell senior had sufficient proof of his status, witnesses and it was all done legally, then I suppose it could happen. But if, God forbid, it does happen, I will contest that as long as the breath is within my body."

There was a knock on the door that made everyone jump. Sergeant Rickman answered it. The receptionist stood there with a large parcel in his hands. It was addressed to Mr Gail.

"Mr Gail, a private courier just delivered this by hand. He refused to deliver it up here because he said he was too scared to use the lift because of his claustrophobia. He said to make sure that it goes straight to you and asked that you open it up in front of your esteemed guests because it contains evidence from a crime scene that would be relevant to the enquiries you are conducting."

"Ok. Thank you."
He tipped the receptionist and then put the box on the table. He looked at it as did the others. There were no markings except a typewritten address and no return address.

"That looks a little bit iffy if you ask me Sir," said Constable Jansen. I would be a little wary whilst opening that, you just never know these days Sir."

Sergeant Rickman offered to do the honours but Gail poo-pooed him away and very carefully started to slit open the tape on the parcel. Rickman shouted at him to stop.
"That smell Sir, there's something in there that's not right Sir. I can smell death."

"I believe that you're right Sergeant," said Copperstone. "I would rather you didn't go any further Sir. We may be better off calling SOCO, just in case. We may compromise any evidence in there or maybe trip a fuse? Mind you, I would feel a fool if it was half a pig."

Suddenly, Tancred's office phone rang and they all jumped. Gail walked over and picked up the receiver.

"Hello, this is Mr Gail. I'm afraid that Miss Tancred is unable to come to the phone. Who is calling please?"

"There used to be a show on the telly years ago and the question was to either open the box or take the money." There was a cackle and then the caller hung up.

"Open the box or what? Hello… hello… who is that? Hello."
Gail put the phone down and repeated what the caller had said to the bemused listeners.

"It's that bastard Bernard Tell, said Copperstone. He has been watching and listening to us, the same as he has been doing all along; knowing our every move."

Gail went back to the table, lifted up one side of the box, then gently lifted the other side before looking into it. There was indeed a funny smell emanating from within. There was a newspaper covering whatever it was beneath it. He lifted the newspaper and stepped back sharply, falling over the chair that he had forgotten was behind him.
Sergeant Rickman looked into the box, held his hand over his mouth and looked at Kearney.

"It appears to be two hands Ma'am." He looked at his own hands and turned them over. "It looks like two right hands. I'll call SOCO in and they can examine them. They may be from a corpse that someone, possibly Bernard Tell, has dug up.

The five people sat in another room waiting for SOCO to turn up. They examined the box but took everything away with them for further examination.

“I don’t believe that there is anything more that we can do here,” Copperstone said. “I feel that we have all that we are going to get. I thank you very much, Mr Gail, for your forthright assistance and for sharing with us your personal sadness. Please forgive me for acting like a child Sir. We will go back to our station and follow up on the information that we have. Thank you, Constable Janson and Sergeant Rickman.

Chapter Nine

Wednesday 6th July 10-00
Duns Town Police Station

Detective Chris Marlow stared at the vast pile of paperwork that was in front of him. There was a danger of it toppling over. He was sure that the pile was getting higher by the minute despite him working twice as fast as he normally did.
He looked around at the other detectives and saw that their piles of paperwork got lower as their ranks got higher. He knew that paperwork was an important part of police work and normally he would get on with it without a second thought. But there was physical policework that needed to be done and questions, that had not yet been answered, needed chasing up.
He looked over at Claire and Leanne, who were busily chatting as they went through their own miniscule piles of paperwork. Multi-tasking, they would call it, but concentration on the job in hand would help to reduce everyone's mountain of boring paperwork.
He looked at his computer screen and the bullet points, that he had typed there, stared uncomfortably back at him.

- *Who was the intended victim at the Crown Court, Tell, Lee-Winton or Dolan?*
- *As yet, no bullet fragments have been recovered from the external wall of the crown court.*
- *Were there any bullet fragments found in the victims' bodies?*
- *Tell's laptop? As yet no result?*
- *The bedsheets of Tell. and Lee-Winton. No results?*

- *The diary and journal found at the Hood's residence?*
- *Miss Tancred. Why was she still a virgin despite being found naked and strangled? Why was she killed?*

Kearney and Copperstone were away in London, searching for answers but he was getting frustrated at being, he thought, totally ignored. He toyed with the idea of walking out and seeking answers of his own. But he was just a lowly Detective Constable, at everyone's beck and call; despite him being the one that had found important evidence.
He stared at the screen. The bullet points seemed to be getting bigger and then smaller again as if trying to make him do something about them.
Claire and Leanne, it seemed could come and go as and when they pleased. He knew that they were a great investigation team but fairs fair. Maybe he should bite the bullet and talk to them or ask their advice. What was the worst that could happen? They were both adults and beyond name-calling and rank pulling.
He printed off a screen-shot and went over to Claire and Leanne.
Claire saw him suddenly standing beside her. She looked up and asked him to move out of her personal space. He apologised, not realising that he was that close.
"What's on your mind Chris, you look a little puzzled, are you ok?"

"I'm good Claire but there is still so much physical work to do and we are all stuck here like office personnel. I have a few questions that I would like you and Leanne's advice on."

"Ok Chris fire away. Let's see if we can put a smile on your face."

"Well it's the lack of answers that are the problem. Why are we not getting answers from the autopsy or SOCO, about the tests that have been done on our victims? It seems that nobody is saying anything about it…"

Claire was just about to answer when her phone rang and her face visibly dropped.
"Well Chris as I was just about to say, these things take time for a very good reason. Mistakes cannot be made and yes it would appear that no one is talking about it but from the work that you have done, things were actually moving. That phone call was from Cyber Forensics. The laptop had been completely wiped, by a software program that cleaned everything except the operating system. Apparently, the software is freely available on the net. So, unfortunately, we have to scrub that idea. What else is bugging you?"

"It's the original shooting. As yet, we have no idea who the actual victim was meant to be out of three people. There is nothing from forensics about the type of bullet or gun that was used come to that. But there is a burning question that is really is bugging me.
Excuse me for saying this the way it's gonna come out but why was Miss Tancred still a virgin? I know the original reason. But she was naked when she was killed and you would assume, I'm going by previous crimes here, that

being strangled by hand is a very personal thing. From some of the cases that we have seen, it is a sexual thrill but whether it happened like that or not I don't know?
I have to say that from all accounts Miss Tancred was, despite her age, as horny as hell. Whoever killed her must have known that she was a virgin and was not tempted by that. Or, were they just not into sex?"
So, am I asking the wrong questions or am I being swerved off course?"

Claire and Leanne looked at each other, their mouths were in the open position and silent.
"Bloody hell Chris, I don't think that anyone has seriously asked that question and it's a bloody good point to make. If Lee-Winton killed her, the thought may never have entered his mind because he is gay. Whether he is bi-sexual or not I don't know. Then this Bernard Tell, he may be bi because of the supposed sexual liaisons with young boys but he has had girlfriends we believe. So, Chris, I will pass on your question to Copperstone when he returns.
Have you any more questions like that Chris? I'm surprised that we never noticed that."

"Well, there is just a teeny question and I don't want to insult your intelligence but I really don't know. Does anyone know where Lee-Winton's parents live?"

"Jesus, Chris you are in Sherlock Holmes mode. But no, we haven't as yet got a warrant to get information on Lee-Winton. We hope to have a bit more info' though, when Kearney returns."

"I could find out easily enough and go and look at the premises from a discreet distance Claire?"

"Don't do anything until Kearney and Copperstone return or as soon as they call me. I will pass on your concerns and see what they say but give them a couple of hours until they do call me. Well-done Chris, you are destined to go far in this job. Now, take your mind off of it for a couple of hours and sort out some of that waiting paperwork. I promise that you will miss nothing."

Marlow walked back to his desk a little awkwardly. He knew that Claire and Leanne were talking about him, but, despite the awkwardness, he felt ten feet tall.
He concentrated as best he could on the now shrinking pile of paperwork. He felt even better when Leanne came over and lifted up a few folders. She winked at him and carried them away.
After a few hours his mind, once again, started to wander and Lee-Winton came crawling back into it. He looked to see if anyone was watching and Googled Lee-Winton. There was a glut of information concerning many names of that ilk, mostly belonging to the USA.

He concentrated the search in the UK and very soon, after putting in different questions relative to his search, he came up with the Lee-Winton that he was looking for. But what he found was not exactly what he had bargained for. Before he continued with his search, he printed off a picture and the story of Duncan Lee-Winton. Then he headed towards Claire with his find.
"What else have you found Chris; I can tell you have something by your smile."

"What is Lee-Winton's Christian name Claire?"

"Oh, it's… erm it's…I'm sorry Chris, I don't think that we ever asked it. Why?"

'Would Duncan Lee-Winton ring a bell by any chance?"

Claire looked at Leanne, who was nodding. Chris handed the picture of Duncan Lee-Winton along with the print-out of the story to her. She shook her head and returned the picture to him and then looked at the story.
"The guy in the picture is black, Chris. Our Lee-Winton is white and his parents are still alive as far as we know; so, this could not be our man."

"Read the story Claire. It says that his parents, who were both lawyers, died ten years ago in a car crash; while he was away studying law at Oxford University.
I have checked with the Law Society and although Lee-Winton is a common name, there are no other Lee-Winton's of his age group practising law from this area. So, what happened to this guy then? I searched for Lee-Winton in the more common search engines and it was only then that I noticed the name with reference to an RTA, that happened suspiciously, less than ten miles from here. Sara and Sidney Lee-Winton's bodies were both taken to South Africa for burial; where Mr Sidney Winton's only relative lived. Mrs Sara Winton came from the same village but she was an orphan and had no relatives. All other searches for Mr Duncan Lee-Winton drew a blank."

"Sorry, Chris, I don't think that I can agree with you on this. It sounds a little far-fetched. Even more so because of the colour difference and what would be the motive; money, identity theft? I think, to be honest, with you Chris that is a very complicated case to prove. So, once again, leave it with me and I will throw it to Kearney when she returns. She may go all out for it I don't know. Sorry mate."

Once again, Detective Chris Marlow headed back to his desk. He felt a little dejected but he wasn't finished with his new pet project. He was willing to search many different avenues and would never give up. But luck was on his side and he managed to find the address of Mr & Mrs Lee-Winton, at the time of the accident. It was closer than he had imagined. Once again, he printed the information, only this time he kept it to himself.

Claire received a phone call and relayed the information to Leanne. They both stood up and headed towards the door. She looked at Chris.
"We have to pop out for a bit Chris. By the time I get back, Kearney will be here and we can present her with your findings. Can you answer my phone if it rings and take any messages for me? Cheers mate."

Chris had no chance to say goodbye before she was gone. He sat there silently, looking at his screen and then over to Claire's empty desk. He sighed and his shoulders slumped. He looked at the reduced pile of paperwork. He knew he had to finish it before Kearney came back because she would no doubt pick on him for not doing what was expected of him.

He took a deep breath and once more got stuck into the laborious task. But at the same time he glanced frequently at the computer screen and every now and again, he would key in another search then print off a copy of the result.

It was three p.m. He had finally finished all the paperwork that he had in front of him. There was no sign of Kearney, Copperstone, Callison, or Gavin.
He looked at the results that he had printed off and heard Kearney's voice, in his memory, saying that there was no room for people playing lone wolf and looking for brownie points. He was a team player but at the moment he was missing the team.
He took a deep breath. He made a choice there and then, regardless of the outcome. He was a copper and he would do what a copper was supposed to do. He would go and physically watch the comings and goings at Lee-Winton's parents' house, whether they were the right people or not. He had made up his mind that something was definitely amiss with the news report of the Lee-Winton's tragic accident. But he didn't know exactly why he thought that. Maybe a true copper's gut, a copper's instinct, he told himself.
He looked around him to see if anyone was watching and then made a phone call.
The person at the other end answered gruffly.
"Yes, who is it?"

"I am getting closer Sir. As soon as I am sure I will make all the arrangements."

"No! Just call me and I will make the arrangements. There cannot be a repeat of what has happened. I have special

people standing by, waiting for the call. You go and detect Marlow. Use that inquisitive nose, to find what I am looking for and then blend in amongst them. Don't call me again, unless it's good news."
Marlow heard the line go dead, he smiled and shook his head.

He decided to go to the home of Lee-Winton. He parked his car near enough, but not too near, to the Lee-Winton's house. He sat in the back seat and kept as low as he could. Now and again, lifting his head to look through the binoculars that he had brought with him. He cursed himself for not bringing a camera but it was too late to do anything about that now.
His phone rang. He put it on silent without looking to see who it was who was calling him. He assumed that it was Claire wondering where he had gone without her permission.
The windows started to mist up so, he opened the passenger window enough to let fresh air into the car. He started feeling drowsy and realised that this might not have been one of his better ideas. He thought about cancelling the whole stupid thing but he succumbed to sleep before he could move.
He was dreaming of a place near a beach, in a far-off country, surrounded by scantily clad girls all wanting to be photographed with him; a famous British copper.
The paparazzi were taking hundreds of pictures of him and the many young women, fighting to get close enough to be pictured with their hero. It was a most enjoyable place to be in the middle of but it suddenly started to get a bit claustrophobic.

He was searching for a way out and finally managed to squeeze his way through the hot sweaty bodies and jumped into a car. He put his foot down but what was that noise? What was that metallic knocking sound? He drowsily opened his eyes and saw a shadow in his peripheral vision. He turned his head towards that shadow and his mouth fell open.

Chapter Ten.

Wednesday 6th July 13:45
Duns Town Crown Court.

Claire and Leanne, walked into the Crown Court building. The first thing that they asked was if Lee-Winton was on the premises? The answer was a resounding *no!*
He was not in their good books, of that there was no doubt. He had cost thousands of pounds in lost cases for the prosecution and at the moment his name was toilet paper. Claire told the receptionist that she had a call about a parcel that they had received in her name. A security guard took the detectives to an interview room at the back of the Crown Court.
They walked into the room and saw the parcel sitting on a table. On the parcel was a hand-written note that said.
'To Detective Inspector Claire Callison. Care of CPS. Private and Confidential. For her eyes only.'
She looked at it and then turned to the security guard who was looking at her suspiciously.
"May I ask if this parcel has been x-rayed officer?"

"I'm afraid not Miss. The machine has broken down. All of our mail has been directed to airport customs until repairs can be made."

"So, did it not enter your mind officer, that this parcel is a little bit *suspicious*?"

"Of course, it did Miss. But it is addressed to you and not the court. So, I'm afraid we had to wait until you had seen it and then we can make arrangements to remove it to customs for x-raying."

"So, what if there is a bomb in there? Waiting to go off as soon as we got here?"

As she said that the three moved away from the room and stood around a corner glancing every now and again at the parcel with great trepidation.
Callison called it in and waited for the bomb squad who arrived after two hours; during which time the court had been completely vacated. They carried a mobile x-ray machine. She watched as the squad sent a robot in to take pictures of the box and its contents. It was soon plain to see that it wasn't a bomb but what looked like a pair of human hands.
Claire thanked the squad and called in SOCO to examine the parcel in case there was evidence that would get compromised.
"Jesus Christ! What the fuck is going on? Why would someone send a pair of human hands to me? If they are in fact, human"
SOCO turned up and they carefully examined the parcel. They opened it and confirmed that there were two human hands but they were both left hands. There was no note except for the delivery address. They took the parcel away for further examination and fingerprinting.
The parcel had been delivered by a private courier and CCTV caught a minute section of his face; that peeped out from under the baseball cap that he wore. He knew where the cameras were and tried to avoid them.
Leanne stared at the pictures that were produced from the video.

“If that isn’t Winton, I’ll eat my untattooed underwear,” she said.

“I’m afraid I have to agree with you on that one Leanne. What’s the bastard playing at? Now we have more shit to follow-up. Let’s get back. Hopefully, Kearney will hopefully be back and we can discuss Chris’s ideas with her.”

Wednesday 6th July 16:55
Duns Town Police Station

Claire and Leanne returned to the police station, and found Kearney and Copperstone, standing in front of a whiteboard, with a handful of detectives. There was a picture of Lee-Winton wearing a baseball cap but he was showing more of his face than he did on the Crown Court CCTV. Kearney stopped talking when she saw the two detectives heading towards her. They went straight to the whiteboard.
“Lee-Winton… How did you get that picture so quickly Frances?”

“So, this is the infamous Lee-Winton? We hadn’t actually seen him before but thank you Claire. Yes, Mr Winton took it upon himself to deliver a parcel, containing two right hands. They were taken away by the Met’ SOCO. As I understand it you have received a similar parcel delivered to the Crown Court, containing left hands?”

“Yes, the bastard is really taking the piss. So now could I have a warrant for him. I want to check his locker and get details of his services with the CPS.

Detective Marlow has come up with a couple of good points as I am sure that he has told you?"
She looked around the room and was shocked that he wasn't there.
"Where is Marlow? He was so excited about his find, or have you sent him out?"

"He wasn't here when we returned at about four p.m. ish. I actually tried ringing his phone but he isn't answering. So, what exactly was it that he found?"

She looked around to her desk and saw the paperwork that Marlow had given her earlier. She picked it up and showed Kearney, who pondered over it; then shook her head and smiled.

"So, Marlow thinks that Lee-Winton is this black chappie and what then exactly Claire? His question about Miss Tancred still being a virgin after her attack is indeed a valid point and something that we should have asked before. So, where would he have gone if he were so excited about telling me about his Eureka moment?"

"I have no idea. I told him to stay here until either you or I returned. Maybe he went out for a snack or something. I'll call him now Frances."

Claire tried calling Marlow's mobile number a couple of times without success. She was about to go and look for him when Kearney received a call herself and stopped her on the spot.
"I have just been informed that we have two suspicious items on the back of a truck; that has been dumped at a

disused service station. Uniform are there and SOCO are on their way. There are reportedly some foul odours coming from them, although they have been sealed. Can you go and see what is happening Claire, and keep me informed? If you hear from Marlow tell him to get his arse back here, pronto!"

Wednesday 6th July 18:10
Stanton's Service Station

Leanne was driving and as they neared the garage, they saw a crowd of people; pushing and shoving trying to get closer to the truck, in the hope that their thirst for blood could be quenched.
Leanne pulled as close as she could and put on her Siren. The crowd jumped in shock at the sudden noise but only momentarily. They went back to pushing and shoving.
Claire climbed out of the car and bodily pushed her way through the throng. She saw two police constables half-heartedly trying to keep the onlookers away.
She signalled to Leanne to force the car in between the truck and the crowd, which she did to perfection. Claire held up her warrant card and ordered everyone to stay back or risk being arrested. She told the uniformed coppers to get more men but as she did so, a transit van pulled up with reinforcements and forced the throng back. SOCO turned up just after them and all the vehicles were used to block access to the blood hunters.

Claire spoke to one of the uniformed officers who was first on the scene.
"Ok, Constable can you tell me what is going on and who reported the truck?"

"It was an unidentified male that called it in, saying that there were bodies inside the drums that are on the back of the truck. When myself and Constable Draper turned up, there was already a handful of people trying to pull off the tarpaulin but the smell coming from the drums kept them at a distance. Then a new group turned up and the struggle started again. We struggled, as you saw, to try and restrain them."

"Yes, Constable I saw that. Now, I want you and Constable Draper to ask those people how they came to be here and get as many names as you can… and proof of ID, if possible. Could you do that please?"

Jack Samms, Duty Medical Officer, came and spoke to Claire.
"We noticed that the filler cap on one of the drums had been removed. Possibly by one of the onlookers, I guess. The release of gases inside has forced out the putrid air that had hung about but saying that, they are not that easy to open; unless you have the proper device to open them with. They are apparently brand new and freshly painted in that bright yellow colour. You need sunglasses to look at them.
Anyway, we believe that they both contain bodies. One of them certainly does. We have to take everything as it is to our special lab. The lid, of each drum, is sealed by a special bracket or latch that is easier to open than the filler cap but we cannot afford to open them here. It has to be done under laboratory conditions in case of contamination. But we have done tests. I believe that the one we have looked at, has been in those drums for at least a week but I believe that we will never know for sure. I would hazard a

guess that chemicals had been used to assist the decomposition. The condition of the bits that we could see indicate they are probably turning to soup but we have DNA from the open one. So, I will keep you informed of what we find as soon as we find it.

Leanne called up the service station's security company and asked how long the truck had been parked there? She was told that it parked there yesterday, Tuesday 5th July at 20:00 hrs. CCTV picked up a man leaving the truck and disappearing. His face was not visible and he purposely shied away from the camera. She took their address and asked them if they could copy that video and also the recording of the shenanigans of this afternoon.

"We think that somebody climbed on to the truck and opened one of the drums. Hopefully, you have him on video too because he or she would have needed a special tool to open it."
She arranged that someone from her office would come and collect them.

Claire called Marlow's mobile number but once again he didn't answer. It just kept ringing before going on to voicemail.
"Something is up with Chris Marlow Leanne. He always answers his phone on the first or second ring. I want to know where he is. This isn't like him at all and he wouldn't purposely get on the wrong side of Kearney."

"I don't think for a minute anything is wrong Claire. He has been working very hard the last few days and maybe he's just left his phone in his car and gone to find some jollies somewhere. He is a young man and that's what they do…sometimes…apparently."

"Maybe you are right, bless him. But he will certainly have some arse-kissing to do when he shows up."

Claire called Kearney, reported the service station findings and asked about the search warrant for Lee-Winton. She was told that it would be ready tomorrow at 10:00 and would include the CPS office. As soon as his bank details were revealed another warrant would be issued for that. Kearney told them both to go home. They did as they were told but made a detour and called around at Marlow's home. There was no reply. His car wasn't in the drive. Claire posted a note through the door, asking him to get in touch with them. Whatever the problem was, it would still be solved.
Maybe he is at his parents, Leanne, for whatever reason but I don't want to start worrying them until we know for sure that he isn't lying in someone's bed with the father of all hangovers. We have all been there until we finally accept that there are no answers in a bottle."

"Dirty little shit is probably banging someone instead of covering Kearney's arse in kisses," Leanne said, before breaking out in laughter.

Thursday 7th July 10:30
Duns Town Crown Court

The personnel manager at the office of the CPS was more than helpful and showed the two detectives all the personal information of Duncan Lee-Winton.

Mr Lee-Winton started employment, directly for the CPS, in 2007. He had been a very successful and confident addition to their department from day one.
They supplied his original C.V., that he had sent them, along with his application form which stated his academic credentials.
His address was given as Blue House Apartments. His parents address as 34, Cutenhoe Gardens, Duns Town. His parents, who were both retired lawyers, were now living in South Africa for six months of the year and then back to England for six months. His Parents names were Sara and Sidney Lee-Winton.
Claire looked at their names and remembered that Marlow had mentioned the same names when he spoke to them yesterday. Now, pieces of the jigsaw were becoming a little clearer but far from being placed together.
They found nothing else that could help them. Lee-Winton's office was empty. There was no laptop, no personal paperwork or anything that gave any indication that he, in fact, worked there. His locker was also empty.
Claire left the CPS offices and called Kearney.
"On my desk are the details that Marlow found about Lee-Winton's parents. It is the same people apart from there being a colour difference. I have emailed his bank account details so, if you could sort a warrant out for me, I would be grateful."

"DCS Copperstone has said that he will be looking at his bank details. I would like you to go to Lee-Winton's parent's address and see what you can find out, from the neighbours. If you find that a warrant is justified for that address let me know as soon as you can."

“I don’t suppose that you have heard from Marlow, have you? He is still not answering his phone and I am bloody pissed off. I called at his home and banged on the door. There was no answer and then I noticed that the car wasn’t there.”

“I must admit Frances I am a little worried about him. Especially now that we are getting more information about Lee-Winton. I hope he hasn’t gone off and got himself into trouble. I know that he was excited that he had found something but I’m not sure if he went off half-cocked looking for answers.”

“I’ll give him until lunchtime and then I’ll take it further. Get on with your search and stay close to your phone.”

The two detectives arrived at 34, Cutenhoe Gardens, the home of Mr & Mrs Lee-Winton. It was a beautiful Georgian house that had not been spoilt and modernised in any way; including the wooden windows, which was in total contrast to the neighbouring houses. Several owners had wasted time and money, changing the appearance of their homes but at the same time robbing them of their character.
There was no drive on the premises but there was a lovely well-kept front garden. It was a kaleidoscope of colours that someone had shown love and devotion to, over many years.
Claire thought that the Lee-Winton’s really existed and Marlow had indeed been mistaken. She went into the garden of the premises and rang the bell. There was no answer. She knocked on the wooden door, a little harder than she had intended, but still there was no answer.

Leanne checked the side gate. It was unlocked. She went through and noticed that the rear of the garden was in complete contrast to the front. It was like a jungle with shrubs, trees and bushes all intermingled, amid grass that was standing waist high. She knocked on the back door, which had a thick coat of dust and grime and looked as if it had not been used in years. She rejoined Claire and shared what she had just seen.
Claire saw a neighbour peeking through the curtains and went and knocked on her door.
A woman's voice behind the door asked who they were and demanded to see ID, which they both posted through the letterbox. The woman went to her living room window, pulled back the net curtains and compared the ID pictures to the two women standing at her door. Satisfied that they were who they said they were, the old woman opened the door, returned the IDs and asked what they wanted.
"I'm sorry to disturb you but we are trying to find out about the people who live next door. Could you possibly help us by answering a few questions Miss…?"

"It's Mrs Janet Higgins. Please come in. I can see the curtain twitchers already."
Mrs Higgins guided them into the living room and asked if they would like tea or coffee. They both declined. Mrs Higgins sat down and prepared herself for the questions.
"Claire smiled at the woman, who it seemed spent her time cleaning the spotless house.

"Forgive me Mrs Higgins, we are trying to find out about your neighbours, Mr and Mrs Lee-Winton I believe is their name. Would that be correct?"

"Those poor people. I cried when I heard what had happened to them, as did many of the neighbours who have since moved away or passed on. They were killed in a car accident. Young Duncan was in pieces the poor man. I don't think that he ever got over it. They were a very close family and got on with everyone around here. My goodness, I used to babysit Duncan when he was little. Such a beautiful baby."

She stopped talking, stood up, went across to the mantlepiece and took down a photograph. Then she returned to her seat beside Claire. This is my husband and me with Sara, Sidney and little Duncan. We were all so happy and carefree then. It seems so long ago but I think it was only nine or ten years ago, something like that when it happened."

Claire showed Leanne the picture, she took a good look and then returned it to Mrs Higgins.

"So, Mrs Higgins the garden is in such beautiful condition and must require so much time and attention. Do you know if Duncan is still living there?" asked Leanne.

"My husband and I do the garden in memory of Sara. She had spent many hours learning from us about flowers and shrubs; she was like a sister to me and my Albert and Sidney would go and sit in either his or Albert's shed with a few beers and talk about sport and whatever else men talk about in those situations." She smiled at the memory. "The back garden… well I know that you have seen it and Sara would have been heartbroken if she were alive to see it. Duncan… well to be honest, we only saw him once or twice before he left for the funeral service that they had in South Africa. We had a memorial service of our own for the family which he attended and stood up and thanked us all. He promised that when he returned from Africa, he would celebrate their lives and their death as only African's can."

"So, who lives there now Mrs Higgins would you know?"

"Well, it's the strangest thing but there are two men; one is young and the other man is older, like maybe his father. There are similarities but we have only seen him a couple of times and not really close up. We don't know his name. But the strange thing is that they are related to Mr & Mrs Lee-Winton. The young man is called Duncan Lee-Winton, isn't that a coincidence? But they are white people and no sign of dark skin or anything. I know that it could be as a result of marriage but… I… I don't know and I don't wish to be a racist or whatever the term is. The young man seems nice enough though. I believe that he is a lawyer and he is there a couple of times a week… Oh, come to think of it I saw the older man. He was chatting to a young man that was sitting in a car just up the road. He climbed into the passenger seat and they drove off. I waved as they passed by."

"Could you remember what the young man looked like Mrs Higgins?"

"Err… well he was very young actually but everyone looks young to me these days." She laughed. "But he had short hair at the sides and a bit longer on top. Very old fashioned I thought at the time… oh… and… he wore a tie, a red tie but that's all that I can tell you. I'm sorry. Oh yes, the car was a dark grey Ford. I don't know what model. I just saw the Ford badge as they came close."

"That's perfect. You have been very helpful but one quick question. Does the young man own a car, do you know or have you seen any strange cars parked outside the house?"

"Err… yes actually. Friday, I think it was. I saw a Range Rover but I can't remember the colour and there was a little grey hatchback I'm not sure if it was on Monday or Tuesday. Both cars were only there once. I can't remember any other cars but Duncan has a pushbike that he rides around on usually."

"Thank you, Mrs Higgins. You have been very helpful. If you remember anything else that seems strange could you call me on this number, anytime at all?" Claire gave her a card with her details on it and then left the old woman's house. She heard her lock and bolt the doors.

"I wish all people were as security conscious as she is," Leanne said.

"Well Leanne, it looks as though Marlow was right, and that the Lee-Winton's have had their identities stolen. But that raises yet another question. Whatever happened to the real Duncan Lee-Winton? What is worrying me more is Marlow. Was that him in the road and Bernard Tell who kidnapped him?"

"It certainly sounded like him from her description. I think we should drop everything and report to Kearney and get a search warrant for the Lee-Winton's house. I'll drive. If you get a hold of Kearney and tell her what we just found out and tell her we want the warrant straight away… possible officer down scenario."

Leanne put on her Siren and flashing lights and headed towards the station. Claire reported to Kearney and said that she wanted the warrant ready so that she could head straight back out and back to where they had just left.

The journey seemed to take forever, despite it being only a couple of miles away. Claire tried calling Marlow again without success.
They eventually arrived at the station and were about to go into Kearney's office when Claire's phone rang. She looked at the caller ID, it was Marlow.
"Jesus Marlow! Where the fuck, are you? We are worrying our fucking guts out, wondering what happened to you."

"I'm afraid it isn't Marlow," a strange voice said.

"Is that you Bernard Tell? Where the fuck is the detective you kidnapped?"

Kearney saw that Claire was yelling at someone on the phone and went to investigate. As she got closer, she felt the tension in the air and saw the look on both Claire and Leanne's faces.

"This is Jack Samms Claire. I believe that I have your Detective Marlow's phone."
"You… but how come you have it? Did he leave it there?"

"No Claire. As far as I know, Detective Marlow has been nowhere near here. There would have been no reason for him to be here."

"So, tell me Jack, where did you find the phone? Please it's important."

"Err…The phone was inside one of the drums. It was wrapped in a plastic bag. We only found it because you were the last one to call him. We heard the ringing amongst all the… remains of whoever was in the drum. We know that it wasn't Marlow inside the drum but whoever it was had their hands chopped off. I think that the phone was put in the drum yesterday between the last time you saw him and the time that the police were called."

"So, what about the other drum Jack? Have you looked in that one yet?"

"There is a build-up of gases inside the other one and I assume that it contains the same as what was in this one. It certainly doesn't contain Detective Marlow. I can only open it in a specially air-sealed room. I will let you know what I find."

"Thank you, Jack. I apologise for mouthing off at you. I'll be in touch."
Claire noticed the concerned faces standing around her, wanting to know about Marlow. She sat down on a chair and told them about the conversation that she had just had.

"We need that warrant Frances. We need it now. That bastard Lee-Winton or his father has kidnapped Marlow and we have to find him now."

A uniformed officer ran to Kearney and gave her a document. She looked at it and then passed it to Claire.
"There is the search warrant, Claire. I'm sending a uniform squad with you, along with SOCO to search the back garden. I will get CCTV all over this town looking for Marlow's car. Nothing else matters."
She looked at the remaining detectives in the room, they were waiting for the ok from her; wanting to do their bit and search for a colleague, who was in an apparent hostage situation.
"Ok guys. Drop anything that is not too important. Go and find him and pay your snouts whatever they want. I want Marlow back here, happy, healthy and ready to feel my boot up his arse." She smiled and tried to cover the falling tears.

Chapter Eleven.

Claire and Leanne arrived back at 34, Cutenhoe Gardens, along with a posse of uniformed police and SOCO technicians. They rang the bell and knocked hard on the door but received no response.
A burly police officer turned up with the big red key as it was known and battered the door down in one movement. At exactly the same time, another big red key gained entrance at the back door.
Claire walked into the living room and was surprised to find a mountain of dust and cobwebs. They covered every nook and cranny, except for a table in the centre of the room. It was clean and had papers scattered around. She looked at the papers and found them to be related to various bank accounts in the name of Lee-Winton.
Leanne and a couple of uniformed police searched upstairs but they had found nothing except cobwebs and dust. The kitchen area was clean as was a nearby downstairs toilet but there was no sign of Marlow.
Leanne rejoined Claire, looking like an advert for Christmas. She was covered from head to toe in cobwebs it looked like tree trimmings.
She knew that her partner was scared stiff of spiders, but at this time all that mattered was Marlow. Claire helped brush off as many of the cobwebs as was possible.
Leanne's face showed the sadness of not finding Marlow.
"I don't think that there is any point in looking any further Claire. He's not here and I don't think that he ever was. The garden is untouched. It looks as if this house has not been cleaned since the previous owners died."

"I know Leanne but at least we have found that there is some sort of scam going on. There are about ten different bank account numbers here; with direct debits for utility bills and council tax in Lee-Winton's name. But I can't see what I'm looking at, we have to pass that on to financial forensics and to Copperstone."

Claire spoke to Kearney and reported that they had found nothing except some financial documents, which she would send to Copperstone. Hopefully, he could tie it up with his bank investigation, so that it would open further avenues for investigation.
"But Frances. I have been thinking about it and it still bugs me that there is nothing concrete against Winton-Lee, except circumstantial evidence that even an everyday common or garden solicitor could explain away. If we could get him into the station, we may get something out of him. But at the moment he is the least of my problems. I want to go out and search for Marlow."

"Ok, Claire. Put someone in charge there and get them to search the interior of the house properly and also the garden. Get metal detectors if necessary, in case the real Lee-Winton is buried there. I am going to make a call or two; just in case he was murdered in South Africa or to prove that he returned to this country, after the funeral. Send that paperwork to Copperstone ASAP. Good hunting Claire."

The citizens of Duns Town had never seen so many coppers in the town. Even coppers from nearby towns were drafted in, in the search for their fellow officer.

All through the rest of that day and throughout the long night, the search continued. Weary police officers and caring citizens refused to go home. There was always one more place to check, one more idea of where he could be. But the ideas, the places, and the searchers were exhausted. There was nowhere else that they could think of to search.

Friday 8th July 07:30
Duns Town Police Station

Detective Claire Callison, entered the detective's room, followed by a few other tired, dejected detectives and uniformed officers. Lastly, bringing up the rear with a selection of refreshments donated by the nearby café, came Detective Sergeant Leanne Gavin.
Kearney turned up and looked the worse for wear; more so than the other detectives. She had been out all night looking for Marlow's car. Her footfall was heavy as she walked past Claire and gently patted her on the back. Leanne offered her a coffee and she drank it regardless of what it was.
A Constable walked up to her and gave her a blown-up picture that Leanne had managed to take the day they had almost caught Bernard Tell. She looked at the picture and after a few minutes, she summoned the strength to stand up. She faced and addressed the tired officers.

"Ladies and gentlemen. This picture was taken by Leanne and she and Claire believe that this person is the suspect, Bernard Barton Tell. It's taken this long to produce because the enhancement machinery, that we have, never came close. So, we had it sent to our bestest friends at the

Met' and they had, it seems, forgotten about it. But I called them yesterday and here is the result. Not brilliant by a long shot but it's more than we had. You can see a portion of his face and we have video of the same man that we have taken pictures from and will be up on this board within the hour.

Look at his picture, look at his face, touch it, taste it, smell it, burn his likeness into your brain. We know that he has been watching us. He may be watching us at this very minute, laughing at us because he has taken one of us. But we are not going to give him a cat in hells chance because we will catch him before he hurts Detective Chris Marlow. Take deep breaths my fellow officers. Take in the oxygen and let your brains do what they are good at. He is closer than you think. Don't look over your shoulder, look over your colleague's shoulder and you will see him. There are two of them. Find one and the other will be close by. All I ask is just a few more hours from you, a final spurt home. We are finding out more. But it is not enough!"

She was interrupted by DCS Copperstone, who came into the room.

"Excuse me for interrupting you Frances but I have just heard from Jack Samms. The severed right hands that were sent to us both match the two bodies that were placed inside the forty-five-gallon drums. Well, one hand each to be precise; they matched exactly to the bodies and the prints on the hands match our missing petty thieves, Richard Starkey and Gordon Grafton. Confirmation of DNA samples proved, without a doubt, that everything matches up. So, we can scrub them from our searches. They no longer matter."

Claire stood up and faced Copperstone.
"They no longer matter Sir. They no longer matter? I'm sure that their families and friends would think otherwise. Despite what they have done they were murdered by somebody and I believe that somebody is Bernard Tell. We don't know what part they played in all this but like the others Sir, they are victims and we must treat them as victims." She sat back down and waited for the shit to hit the fan.

"Of course, you are absolutely right Claire and I apologise for the way that I came across. They are indeed victims. We must find this man and whoever is running with him. Thank you."

Copperstone was a little red-faced as he handed back the proceedings to Kearney, just as the CCTV videos were ready to show. He stayed where he was ready to look at the suspect, at the same time talking to someone on his mobile phone.
Kearney switched on the player and the suspect came into view guarding his face with a hood and a hat. The next section of the video showed a man climbing on to the truck, pulling the tarpaulin off and then doing something which was hidden by his body. But as he backed off the truck the filler cap of the drum was in plain view and had been removed from the drum. Then the police turned up. The man jumped off of the truck and mingled with other people. As the crowd gathered the man disappeared and was nowhere to be seen.

"Not exactly what I was hoping for," Kearney moaned. Claire came over and asked Kearney to replay the video, which she did.

"Leanne, come and take a closer look at this video and see if you can follow the man that jumps off the truck?"

Leanne watched carefully and played it again.
"I remember that man, he purposely stared at me, then moved off. As he moved away, he took his hoodie off and disappeared."

"That isn't far from the town centre. Can you call your cousin, Cherise Day and ask her if she picked anything up from there? Give her the time. We may be lucky and even more if she caught him dumping the truck there."

"So, Claire why do you think our suspect placed Marlow's phone in the drum instead of destroying it?" Copperstone asked.

"It was you that said he was fucking with us and as a result of what you said, I laid a trap but lost him. It's a joke to him. I think that he has lost the plot and I can't think, for the life of me, how those two murdered petty thieves come into it."

"I think they could be your proverbial red herrings Claire," said Kearney. "He thinks that he is more intelligent than you, or the whole police force, because he has access to all of us. He has cameras everywhere and probably sniggers like a schoolboy when he sees a pair of our knickers going up and down. He is a known pervert

don't forget. You blokes are no safer either, remember that!"
Copperstone was still talking on the phone and reminded, whoever it was, that he wanted action to fix the problem that they had previously discussed. Then he put his phone away. Leanne returned to the office and told Claire that Cherise had said that it was just beyond their range. But she would get her team to look out for the truck between the times that were given to her.

Claire's phone rang. She looked at the caller's ID, it was a withheld number. She was about to ignore it as she usually would but then changed her mind.
"Callison here, who are you and why are you withholding your number?"

"It is I, Claire. The one who you are trying to find but are not bright enough to do so. How the hell did you make DI? It certainly wasn't doing police work. Maybe it was undercover work? You know what I mean, kettle on knickers off sort of thing."
Claire signalled to Kearney to listen in and trace the call.

"What do you want Bernard? I'm too old to play your childish games."

"That is very astute of you Detective but it's no use trying to trace this call. I am, contrary to Kearney's speech, far superior in intelligence than you could even get close to understanding. Kearney will come back in a second and tell you that you have to keep me talking. I have no problem with that Claire. So, how are you holding up in the search for that nasty and selfish Marlow chappie?"

"Where the fuck, are you Tell? You bastard! Where is Marlow?"
Suddenly all the screens lit up and Claire was on every one of them but not full faced. The screens flashed and then she was facing forward on the screen. Everyone could hear both sides of the conversation.

"Claire, using unnecessary language like that is a sign of not being in control, a sign of weakness. Not being able to speak English in a civilised manner, when under stressful situations, presents you as a lowlife and not as the failed teacher that you are. I would imagine you were better off learning from the half-wit children that you chose to stand in front of and profess knowledge.
I have purposely left signs that a blind man could see. Marlow was more than a lowly Constable. He learnt fast and he would have soon overtaken you all; who are staring at the screen in wonderment."
He laughed as he changed the screen to show the other detectives looking around them.
"It's simple schoolboy technology Claire. Nothing special." The screen returned back to Claire's face.
"I thought that Marlow was a gifted detective and I really had no intention of harming him until he opened his mouth and pissed his pants. He knew who I was and somehow thought that I was going to kill him but he was supposedly a good guy or so I thought. His allegiance was to someone who will soon be the next… well I was going to say victim there for a second Claire but it would not have sounded right. But I will get back to him another time, another day.
You all think that you know exactly what is going on out there and I will take this opportunity to tell you that it has

absolutely nothing to do with money… well not as far as I am concerned anyway. So, Copperstone it's back to square one for you and your cash chasing. There will be no more clues left lying around. There is absolutely no point. You walk past them, ignoring them and assume that you have all the answers.
I have killed people, Miss Callison. Greedy, lying, thieving people but the one person I never killed was Petra! Yes, I know that you don't believe me. I can prove it but what would be the point? The person who actually killed her is now where he belongs.
I am not a decent man Claire, far from it but I am a fair man. A killer yes but a fair man. But you will find that out eventually.
So, I see that tracing my call has died a death. Are you taking all this information on board Claire, please answer me and then we will work out a formula for returning Marlow before it's too late?"

"I'm listening to you Tell and so far, it's all been about you. I am picking up your selfishness and very little else. Just tell me where Marlow is and if anything happens to him I swear that I will kill you with my bare hands and that son of yours."

"Son of Mine? Ha. How easy it is to deceive you and send messages that you really want to hear. I have no son. But I truly do believe that you would take my life for Marlow's life; even though you really don't know anything about him.
But I will tell you that he offered both you and Cherise's details if I let him go. I was aghast with that suggestion. I swore up until that point that I would not harm him. He

squirmed and screamed like a little girl but then he pissed himself as well and that sort of made my mind up for me. He was equally upset when I told him that I already had all your details and always knew what you wore underneath. To be honest, I could have given him a price for that information and in any other situation, he would have gladly paid me. I know that is not what you wanted to hear but… shit happens. Believe me Claire, there is much more that you should know about your colleague Chris Marlow.
But because I am getting a fondness for you Claire and you also Leanne; it is only fair that I give you a clue to Marlow's whereabouts. But I will give you only one clue and I'm sure that even a child could do this. Marlow would have been able to work it out but there is not a lot of time. He may frighten himself to death.
This will be fun watching you flap around like headless chickens. Remember to 'dig deep' and pool your resources."

The screens went dead and then there was complete silence.
"What was the clue? He never gave it," shouted out one of the detectives.
"*Dig deep and pool your resources*. That's the clue," Claire shouted out.

"But that sounds too easy, too fucking obvious. So, we have to turn it around and look at it differently," said Kearney.

"Maybe not," replied Claire. Maybe it's a bluff because he knew that we would guess that it was too easy.

Remember, this bastard enjoys playing games with us and he would laugh at us if we failed to see what was staring us in the face."

"So, where do you think that it is?" asked Copperstone. Claire looked around at the screens. She knew that Tell was watching her. She picked up a pen and a piece of paper and wrote down where she thought it was and handed it to Copperstone. He looked at it and shook his head in disbelief.
"Surely not. That is one of the first places that we would look."

"Well it appears that nobody has looked there so far and I am going to check it out. C'mon Leanne, let's go and get Marlow. You other guys can stay here and either pool your own resources or just follow me."

Five police cars left the police station with their lights flashing and Sirens beeping, forcing traffic to pull over and give way. The five cars contained a total of fourteen officers and only one of them knew where they were going.
"Ok, Claire. I admit that I'm a thick bitch. So, where the fuck are we are going?"

"Somerfield Wood, the building site that was closed down."

"How does that compute? "Dig deep and pool your resources," he said. What's that got to do with a building site?"

"It was a double clue and that was the second part. The first part was *flapping around like headless chickens*. It was meant to be a slaughterhouse for chickens and then they changed the plans to include all animals. But unfortunately for the investors, they found an underground spring. They decided to refuse all planning permission, let the hole fill up naturally and then turn it into a leisure park with a natural swimming pool."

"Fuck me Claire, that was bloody hard. I never would have thought of that."

"Yes, you would have. You and the others just overthought the situation. He was hoping that we would ignore the obvious but chickens hatch and counting come to mind at the moment. There is no guarantee that I am right and shit will certainly come my way if I am wrong."

"You have convinced me Guvnor," she laughed.

The convoy approached the building site and a security guard came out to see what all the ruckus was about. "Just open the gate it's an emergency," Claire shouted out.

"What sort of emergency Miss?"

"Just open the fucking gate or you will be the fucking emergency," Leanne shouted out. The security guard ran back inside the building and lifted the gate up.
The convoy, once again led by Claire, drove down the steep and winding road and eventually came to a stop. Claire and Leanne got out of the car and looked into the small lake that was almost up to the roof of Marlow's car.

On top of the car roof was a bright yellow forty-five-gallon steel drum, that wobbled slightly as the car slowly moved in the water.
Claire and Leanne were joined by their colleagues, staring at the car of one of their own that was near to tipping over. Claire took her shoes and coat off and Leanne followed suit. They dived into the cold water and swam towards the car. As they got nearer, they realised that the car was in danger of tipping over at any moment.
They tried opening the doors but they were locked. They needed water to fill the car for stability but at the same time had to keep the car from moving and dislodging the drum off the roof because they were both sure that it would sink.

Leanne dived down into the cold, dark, murky depths of the excavated site. She was gone for what seemed an absolute age but then returned to the surface coughing and wheezing with a rock in her hand. They tried to work out which would be the best window to break first but to do that they would have to know what the car was resting on. Claire took a deep breath, dived into the depths and blindly felt around the vehicle. It was almost touching the ground on all four wheels but she favoured the driver's side. She swam back to the surface and told Leanne which window to try and break.
Leanne used all the strength that she could muster and smashed the side quarter-light window. The car filled up with water, steadying it enough to be able to climb on. Claire carefully climbed onto the roof of the car and saw that the filler cap had been removed from the drum.
She saw the locking clasp that held the lid on. She tried to open it but her hands were cold. She felt the car rocking.

She noticed that more officers were swimming towards her then she heard a moaning noise coming from inside the drum.
"He is still alive but I can't open the clasp on the drum. I need help."
A young constable climbed up, joined her, managed to open the clasp and remove the lid of the drum. Marlow looked up at them. He was talking gibberish and shaking. His hands were all bloody and his knuckle bones and fleshless fingers shone through the broken skin.

The plan to get him out of the drum was harder than it looked. They had no idea if he was injured or not apart from his hands but they had to get him out and into the waiting ambulance that had just turned up.
The Constable who was the first to arrive, Mick Cobbly, suggested lying the drum down and pulling him out. They had no other choice so that is what happened.
The drum was laid down onto the roof. Mick held Marlow's arms and the others pulled the drum away. It was easier than they imagined. All that remained was to get him to the ambulance as soon as possible. Six of the strongest swimmers, carried him on their backs together and swam slowly and easily towards the waiting ambulance. Claire and Leanne followed close by; both offering words of encouragement to the swimmers and Marlow who was far away in a different world.
The two women detectives received a round of applause from all the officers concerned. They clapped back in return, jumped into the car and followed the ambulance, with the heater set to the hot position.

Kearney and Copperstone were waiting at the hospital when they arrived. They took Claire and Leanne into a private room and made them hot drinks.
"How on earth did you work that out Claire?" asked Copperstone.

"Just a lucky guess Sir, just a lucky guess."

"I think that it was much more than a lucky guess Claire," he said. "May I suggest that you both see a doctor and then go home," he added.

"Consider it suggested Sir," laughed Leanne. "Thank you, Sir but we will wait and find out about Marlow if that is ok?"

"I'd like to get you out of those clothes straight away first Claire…I'll erm… I'll see if I can get you something to change into," Copperstone said and promptly disappeared to probably hide his embarrassment.

One of the doctors turned up and told them that Marlow was ok, apart from needing plastic surgery on his hands. He was probably in a state of shock. He was not responding to the usual tests so they would keep him in for a few days.
"I understand that he was locked inside a forty-five-gallon drum. Is that true?"

"Yes. That is what happened and we don't know how long that he was actually in that drum," answered Kearney. "At least twenty-four hours we believe."

“My God. How can anyone put a fellow human being through that amount of suffering? I would say that he will certainly require counselling after this shock. He almost certainly believed that he would die. I imagine. It would be impossible to understand what went on in his mind, bloody impossible. The good thing is, he is young and fit and I believe that he has many friends that will help him to regain his mental and physical strength.”

Claire and Leanne sat there waiting with a blanket over their wet clothes, drinking strong coffee, worrying about the effect that this experience would have on one of their own.
Copperstone turned up with a selection of clothes that he had gathered from the Salvation Army Shop. The two detectives politely declined his offer and finally gave in to tiredness. They both decided to go home.

Claire drove Leanne home. She was a bit fidgety. She kept opening the window and sticking her head out of it and taking deep breaths.
Claire had seen her friend and partner like this before and hoped that it would pass over in a few minutes. The deep breathing helped usually but then she realised that it wasn’t going to happen this time.
“How bad is it Leanne? Are you ok?”

“No, Claire. I keep imagining what it must have been like trapped inside that drum and not being able to move. I…I… my legs are … I can’t move Claire… I can’t move.” She burst out crying and her whole body started shaking uncontrollably.

Claire stopped the car, put her arms around her friend and tried to comfort her. She knew that Leanne suffered from claustrophobia but this was by far the worst that she had ever seen her. She would take her home and stay as long as was necessary to help her friend and partner deal with her breath stopping, frightening, nightmare.

Chapter Twelve.

Saturday 9th July
Leanne's Flat

Eventually, Claire managed to get Leanne to sleep. She gently removed her friend's clothes and washed her body with a warm flannel, like a mother with a sick child. She removed the cushions from the sofa in the living room and laid them on the floor next to her friend. As she laid down, Leanne reached out and held on to her hand.
Claire had seen Leanne break into a nervous sweat, a couple of times when faced with situations involving small spaces. She would do her duty and bravely enter these situations; to children, animals and anyone who needed help. But it was always after the event that she would get upset. Last night was the worst that she had ever seen her friend. But under the circumstances, anyone would get breathless at the thought of the confinement that they had both witnessed.
She didn't get much sleep. She opened her eyes every time that Leanne whimpered; patted her hand, talked to her and comforted her.

Claire felt the warm sun in her face and knew that she would get no more sleep. She felt dirty and desperately needed a bath. There was only a shower at Leanne's flat but 'needs must' she told herself. She stayed under the powerful, pulsing and invigorating shower until she felt that all the dirt and remnants of yesterday's horrific discovery were washed off of her body.

She helped herself to a change of clothing. Then she put her own and Leanne's dirty washing into the washing machine and started cooking breakfast.
She was no stranger to Leanne's flat and vice versa. They each knew where everything was and they had similar likes and dislikes which made working together easy and enjoyable.
Leanne woke up to the smell of bacon cooking and got up and into the shower. She dressed and walked sheepishly into the kitchen and smiled at Claire.
"I'm sorry Claire, was I that bad? I can still feel the pain in my legs. I honestly felt as if I was crippled."

"Well, you know the rules Leanne; don't think about it. Think of something or someone nice or even diving into a full English. Remind yourself that you need to go shopping, there wasn't that much in the fridge, there's even less now."

"I know I just keep forgetting to go shopping, the Chinese takeaway is nearer." They both laughed trying hard to force yesterday further into the past.

"So, how do you feel about getting back to work this morning? I think that we should go back to the beginning; ask each other questions, like we used to do and a session of what-ifs. We need to kick arse Leanne to make ourselves feel better."

"I'm good with that, after I get through this mega breakfast. Thank you."

Claire called the hospital and was told that there was no change in Marlow's condition. He was not responding to medication. He just stared blankly and was constantly shaking, especially his hands. He was making funny noises. His parents were sitting with him. Claire didn't relay the details to Leanne, she just told her that there was no change.
She knew that Leanne usually took a few days to get over her claustrophobic attacks and no one else, except Kearney, knew about them.
They arrived at the office and went directly to Kearney's office. She knew, without being told, that Leanne had had an episode. She said nothing.

"Ok Ladies so what do we know? Nothing seems to be moving, although I have received information from Immigration; Mr Duncan Lee-Winton never re-entered this country from South Africa. I am waiting for the South African Ambassador to make enquiries and he will get back to me…eventually. So, back to square one."

"That's the main reason we're here to be honest Frances," said Clare. "We think that we should go back to the beginning and see what we have missed. We understand that there were no bullet fragments found on the victims of the Crown Court shootings. Although, we have yet to get the autopsy report. We still don't know who the intended victim was either!
Lee-Winton has disappeared suspiciously and Bernard Tell has us all set up on candid fucking camera. We have a total of six bodies, seven with Mrs Hood, but we are putting that down as accidental or misadventure, as they say. So, Frances we have absolute Jack to go on; and if

that isn't enough, Bernard Tell is trying to turn us all into canned soup…"
Claire realised what she had just said and looked over at Leanne, who covered her face but then looked up and smiled.

"It's ok Claire, I'm good. Slightly gone off soup at the moment though." She laughed.
Kearney saw Claire's mistake and instantly started to answer her questions not giving Leanne time to think about it.

"As for the 'Candid Camera' quip Claire; the building has been physically swept and wireless cameras were found. They have all been removed but there is no evidence of who installed them and where they actually came from."

"Bernard Tell said that it was 'schoolboy stuff.' We know, darn well, how easy it is to get surveillance gadgets from the internet but there must have been somebody close by that installed it."

"I wouldn't have called it 'installing' Claire. All it consisted of was a pronged gadget that easily clipped onto wires, using a pair of pliers. Those wires are already part of the server system and could only be found by a physical search."

"So, have they all been removed? Has the station had a clean sweep as well as the changing rooms because I certainly won't change in there anymore?"

"Oddly enough Claire, there was nothing at all found in those areas. They were clean but everywhere else looked like it had suffered a virus attack from little one-eyed monsters."

"Can I see what they look like? So that Leanne and I can check our own homes for the pervert's cameras. To be honest, I will never feel comfortable in this place again because they were put there unchallenged. Who is to say that they are not already back there?"
Kearney gave the detectives a gadget each.

"We have installed cameras of our own and we will soon catch anyone who tries to hook up with the server or the main phone lines. The installation engineering company insist that all their operatives have filled in the 'Disclosure and Barring Service' form. They have all been checked. Anyone not registered with the company cannot enter the system without logging on, with a sophisticated password system, that is immediately identified by a master encryption identity device."

"It still reminds me that 'Big Brother' is looking over my shoulders and waiting for me to drop my knickers, along with that pervert Tell," Claire said laughing. "But how do we know that these gadgets are not still sending information out?" she said, sticking her finger up in the air while turning her seat in a circle.

"Ok, ladies. Let's get back to basics," Kearney said. "I have received some bad news about the DNA from the sheets at Winton and Tell's flat. The samples have been compromised. They are doing a third DNA check and will

let us know; although to be honest it isn't going to change things. We know that they were sleeping together. So, where do we want to be? We know that Bernard Tell killed William Tell, who we now know was his half-brother. Dermot Dolan, along with Robin Hood, were both killed for giving him a, well-deserved, arse-kicking. We can't, as you have said, count Mrs Hood but I will try and throw it in for good measure.
Petra Tancred… he was obviously responsible for that killing, despite his claims to the contrary. Also, the two petty crooks, that we know very little about. Exactly how they are involved, we don't yet know but because they are dead, we have their prints and DNA that link them to weapons associated with the case, they are by default, involved."
"I had the statement from Leonard Gail transcribed. Take a copy each, read through it and give me your thoughts on Monday. I need another couple of females looking through some of what he says. It certainly doesn't ring true to me. He is hiding more than he is telling. Maybe we should start working this case backwards and find out what Starkey and his mate were really up to? Money still talks and there are enough snitches out there, who need money for a fix. So, I think we can start sniffing around the town until anything concrete comes in."
The two detectives flicked through Gail's statement and shoved them in their bags.

"Great stuff Frances, I'm in favour of that. There must be information out there because they were well known by all the other petty thieves that share their information. We just gotta find the right intel," Claire said looking a bit happier when she saw Leanne's eyes light up, at the prospect of a walk around the town talking to the low-lifes and a bit of therapeutic shopping.

The low-life, in the town, were in fact a group or groups of petty criminals and homeless people that the detectives usually got on really well with. They almost all had interesting personalities and were good at whatever illegal skill that they had. They were, as Leanne called them, 'honestly dishonest.' These people; the thieves, the scam artists and codgers, were where they were for many reasons. Sometimes, those reasons would never be told. They knew that if they got caught breaking the law, it was part and parcel of their occupation and they would be rewarded by getting a bed and three meals a day. Crying and stamping their feet would do very little, to gain the sympathy of a Judge. But who knew that for sure unless it was tried. 'Honestly dishonest' …what you saw was what you got. Unless of course, you were a victim.

Claire and Leanne wore casual clothes and assumed the identity of normal shoppers. They blended in amongst the normal Saturday bargain hunters, in the packed town centre. They headed for the most likely places, where they would come into contact with people who could help them, in gaining any information about Richard Starkey and Gordon Grafton. But word had soon got around that the detectives were on the prowl and they themselves were being watched. It seemed that the 'low-life' had obtained built-in radar. They disappeared as soon as they were spotted. Even their own snouts were hiding from them.
"It looks as though we have been marked out Leanne, so we may as well just relax and do some shopping for real."

"I thought that's what we were doing already," she laughed.
So, the two detectives carried on doing what came naturally to them and had enjoyed some retail therapy. They both, at various times, spotted the small-time villains but they pretended that they were not interested. They were careful to stay well away from them and gave them time to relax and to get used to the coppers being there, innocently shopping.

Very soon the two detective's arms were full of bags. They became easy targets for bag snatchers and pickpockets. Leanne gave the sign that they had just been marked out by one of the thieves. Their aim was to try to distract one of them and steal the other one's bags, whilst they were both in a state of shock.
Claire was the distraction and Leanne knew that it was her bag that was going to be snatched. They played along with it and waited for it to kick-off. There was a crowd of people heading their way. They knew that this would be the time that the thieves made their move.
A man had purposely made a clumsy attempt to grab a hold of Claire's shopping bags. She shouted out one word.
"Now!"
The other thief went to grab Leanne's bag but they were surprised when both the women dropped the shopping and grabbed hold of them instead. The two men were struggling but they were the ones who were surprised. The women soon had them cuffed. Passers-by helped to pick up the shopping bags that actually had real shopping in. Security guards soon turned up and helped march them off to the holding cell in the middle of the shopping centre.

The two men sat in the cell, cursing their luck and each other for getting caught so easily. They looked up at Claire as she stood the other side of the bars. She introduced herself and showed her badge.
"We knew you were coppers. We could smell ya when you first came in here. You were lucky that you caught us at the last minute because we were held down by the crowd. You attacked us for no reason. Now let us go. You can't hold us because we haven't done anything wrong. In fact, we can sue you for wrongful arrest."

"Oh, you are so wrong Mr Frankie Fox and your mate Nigel Swanson. We knew what you were going to do before you did. My God, no wonder you keep getting caught. Jesus, I have seen some amateurs in my time but you take the biscuit… well you would if you didn't keep getting nicked."

"You will be sorry when I get my solicitor on to you for assault, wrongful arrest and false imprisonment."

"See all this shopping in front of you Mr Fox? You tried to rob me and my friend and it was in your possession. So, how is that wrongful arrest? Also, assaulting two police officers in that action. Oh, and resisting arrest. So, where does wrongful arrest come into it?"

"You are framing me. It won't change the picture darling. I demand to see a solicitor now, this very minute."

"Frankie baby, you know how this works. You know that we can make a deal. You scratch my back, as they say.

You either walk away from this or get a first-class ride in a limo to jail. The choice, Frankie baby is all yours."

"You fucking bent bitch. What's the deal then and I might give it some thought."

"Richard Starkey and Gordon Grafton."

"Who the fuck are they? I ain't never heard of them."

"Oh dear, Frankie. Are you sure about that, I mean really sure?"

"Nah, never heard of them. Get me my brief… Now!"

"Oh, that is a real shame for you. I tried to hide this bag that was found on you. What is it Coke? H? It doesn't smell very nice; how much is there? A couple of years' worth, maybe more?"

"Everyone knows that I don't touch any of that shit. I ain't no druggie. Go get me my brief."

"Ok Frankie, this is the last chance. Tell me what I want to hear or go rusty in jail."

"Fuck off bitch. Ya ain't gonna frighten me into your bullshit."

"Even if I tell the prison guards you are both *kiddy lovers*."

The man sitting next to him in the cell started arguing with him and started to punch him about.
"What do you want to know exactly?" asked Nigel Swanson.

"Everything, absolutely everything about them and then you are both free to go."

"I just think that you are totally out of order threatening us with what you know is a death sentence," Nigel Swanson said. He was trembling with anger. Claire knew that if he could have broken through the bars to get at her, he would have done so.

"We have always put our hands up when we have been nicked. But you, ya fucking mercenary bitch, have done yourself no favours with your attitude. As soon as we're both released, we will make sure that none of your snouts will ever tell you fuck all. I want it in writing that we will be freed today, the minute we give you what you ask."

"I'm afraid that I can't give you anything in writing Mr Swanson and you know that. I suggest that you control your temper and start breathing properly or I will walk away. This deal now depends on your co-operation. There are dead bodies out there and the tally will just keep growing, until you help us to find the murderer of Starkey and Grafton."
The two men sat there silent, motionless and open-mouthed; not quite believing what she had just said.

"Murder?" said Frankie, "you never said anything about them being murdered, when is that supposed to have happened?"

"Oh, so you do know them, or should I say *knew*."

"Look Detective, of course we knew them. If you had said that earlier we wouldn't have had to go through this fucking pantomime. Now what happened to them? They were mates of ours," Swanson said sadly. Claire nodded to one of the guards who brought coffee for the pair and let them out of the cell.
"Look Miss, you know how this goes. We always argue the toss with you coppers and there is usually respect from both sides. But you lady, you need a joint personality and attitude transfusion. Now tell us exactly how they died and we will help you," Frankie said.

"I'm afraid that there is no easy way to tell you this." She asked Leanne to leave while she told her story to the men. Claire said, as she sat down in front of the two men. "Richard Starkey and Gordon Grafton were both murdered… brutally murdered. They err… they both had their hands severed, sawed off at the wrist and were… and were…still alive when it happened. Then they were put into a forty-five-gallon drum, the lids were closed on them and then they were sealed. We err… we believe that they were both alive when the drums were sealed. The Coroner told us that there were scratches, dents and bits of bone stuck to the lid. They tried to punch their way out before they eventually suffocated."
Swanson jumped off the seat and vomited into the corner of the room. Frankie went very pale and almost passed

out. Claire took a hold of his arm to stop him falling. It took a while before both men were well enough to talk but Claire told them both to take their time. She arranged for a doctor to check them over and they were then removed to more comfortable surroundings. When they were ready, they called Claire and Leanne, who had just rejoined them.

"All we know," said Frankie. "Is that they were following someone but they never gave any names, just hints really. They said they were working for some guy who would pay them fifty big ones, to get as much shit as they could on the guy they were following. He apparently kidnapped his own father and was keeping him imprisoned and drugged up somewhere. They had to find the father to get the money. They bragged about it to anyone who would listen but they never gave the full version… never said who the job was for or who the guy was that they were following…
No…I'm lying, sorry he was called Mr Bee. The one they were following, that's what they called him, Mr Bee. It was Mr Bee this and Mr Bee that, that's all we bloody heard from them. But there was nothing else that they told us. Nothing we can give you I'm afraid, to help you catch the bastard wot done them in."

"We did hear that your friends had not been seen for a couple of weeks," said Leanne.

"Sorry sweetheart, time means nothing to us, every day is the same; yesterday, today, tomorrow, all the bloody same, excuse my French."

"Can you give us their address, so that we can look for clues?"

"Ha, that's a good one, their address! They are like us, we ain't got no address. We squat in different places every night. We keep getting moved on, by your lot and private security companies. Starkey and Grafton swore that this money, that they were gonna get, was gonna buy a caravan at Southend and we could go and spend a few days with them, every now and again. They told us all, all their mates, they could come and have a good piss-up and somewhere to sleep for a few days. But it didn't happen and it ain't gonna happen."

Claire had all that she was going to get. She apologised to the two men and offered them £40. They refused to take it. "We volunteered to speak to you once we knew what you wanted and why. It was our friends that copped it. We are not and never will be, paid snitches. But if we hear anything, we will make sure that we come to you. We don't want your money. We don't want fuck all off of you… Now I would be obliged if you let us go," said Swanson. They watched the men leave the shopping centre and almost felt sorry for them.

They carried their shopping back to the car park and put it in the boot.
"I suppose we had better do a bit of grocery shopping while we have the time. Have you got any ideas from what those two said, Leanne?"

"It could be anyone at all looking for Bernard. Someone related to his father or a business partner? I don't know. I think we will have to talk to Kearney. She spoke to Miss Tancred's lawyer and I believe that she heard quite a lot about their business. So, shall we do the shops first and Kearney second?"

"No Leanne you drive towards the supermarket and I will talk to her. I don't want to go back to the station. It's like a monster that wants to trap us there and never let us go." They both laughed.
Kearney never answered her office phone. So, Claire decided that Monday would be soon enough. The two detectives were happy enough to go and do their grocery shopping and let the criminals have a day off.

Chapter Thirteen.

Saturday 9th July 12:30
Mayfair Towers, Paddington.

Detective Chief Inspector, Oscar Evesham, arrived at The Mayfair Towers building and noticed the large removal van. It was wedged into the special loading bay, designated for deliveries and collections for the apartment's residents and service staff. He peeked into the back of the truck and saw the ranks of filing cabinets, printers, and copiers.
Three men, pushing a loaded trolley, gave him a funny look as they loaded up the trolley. He stretched to have a better look at the contents of the trolley. One of the workers headed towards him menacingly, asking what his game was. But a flash of his warrant card stopped him in mid-track and he returned a smile.
"Excuse me mate. I assume that all that office equipment is from Apartment 9a? It's ok, I am on my way up there now. I just wanted to know if you were almost finished, before I go to see Mr Gail."

"Yes officer. It is from 9a and that was the last load. We are all done. Mr Gail said that he was expecting a c… police officer to call." He smiled awkwardly then shut and locked the rear doors of the removal van and drove away.

Evesham walked into the reception area, asked for Mr Gail, Apartment 9a and said that he was expected. He showed his warrant card as ID.

"I believe that he is expecting you Sir but I will just check if I may?"
The receptionist called Mr Gail and announced that the Chief Inspector had arrived at the reception desk; Mr Gail told the receptionist to send him up.
DCI Evesham rang the bell of 9a. The door opened, Mr Gail introduced himself and invited the police officer in.

"You were lucky that you phoned me when you did officer. I was in two minds whether to book a round of golf this afternoon but as you said it was very important… Well, we are here now; it seems strange because DCI Kearney seemed to be happy enough when she left. Excuse me officer but you seem vaguely familiar to me have we met before?"

"Oh yes Sir, many years ago when I was a constable. My colleagues and I were always in different courts with villains of all sort. I used to see you with Miss Tancred and Mr Tell; they were very good. I used to sit and watch them plead their cases in my own time. It was a skill that I assume many lawyers are sadly missing in this day and age Sir."

"Yes indeed. You are correct in your assumption officer, which I of course share with you. But can we talk about why you are here; is it because you have found out new information as a result of DCI Kearney and DCS Coppertone's enquiries? Have you had any new information on the disappearance of Mr William Tell and the murders of his son and his business partner Miss Petra Tancred?"

“Excuse me for asking Sir but are you selling up this apartment after the sad loss of Miss Tancred?”

“With respect officer, I hardly think that is any concern of yours. I have just asked you a question and you are here, I believe, to inform me of your progress are you not?”

“Forgive me Sir but the question that I asked is of concern. We may not be finished with our enquiries here. But yes Sir, I have new information regarding them, which I will come to shortly. But firstly, I need to know if you are acquainted with a Mr Richard Starkey and a Mr Gordon Grafton; both from Duns Town?”

“Erm… no, I’m afraid that those names do not ring any bells officer. I’m sorry.”

“So, you would have no idea about a payment of fifty thousand pounds, that they said you would pay them for any information on the whereabouts of Mr William Tell senior? I ask because that is what they have both written in their statements.”

“Fifty thous… my goodness officer I have absolutely no idea what you are talking about! Fifty thousand pounds, that is a fortune. No, I’m sorry officer.”

“That is perfectly alright Sir. I knew that they were a pair of lying scumbags, who would say anything to cover up a murder.”

“Murder! Whose murder were they trying to cover up? Is it Miss Tancred or William Junior? Please tell me officer.”

“I’m afraid that it was neither of those people Sir. It was a male, who we believe goes by the name of Mr Bee. Through our investigations, we believe it to be Bernard Bartley Tell. But we have no other information about him except for the surname Tell. We think that it is connected somehow to the other murders”

“Bernard Barton Tell, you mean officer. He is the disowned son of William Tell senior. A more perverted piece of shit you will never find. But if he is dead then Mr William Tell will never be found. Can you talk to these men and find out if they had done what I… if they know where Mr Tell senior is?”

“We were going to charge them with murder Sir but at the moment we have insufficient evidence. They changed their original story and now say that they found the body of Mr Bee. They stole documents from him and among those documents was an address of the care home. We fingerprinted Mr Bee or Bernard Barton Tell and as yet we have no match. Would you know Sir, if he had ever been in trouble with the police?”

“No, is the short answer to that. His father refused to involve the police in his son’s perverse activities. He sent him away and then he disappeared. Now, what about this care home?”

I’m sorry Sir, it is a little dry in here. May I have a drink of water please?”

“Oh, excuse my manners officer. Allow me to get it for you. Would you like some ice with it or would you prefer something a little stronger?”

“No, thank you. I am on duty and I have a vehicle downstairs. But ice in the water would be perfect please.” Gail, delivered the drink and sat down.

“Now officer as you were saying.”

“Well Sir, as a matter of course, we made enquiries about the care home. We believe that we have found a man who could possibly be Mr Tell senior but we have no idea what the real Mr Tell looks like Sir. The man in question, is booked in under the name of Peter Tancred Sir. So, you may understand why this led us to you, in spite of the two men changing their story.
The two men gave us an indication, where the man you are looking for was found. It is a private clinic in Hampstead Heath. The man in question had been heavily sedated, by his own doctor, who visited frequently. But I’m afraid we cannot locate this Doctor. The man is now being treated by a police doctor and is slowly coming ‘round. It would help us if we can draw a line under this part of the investigation. We would like to arrange a legal and proper identification of the gentleman; is there anyone of his relatives or close friends who could do that Sir?”

“I will gladly do it officer and I would like to arrange for his own doctor to take charge of him, if it is indeed Mr Tell. When can I see him? It is of the utmost importance that we get him to a safe place before anyone can force him to change his will.”

"I see Sir. You mean this Bernard chappie and you believe that Mr Tell is in imminent danger. Is that what I understand Sir? Even though this Bernard Tell is dead Sir?"

"Yes. Indeed, he is. Of that there is no doubt. But Bernard had a son, who is going by the name of Duncan Lee-Winton. A poor young man who was murdered, probably by them, ten years ago." He was interrupted by Evesham before he could finish his sentence.

"I'm sorry Sir. You cannot go around making unsubstantiated claims like that."

"Yes, of course. You're right, I apologise for my outburst. Do you think that you could possibly take me to this care home now officer? Then I can arrange emergency transport to Mr Tell's own private care home?"

"Why yes Sir. Of course, I can Mr Gail. It is not a problem Sir. In fact, I was hoping that you would ask me that. I will take you and then it will be another job that I can tick off my never-ending list of enquiries. Thank you, Sir. Now, if you would like to get your coat and anything else that you need; my car is in the main car park. It isn't the luxury that you are used to Sir but it is all that they will give us."

"I promise you officer, that if this is Mr Tell, I will personally buy you a luxury car. It will be the envy of all of your colleagues."

"That is very kind of you Sir but we are not allowed to take gifts of any description. But thank you again."

"You tell me the name of your favourite charity officer and they will be richer overnight."

"You are indeed most kind Sir. Hopefully, you will meet up with Mr Tell."

The two men got into the lift and exited at the reception area. Everyone that they passed spoke to Mr Gail and his friend. But Mr Gail expressed his apology and told them that he was in a desperate hurry.
They arrived at the police officer's car and Gail looked at it in obvious dismay.

"I'm afraid I see what you mean officer. It is a bit battered but it has… well, I'm sure that it has many good memories of the bad guys that you have caught."

He laughed as he sat in the front passenger seat. As he pulled the seatbelt out, he felt a sharp pain in his thigh. He turned and saw the police officer holding a syringe and laughing.
"*A more perverted piece of shit you could never find*, that is what you said. Guess what Gail? If you look into the mirror at your soul, you could easily have found it."

Leonard Gail took a deep breath. He smiled and then relaxed back into the seat. He felt the nice policeman, clipping his seatbelt in. He saw all the bright lights whooshing past the vehicle in a kaleidoscope of colour and stared at them like a young child watching his first

firework display. He jumped up and down excitedly, as much as the seatbelt allowed him to. But all good things will eventually come to an end.
As much as the colours excited Leonard, they had made him tired and sleepy. The colours had now turned to boring, ugly, blacks and greys. He stuck his thumb in his mouth and sucked on it loudly. His eyes slowly closed and sleep took him.

"Wakey, wakey, Leonard. Sleepy time is on hold for a very short time. C'mon wake up, you parasite."
Gail jumped awake as ice-cold water was thrown over him. He gasped as he was rudely awakened. He opened his eyes and looked around. He blinked a few times to clear his vision then he noticed that his friend and partner was in the bed in front of him and staring at him blankly. Gail tried to move but realised that he had been restrained in a wooden armchair. He looked around and saw DCI Evesham looking at him and he was smiling.

"What in God's name do you think you are doing officer? Untie me at once so that I can see for myself that Mr Tell is *Compos Mentis*. Untie me I say. My God, you don't' have any idea who you are playing with. Untie me now or your career will be surely at an end."

"My God Gail. I never thought that I would get away with it. I thought that you would recognise me straight away. It's just as well you didn't, I suppose, otherwise you would be with your dead cronies. Well, most of them anyway. My Father, yes that is him in the bed. His actions will be very limited for a short time more but he can understand everything that is going on.

I am afraid that you will join him temporarily in gaga land; not in the same bed of course, even though you are used to lying next to him. You are both too old for that now… I would imagine? No, you will have your own bed and you can look at each other and try and talk through your thoughts.
Unfortunately, I have a little unfinished business to take care of. I must put right some wrongs. I will be relieving you of your phone, Leonard. I need it to assist me in my defence, well some of it anyway and then you will both get my undivided attention. It will all be over for you. Hell is waiting. Oh, by the way, there will be a nurse popping in and out. She will look after you and keep you where you will do no harm until I return. You may recognise her; she had a sister long ago. Her name was Mary Mortimer! Happy reunion day, Leonard."

"Bernard come back! Come back here you bastard. Bernard…"

Chapter Fourteen

Sunday 10th July 05:00
Claire Callison's Home

Claire could not sleep and spent the night reading up on the lawyer, Leonard Gail's statement. It made for interesting reading and there was something that made the words from his mouth seem a bit iffy. She read it twice and made notes of everything that he said, she had intended to read it a third time but succumbed to sleep before she completed the first page.
Claire, felt uneasy and she woke up with a start, with the uncomfortable feeling that she was being watched. She tried to move her head but for some reason, she was unable to. She thought at first that she may have had a stroke. She couldn't think why it was impossible to move any part of her body, except her eyes.
She looked all around and saw a shadow, of something or somebody, at the far end of her sight range. It seemed to be in the vicinity of her chair at the foot of the bed. She whimpered softly but loud enough for the shadow to hear her. The shadow moved and she saw that it was a man, who then moved closer to her so that she could see him clearly.
"Please forgive the uninvited intrusion Detective Callison. I would first like you to know that your honour was not in any way compromised. I have no intention of hurting you and I apologise for the condition that you now find yourself in. It was the only way that I would be able to talk to you and that you would listen but it will soon wear off.

In a few minutes, you will be able to move your mouth. When that happens, I will help you to sit up and I ask forgiveness for having to touch you when I do that. But your lips and mouth are dry, I will assist you in moistening them."

Tell saw that she was moving her lips and he very gently sat her up. Then moistened her lips and spoon-fed her water. She was soon able to talk to him.
"Who, the fuck, do you think you are? Breaking into my home you, *fucktard*, murdering, perverted, piece of shit. As soon as I can move, I will kick that fucking shit out of you. Now fuck off."

"Oh, Claire, Claire, Claire. I have told you before that you do not need to use such profanity, such obscenity; you have the power to make men scared of you just by using your normal voice and your good looks. But I never came here to cause you grief. I came here to confess. To tell you the truth that keeps hiding from you and Kearney; who it seems cannot follow through on her own suspicions."

"If you want to confess, come to the police station with me and confess so that we can put your murdering arse behind bars for good and put the departed souls to rest."

"You remind me of someone that was close to me. She could say, in a few words, what others need paragraphs for. Even in her youth she was… she has gone now. Forgive me but she is the reason that I am who I am."

"Please spare me the teary-eyed, lame excuses for your murdering spree. Was your son Lee-Winton or should I say Nathaniel Tell, also responsible for these murders?"
"I have already told you that I do not have a son; Lee-Winton or Nathaniel. Neither of them, exist anymore. He exists as someone else and you will never see him again. I can assure you of that."

"Oh my God! Please don't tell me that you have killed him as well."

"You just do not listen to me Detective. I have just said that he exists now as someone else. Why would I kill someone that I have spent the last thirty-four years of my life protecting?"

"Exactly what are you saying and where is this going Tell?"

"Maybe if you would listen, I could start at the beginning."

"Go ahead Tell. You have my undivided attention, for the moment at least and would your barbaric treatment of Marlow be part of this story?"
Tell bathed her lips again and gave her a drink to lubricate the tongue that would no doubt keep interrupting him.

"My parents, who I remember from an early age, were not exactly the perfect couple. Both of them had been into affairs. I saw many people in my childhood; in all stages of dress, running naked, backwards and forwards all over the house. They often committed the acts in my room.

They were depraved, beyond any description and I was lucky to survive in one piece mentally."

"Yes Tell. You really, fucking, believe that, don't you?" He ignored her outburst and carried on where he left off.

"I worked for my father, whilst I was at university, as a trainee law assistant; learning how to rip people off and get paid for doing so. My parent's depravity became nothing but an embarrassment to me and I had often full-on verbal fights with them. It all came to a head when I found my mother naked with a group of young men, most of whom were my friends. I was further surprised when my father came in with a couple of young girls and joined in the fun. I suppose that was when it all kicked off.
I left my father's company in 1982 and found employment elsewhere. I met the love of my life, Mary Mortimer but she was ten years younger than me. We agreed to wait until she was eighteen before we got married. Her parents were not overly keen but they knew that my intentions were good and I was welcomed into the family. My own parents decided to disown me and I was threatened to keep my mouth shut or face the consequences. I had no intention of saying anything. Why would I? It would only embarrass me.
I started to hear all sorts of rumours about me and my apparently sexually perverse activities, incessant thieving and the numerous other false accusations aimed at me. I truly had no idea what they were on about and I threatened them with court action. I said that I would tell the world of their depravity.
They sent two of their finest men after me; Robin Hood and Dermot Dolan. They easily overpowered me and

almost killed me. God knows, they tried hard enough. Then, they tried to set fire to me and yes, I did see a bright light.
Anyway, I was found by a caring passer-by and was taken to hospital. I was in intensive care for a few months, I'm not sure how long it was really. Whilst there, I received a message from Hood and Dolan that I was a dead man walking or laying in my case. So, with great pain and a hefty bribe; I escaped from the hospital and went back to my Mary's house. She took care of me and cried when she saw my wounds, yet she tended to them with love.
We went to the movies one night and on the way out we were grabbed by Hood and Dolan and taken to a warehouse. I was strapped to a chair and my eyes were stitched open, so that I would witness the hate my father had for me.
Mary was stripped naked and my father came in and raped her, inches away from me, she was a virgin. They walked out laughing and left her lying there bleeding. I was still tied up. Mary eventually summoned the energy and stood up. She then tried to cover herself as best she could and then untied me. She wouldn't allow me go to the police, she was too frightened, for both our sakes. We stayed at home too scared to venture out. I slept on the sofa. After a few weeks we found out that she was pregnant from the rape. We told her father, who was a staunch Catholic and he told her that she would keep the child. When she was eighteen, we would wed but I was never allowed to sleep with her. That was too much to ask."

"So how do you know that it wasn't your child then Mr goody two shoes?"

"I wished that it were mine, Claire but I'm afraid that it would have been impossible. Thanks to the beating I had from Hood and Dolan I had just enough of my manhood left to piss, if I sat down to do it. We made the best of it and I stayed with her throughout the pregnancy. Afterwards, her father threw her out. Another soul disowned by her parents. I would show you the scars but I am still embarrassed.
We lived with her sister for a while until…until she died. My father found out that Mary had a child, a boy and he wanted to get rid of it. Leonard Gail found Mary walking back from the shop and tried to get the babies whereabouts but she said nothing. He injected her with heroin and she died.
I found out, from someone I knew within the company, that Gail had been the one that killed her. I knew then, that it was only a matter of time before the baby was killed. I got the proper paperwork under a different name and took the child, and Mary's sister Martina, to another country. We stayed there until we met Duncan Lee-Winton."

"It sounds nothing more than a romantic fairy tale, Tell. So, you are telling me that the person we know as Lee-Winton is actually your half-brother, William Tell's son?"

"I'm afraid that is the truth Detective. As God is my judge."

"So why would he want his own son killed?"

"My Mother… if I wasn't good enough for my Mother to love, his bastard son would have even less of a chance."

"So, you bought him up as your son, in a different country with a different name. What name did you use Tell?"
"The name that he is using now, is the name that he grew up with and that is all you need to know as far as that goes. You will never find him. He has done nothing wrong."

"Aiding and abetting murder is a crime, Mr Tell or did you forget that part of the law? Maybe you dropped out before you got that far?"

"In this case, it matters nothing to me. I am prepared to look the other way for love," he chortled.

"You could say that it got a little complicated when he fell in love with William. It was a pure bloody coincidence that they met the way that they did."

"I don't believe in coincidences either Mr Tell. Regardless of the love issue, your brother is a criminal in the eyes of the law; whether you think so or not and he will pay the price.
When do we get to the part when you turned from being a lovesick hero into a serial killer? That's the part I am waiting for."

"I assume Claire, that you are the sort of person to look at the back page of a story to see how it ends?"

"You could be right there Tell but I know how this one ends. You are sitting here chatting shit to me and you have not even attempted to cover your face. That means you are

either gonna kill me or bore me to death. Or maybe even surrender!"
"I have already told you that you were safe and that I wouldn't hurt you. Surrendering is not going to happen Claire. I have two little jobs to take care of when I leave here and then I'm gone. You will never see or hear from me again."

"I somehow doubt that Tell because I am not giving up on you. Ok, so let's get back to the murders. Did you kill Miss Petra Tancred?"

"No, I never killed Petra Tancred."

"Do you know who did kill her?"

"Yes, I know who killed her and I took his life when I found out."

"Who was that person Mr Tell, who killed Petra and why?"

"We should pass on that question for the moment Claire and move on; I may just come back to it."

"Did you kill Dolan and William Tell, your other half-brother?"

I did, I killed them both at the same time with a special bullet."

"And was that your intention? Two birds one stone!"

"It was. I wouldn't have got another chance and I worked it all out. It was a beautiful shot and I bet that it could never be repeated."

"But why kill your brother? I can understand Dolan and Hood but why your brother?"

"That's another question, unfortunately, that I will have to go back to."

"Ok, Hood? You made it look like a suicide because of what he had done to you. I can understand that. Well, I can't really because I would have to put my mind into a dark cesspit-like place, to understand why someone like you kills people. So, what about Starkey and Grafton? Why did you butcher them and kill them in such a horrific and evil way?"

"Those two men, although they only had records for petty crimes, were in fact enforcers for Gail. He had offered them money to find out where my father was and it didn't matter who got in the way. They got Lee-Winton and kicked the crap out of him but he didn't know anything. So, I paid them back."

"So, can we go back to when Miss Tancred first came on the scene and what happened after it was suggested that she be a surrogate mother?"

"I'm sure that you know all there is to know but ok. My father, as usual, lusted after Petra. It was apparently embarrassing to everyone. I wasn't there I never saw the goings-on, in spite of Gail telling Kearney the contrary.

My mother saw the danger that Petra could cause her. She could have, in fact, been the new queen. So, my mother decided that she should be tattooed, like her, in the hope that it would put people off of her beautiful body. But it had the reverse effect, so she came up with another idea; it was a humdinger of a brainwave.
She said to my father that as they now had no heir, maybe Miss Tancred would agree to be a surrogate mother. Thus, they could obtain an heir and prevent me from laying siege to their vast estate.
My father almost ejaculated in his pants at the suggestion and they both approached Petra with a deal that would guarantee her riches well into her old age. But my father's elation was soon brought down to earth with a mighty bang. Unbeknown to him, my Mother had drawn up the contract with Petra and they came to the agreement that you and the world already now knows about. My father never stopped lusting after Petra.

My mother died mysteriously but she somehow sensed that her end was nigh and put it in her will that the contract could not be broken by either party. But you know, a lot of people they would think that if my Father were as rich as they say, why didn't he just give Petra the money. Then he would be free to take her as and when he wanted to."

"Well don't stop there Mr Tell. Assume that I'm thick. Tell me why he didn't pay her?"

"Sixty-five million pounds for sex Claire? My Father wouldn't have paid sixty-five pence. He was so tight. He never paid for sex and if he were ever refused it shit would happen. He was not afraid to use physical violence or blackmail to get his leg over. But no way in the world would he spend a penny to buy her virginity."

"Ok, so what happened next in the great Tell dynasty? What am I missing? What is staring me straight in the face that I can't see? I… hang on… oh, shit, oh my God… I have only just realised. Oh, for fucks sake, they were committing incest. They were half-brothers and… Jesus Christ what the fuck?"

"Oh, my goodness Claire. You look so shocked and why exactly would that be? Why are you so shocked? Sex is just a means to an end. It happens, even in Royal families. The princes are shagging everyone and everything that has a hole; brothers, sisters, aunties, uncles, nieces, nephews, Mothers, Fathers. Corgi's, horses, sheep.
It is the way of the world; sex has been the driving force in many dynasties for time immemorial. We are all animals Claire and if I were able, I dare say that I would join you in that snug little bed of yours."

"You would be dead before you could get close enough. You fucking perverted piece of filth. You killed William, your own brother, because he was having an affair with your other brother."

"My God, Detective, your brain is still on the night shift. How easy was it for me to get into your bedroom? If sex were my intention towards you, it would have all been over by now and you would not have felt anything except for a little dampness," he laughed.

"Who my brothers chose to have sex with was their choice. Whatever floated their boat? It wasn't my problem.
Lee-Winton lived here on his own. I had business in our adopted country, so I was backwards and forwards but it wasn't easy keeping an eye on him. As smart as he was, it never fazed him that William was a Tell. One night, under the sheets, he told William about his father raping his mother and killing her afterwards; he would kill him too if they found him. That was the moment that ended their relationship and the shit hit the fan before we were ready for it.
William was in contact with Gail and told him what Lee-Winton had said. Gail arranged for Starkey and Grafton to hurt Lee-Winton, just enough to bring me out of the shadows and fall into their trap. Then they would try to torture the truth out of me. But it is my job Detective. I see the trap before these people even think about it."

"So, what is your job? What happened next in this perverted fairy tale of yours?"

"It doesn't matter what my job is, it is neither here nor there. If anyone else was telling you this story Detective, you would believe them. So, why do you find it so hard to believe me?"

"Because you are a murderer Mr Tell. An out and out barbaric and sadistic murderer. I would go so far as to add perverted to that ever-growing list of adjectives."

"I have killed people Detective but murder? Well, that is different. I have killed killers and punished those who needed it."

"Killing, murdering, it's all the same Tell. The taking of God's lives. It is a mortal sin. So, where did Marlow come into this and why did he warrant such ghastly treatment?"

"Marlow, hmm. He worked directly for Gail and kept him informed of everything that he was a party to. When this is over and you get the chance, look up all the op's that Marlow has been on and the disappearing evidence. He almost snatched evidence from under the nose of Kearney at Hood's home, ask her. He took all the evidence from William's flat and cross-shredded it. He knew that it could not be recovered but he showed willing and brought in the waste-basket full of the shredded evidence. That evidence was the proof that Gail was playing with William's mind and forced him to do what he did."

"What exactly was it that William did, Tell?"

"Miss Petra Tancred was a very good friend of mine and she had been for the last ten years. We became close after we found out that we were pawns in a bigger game. The sixty-five million pounds, that she would get in a few months' time was all earmarked for William, her son. She wanted nothing from it. She had her own money and I am totally self-sufficient. I am self-made. So, between the two of us we were set up.
Petra and I were going to my adopted country and we were going to be married, as soon as she reached her fiftieth birthday. The exact day actually. I had the tickets.

Everything was in order. There was nothing that could stop us, or so we thought.
Gail had kept pestering her for sex. If she gave in to him, he would make sure that when she was tested, it would come back as it always came back, that she was intact. But she kept refusing his perverted advances. Gail actually made her skin creep every time he came into the room. But she put up with it and there was no romance, as he would like you to believe. He is a very lonely man, as was his father.
He knew that something was different about Petra but he couldn't quite work it out. Marlow, unbeknown to me, spotted me at the house in Stundon and reported back to Gail. He was incensed and decided that she should die. The money would remain in the Tell estate. But Marlow didn't want anything to do with it. He was an arse licker, not a killer.
Gail chose another way that would cost him nothing. He would again be able to keep the Tell fortune intact. He told William everything there was to know about Petra. The contract of the sixty-five million pounds and the contract stating that she wanted nothing to do with William after he was born. He convinced William that Petra was just a gold digger and that money was the key to her life and her future. The brain-washing of William Tell junior was a complete success. Gail had lit the fuse, stood back and waited for the fireworks."

"Oh, shit, it was William. He killed his own mother. Is that what you are saying? No, that can't be right."

"William, my half-brother, turned up at her house and let himself in with the keys that were given to him by Gail.

She was in the bathroom, with the radio on. He climbed the stairs and reached the top, just as she left the bathroom. She ran to the bedroom and tried to lock it but he was too strong for her. He strangled her without even blinking and left her naked and spread-eagled against the wall; where she was when you found her. He carried on as if nothing had happened, left the house and drove home."

"How the hell could you possibly know that this happened in the way that you say Tell?"

"We had a CCTV in the bathroom. In fact, every room in the house so that we could see and talk to each other at any time. She was a tease, she always was. But she was mine. As was the last love of my life that was cruelly taken from me."

"So, where were you, when all this was going on? Couldn't you stop it or at least let him know that you could see him?"

"I was driving back from London. I saw him on the video that was installed in my car. I called out to him but he never heard me or he chose not to. I drove straight there and found her in the same place as you and Leanne did. I cried and then removed all the CCTV evidence. I wanted to deal with him before the police did."

"You are fucking kidding me? You loved this woman so much, yet you left her spread-eagled for the whole world to see. I really can't get my head around what a fucked-up family you come from. Your father raped your girlfriend, your brother was fucking his own brother, your brother strangles his mother and you then kill your brother. And your father, what about him?" Tell laughed at Claire so much that he had to sit down.

"You are so fucking gullible Claire," he laughed. "You keep missing the fucking obvious. I lied. Petra was dead, as was the sixty-five million quid that we were gonna share. Although, she knew nothing about that part. She was no good to me now. Certainly not worth wasting another tear over. I was angry but not through grief."

"Why did you take the two women to that house, what was the reason?"

"Oh yes, I almost forgot about that, Claire. It wasn't actually me who had dressed up as a judge. I forced Dolan to inject the women. I forced him to wait there and do nothing and I waited with him. But it was someone else, who was dressed as a judge. He had taken the two women to the house and that person couldn't resist showing them poor Petra; who by now was a little ripe, as you yourself had found out. Anyway, I had to make sure that Dolan had done exactly what I wanted him to do. I wanted him dead but in a spectacular fashion. He believed that all he had to do was stand there and pass a message on to William. But only when he was on his way back into the court. Everything was set up and it all went like clockwork Claire. Fucking clockwork and all because I let my temper got the better of me.
I just happened to have a sniper rifle to hand, a disposable one that is actually specially made for certain governments." He touched his nose and winked.

"Anyway, because of my temper, I almost killed off another fortune when I killed William junior and Dolan. But that, you have to admit, was a world-class shot. I doubt very much if anyone else could replicate it. But now I had to rely on plan "B." There is always a plan "B" Claire. Killing two birds with one stone next, will be a most profitable plan for me.
My father, is waiting with Gail. Ready for me to dispatch and send to the gates of hell but they must pay the ferryman first. That will really piss my dad off."

"My God, Tell, you almost won over my sympathy for you at one point but there is no doubt you are a psychopath, a fucking screwed up meatball. Who was this other man that took those two women Tell. It could only have been Nathaniel?"

"I tell you what Claire. You sit down there and I will clear the case up for you. I'll tell you everything you want to know. You clearly are so fucking slow and as thick as shit. You are supposed to be a detective but you can't see what is right in front of you. Go and detect Detective."

"I don't need a DNA test to see how you are all connected. A fucked-up, perverted family. I think you actually enjoyed your parent's jolly romps more than you have let on. Before you supposedly lost your … whatever it was that you supposedly lost? You couldn't make this shit up in. But if it's the last thing I do, I will find you and make you pay for all these deaths. I will get your perverted brother, whatever the fuck his real name is. He must have orgasmed when William got shot beside him… if your family history is anything to go by. How could he

look into his brother's face knowing that he was seconds from death. He conveniently held back and watched his brother die; as well as conveniently forcing himself to shit and spew to add reality to the murder. I just fucking hope and pray that there are no more of your inbred family out there. I have seen your face and I will find it. Whatever fucking country you are in. You are my bitch and you will always be looking over your shoulder Tell. Just you fucking remember that."
He gave her a drop of water and she spat it in his face. He smiled at her and blew her a kiss. He showed her his hands and pointed to the thin skin like rubber gloves that he wore.

"I have many pairs of these gloves Claire. They contain different superimposed finger-prints of many people. Not one of them will be mine. So, good hunting Miss Callison. It has been a pleasure. Thanks to me you will be a lot more determined, now that you know that I am getting away with murder… sorry killing. I fancy that you will find two more bodies soon and they will be ready packed for you. I try to keep the freshness in but it doesn't work. Do you know what the funniest part is Claire? You do not know who those two bodies will be. You just thought, as you listened to me rambling on, that it would be Gail and my father. Ha, they will indeed be going but I need more fun with you first. Let me see… oh yes, Leanne and Kearney. That should be fun. You may even get promoted when she been turned into soup."

Tell walked out of Claire's bedroom and down her stairs with an exaggerated swagger.

Detective Claire Callison struggled to move but she would have a while yet for the drug to wear off enough for her to call Leanne and Kearney. She wondered why he had let her live, when he could have easily killed her. There was a reason but she couldn't figure out what it was. Her determination would hopefully be enough for her to do whatever she could, to catch this narcissistic psychopath.

Two hours after Tell had left her house, Claire managed to pick up a phone and call Leanne. Leanne, in turn called Kearney. They both turned up with a police posse. Leanne let herself and Kearney in, lifted Claire up and put her into an armchair.
Claire told them both everything that Bernard Tell had told her. Neither of them, were very surprised. Things gradually started to make a little more sense.
"So, he is going to kill Gail and his old man but why hasn't he killed them both before now? There has got to be a logical reason Claire" said Kearney.

"Maybe, he is going to get the old man's will changed and Gail is the man to do it. If they are both together, it could only be for two reasons; the first is that they see each other die and the second… Tell is really a greedy bastard as well," Claire said.

"We haven't got any idea where he could have stashed old man Tell and Gail," Kearney said. "It would have to be somewhere where the old man would get proper medical attention, in case he pegged it before 'Plan B.' But saying that, whether he lived or died, the only person who has the power of attorney is Gail. With everyone dead all Tell has to do is produce a blood sample and get Gail to sign the papers. He isn't worried about his father. Gail would have all the necessary papers at his office and I'm assuming that the blood test has already been done. So, we must get to Gail's office. That's the only place to start."

"But that's in London, Frances. That's an hour away. It's too far."

"Not with flashing red and blue lights. Get dressed Claire and fast."

Claire and Leanne sat in the rear the squad car and were almost flying down the motorway. She looked at the speedo a couple of times and she noted speeds of between 120 and 130 mph. She kept checking her seat belt to make sure that it was tight enough, in case of an accident. The fastest that she had ever been before was 70 mph and that was her driving. It was fast enough for her.
She knew that the driver was very experienced at driving at these speeds but it was certainly nerve-wracking as a passenger with no control. It was a bit like being in a plane and she didn't like that either. There was another car behind her, carrying Kearney and Copperstone. She didn't want to look in case she distracted the driver but she knew they were very close behind her. As they reached the end of the motorway, they met up with two police cars from the Met'. They followed the front car and the other car went behind Kearney's car. The speed dropped slightly as they drove through Cricklewood and after that, it was a blur. She knew that they were headed for Cromwell Street in Knightsbridge. She looked at Leanne who had her eyes closed tight. She was not happy being a passenger, especially having no idea where she was. The seats were

small and cramped. Claire knew that Leanne was blanking off everything so that she would not think about where she was. Claire gave her a light punch on the arm, she smiled and said that she was good.

Finally, they arrived in Cromwell Street and everyone disembarked. The police, in the front car were already at the address and knocking at the door. There was no answer at first, then the door opened and someone started swearing in a foreign language… well Claire assumed that it was swearing.

The uniformed police rushed in and searched the office but there was no one in. Claire noticed that there were tourists with cameras taking pictures and as the coppers returned to the car, they started clapping probably thinking it was staged for them! Everyone jumped back into the cars and headed for the next destination; Cannon Street, Southwark. This was a repeat of the Cromwell Street address, no one in.

They were now on the way to Mayfair Towers, the London home of Miss Tancred.

Claire had no intention of getting out of the car but Leanne couldn't wait to get out. Claire joined her and comforted her.

"Fuck me Claire. I will never knock your driving again and if I do just hit me. I can't even feel my arse. I hope I haven't shit myself?"

They both laughed like a pair of school-girls but they soon stopped when they saw the coppers, leaving the apartments empty-handed. Kearney walked up to them with her arms spread wide and shaking her head.

"I think the bastard is watching us and laughing his arse off. That's me in the shit with the big boss. Maybe I should have asked first?" She laughed half-heartedly.

“C’mon ladies, we’ll get back to Duns Town and I’ll buy you lunch.”

“I’d rather go home and change my knickers first Guv,” Leanne said.
The journey back was the same as going. Leanne had her eyes welded shut, despite the car moving at very slow 70mph.

The car arrived at Claire’s home. Leanne, Kearney, and Copperstone jumped into their own cars and disappeared. They were going home for a shower and to get changed. They would all meet up at 3pm for a late lunch at their favourite restaurant.
Claire crept into her house and nervously looked around her. She searched every nook and cranny for wireless cameras. She couldn’t find any. She pushed her heavy sofa against the front door and moved the fridge in front of the back door; it was still plugged in.
She had a long shower and felt much cleaner but she knew that her once-perfect home had been tainted by that pervert Bernard Tell. A shiver ran down her back as she towelled herself dry. She would never feel safe until he was locked up and the key thrown away. On the way to the restaurant She called into the DIY shop and purchased a CCTV kit that would send a video to the phone if anyone breaks into your home. She bought one for Leanne. She arrived at the restaurant; Kearney and Copperstone were already there sitting at a table but Leanne hadn’t turned up yet, which was unusual because she was never late. Claire joined the others and took a seat then phoned Leanne, there was no answer. Five minutes later she tried again, still no answer. After another five

minutes Claire was up on her feet and almost running towards the door, shouting out
"That bastard has got her!" but then she stopped dead in her tracks as Leanne came through the door looking a bit worse for wear. Kearney and Copperstone were right behind Claire and she heard them breathe a sigh of relief when they saw her.

Claire took a hold of Leanne's arm and guided her towards the table. She was shaking nervously. Claire held her hand and waited patiently for her to speak. Copperstone went to say something but got a kick in the shin by Kearney for his trouble. Finally, Leanne spoke.
"I was just about to leave the house and opened the front door and saw it… it had my name…" she snivelled. "It had my name on it Claire… it had my fucking name on it, right outside my fucking door."

"Ok, Leanne, take a few deep breaths. Do as we have practised, deep breaths and think good thoughts. Breathe deep and think of everything that is beautiful in the world." Claire looked around and saw that other people were taking deep breaths, including Copperstone, who looked like a pregnant daughter's father… deep breaths in and out. Leanne opened her eyes and saw that everyone in the restaurant was looking at her. She looked at Claire and smiled.

"Thank you. There was a forty-five-gallon drum, identical to the one that Marlow was in and it had my name on it, Claire. It also said '*Welcome to your new home.*' Well it knocked the shit out of me. I don't know how the fuck I got here. My hungry belly must have driven the car. That bastard is after us both Claire and we have to get him."

"Should we take you home Leanne and cancel the lunch?" Kearney asked.

"No Guv, you said you were paying and you might forget about it. I'm here now. I apologise for my entrance. You understand that I have a little problem and the death-defying drive around London did little to help me? So, when I saw the drum it lit a fuse. Sorry!"

"Nonsense you have nothing to worry about my dear, I'll pay." Kearney laughed and so did Leanne but it was a forced and strained laugh.
"Maybe you should both stay at my house tonight?" Kearney said.

"I think he has your house marked too, Frances," Claire said. "He seemed to know an awful lot about us all. I bought a wireless CCTV set for myself and Leanne. It picks up on the phone, so you can see who is in your house. I don't know what the range..."

"Not much good if you are asl..." Copperstone was stopped short by another kick in the shins. "Would anyone like a drink?" he asked, keeping his shins out of Kearney's range.

"I have just had a thought, the cameras that were planted at the station. They must have had a short-range because the batteries were small. So, he must have been close to the station to pick them up. Maybe he isn't in London.

Maybe he is somewhere close to that station. Is that plausible?" She aimed the question at Copperstone but he was already on the phone asking the very same question. After a few minutes he put the phone away.

"Yes Claire, it is possible but only if he is receiving on the other side then he can be traced. My friend, who removed the cameras, is working out the possible distance that the cameras can send their signal. But he is not at work so I will get you that information as soon as I can. There will be an engineer fixing up your CCTVs Claire but with a few tweaks which I will tell you about in a minute. Now, who is for a bloody drink while I still have my shins in one piece?"
They sat eating lunch and then Leanne suddenly stared into space.

"What is it Leanne" asked Claire. "Are you ok?"

"Err, yes I'm sorry. I was just thinking about the drum. Where, the fuck, is he getting them from? They are all the same colour yellow and they are all new, so he must be buying them from somewhere local. Have forensics mentioned anything about them Frances?"

"I don't think that we have even got that far Leanne and I'm pissed off that we haven't chased it up. But you can guarantee one thing for sure, arses are getting kicked tomorrow."

Chapter Fifteen.

Sunday 10th July 15:00
Leanne Gavin's Apartment

Bernard Tell, left Detective Callison's house with a heavy heart. He had grown quite fond of her. She was tough, determined and, when it counted, she could be a very hard adversary. He had made up his mind to kill her and put her in a drum but she was too good for that. Her partner, Leanne, had her weaknesses but was, by no means, any less tough than her partner. He knew that they would never meet again. He had indeed been moulded by a fucked-up family. He knew that his father had killed his mother with a drug that was not picked up by the autopsy. Nathaniel Tell had taken his mother's maiden name of 'Mortimer' and was schooled in South Africa with the intention of one day taking what was his and his brother's inheritance. It all fell into place when they met the real Lee-Winton.

Duncan Lee-Winton was in South Africa to bury his parents. They had died in England. When he got there he found that his paternal grandfather had been made homeless because his house had been sold. He started legal proceedings to get it returned. Lee-Winton was regarded as a trouble maker. He befriended Bernard and asked if he could leave all his valuables and documents with him in case he got arrested. He told Bernard of his law certificates and everything related to them; even where the keys were hidden to his house in Duns Town. Duncan Lee-Winton had set himself up as an ideal candidate for identity theft. He also had no idea that

Bernard was working with the South African Secret Police.
Bernard and Nathaniel both liked the man. He had a great personality and he knew so much about the world. He always knew what was going on. Lee-Winton's ongoing war with the authorities was doing him no favours at all. Bernard knew this and told him that he was being watched. But once Lee-Winton had his mind set on something, he was like a dog with a bone. Every time Bernard looked out of the window there was always someone sitting in a car and watching. Always watching. Lee-Winton came to Bernard and asked him to post all of his possessions to England because he felt that he could be caught and thrown into prison, anytime soon. Bernard did as he was asked and only just in time as it happened. Lee-Winton was run over and killed outside the house. Bernard decided that now would be a good idea to follow the documents to England. He informed the secret police of his intentions and they assisted his immigration back to England. But they had insisted on knowing his every move, especially as far as William Tell and his finances were concerned.

Bernard set up Nathaniel as Duncan Lee-Winton until something else could be arranged. Bernard had planned for some time to return to England, to set up his plans for retribution against the family; that had disowned him and attempted to kill his brother. Bernard had left nothing in South Africa. He took whatever money he had with him, knowing that he had access to Lee-Winton's small fortune in England. It was imperative that he had the finances because palms needed to be greased to make his plans a success. People would die but not until everything was ready. He was surprised how easy it was to set his brother up as Lee-Winton with a university place assured. Through hard work, Nathanial would be guaranteed a place of work in the CPS. Again, palms were readily available to be greased, to enable his little brother to assist him in the grand plan of retribution.

Ten years later he had almost fulfilled his wildest ambitions. The people, that had hurt him, were now dead; well there was two to go. But, because shit happened, he would never get the sixty-five million from Petra Tancred. He was pissed off because he had bought and paid for the tickets to South Africa and he lost his temper and blew away his other means to a fortune. So, things were getting a little complicated. He knew that the secret police were after Tell's fortune, financial documents and the many properties that went with it. If they had the means to get it then Bernard would get nothing. He had never minded because he had banked on Petra's fortune. Now he would have to play a card that he never intended playing.

But first, he wanted to leave a little parting gift for Detective Sergeant Leanne Gavin; just to remind her that she was a human; albeit a weak human, when the right buttons were pressed. He had found out her weakness and he would enjoy watching her squirm like she did when she and Claire rescued Marlow. He wouldn't physically hurt her. He didn't have to. He wished that he could make a woman squirm but with love and not fear. He'd never had the wherewithal to do it with. Petra was meant to go with him and watch as they gave him back what he once had and then she would give him what many men coveted. But yesterday was filled with dead dreams. Soon he would have more money than he really wanted for himself and his brother. Buying a small country would certainly have its advantages. He would choose the best plastic surgeons in the world and find a woman that would give him the love that he had been twice denied. Tomorrow's dreams are still alive.

He looked at the video on his phone and saw Leanne in the shower. He took the lightweight, bright yellow drum out of his van and left it outside her flat. He wrote her name on it in red ink and underneath her name he wrote, '*Welcome to your new home.*' He started giggling like a schoolboy as he sat in his car and fidgeted excitedly waiting for the action to start. He could just see Leanne's front door from where he was parked but he also had a video camera positioned outside her front door, just below the gutter in the communal walkway of her block of flats. Leanne opened the door and backed out, with her hand in the letterbox. She pulled the door closed, turned around and walked straight into the bright yellow drum. She fell forwards onto the drum and then pushed herself back towards the door and held her arms up in the air as if they were on fire. Then she started hyperventilating. She tried her hardest to stay standing but her legs had turned to jelly. She could do nothing to remain standing up. Finally, her legs gave way and she sank down onto the floor, frozen to the spot.
Bernard was in hysterics and he was rolling around in the van, holding his stomach that was now causing him pain. Yet still, he laughed. Leanne couldn't open her eyes. Her body refused to let her take control of it. She soiled her pants, which gave Bernard an even bigger thrill as he watched it on the video.

She called out for Claire but knew that she was too far away. She thought that she heard the metallic clunk as the lid was removed from the drum. She was waiting to be lifted into it and could do nothing to prevent it happening. She felt someone touch her hand and she screamed out, loud enough to wake the dead. She managed to open one eye, saw her neighbour on her knees next to her and then heard her call her name. Another of her neighbours had physically taken the empty drum and threw it over the balcony; he assumed that's what it was that had upset her. The woman kneeling beside her, gave Leanne's keys to the man and asked him to open the door for her. She then helped Leanne into her flat and stayed with her until she was close to normal. Leanne was still in a panic but thanked the woman and told her that she would be alright. She asked her to request that the man to put the drum somewhere, so that the police could take any evidence from it.

Bernard was disgusted when he saw the neighbours rush to Leanne's aid and angry with the big bastard that threw the drum over the balcony and damaged it. "Do they have a fucking clue how much they cost?" he shouted and started banging the steering wheel. He watched Leanne clean herself up and still swearing to himself he drove away. He was ready now and in the right frame of mind to deal with his father and Gail.

Leanne changed and dressed. Although she was still very shaken, she tried the breathing exercises she had done with Claire, many times before. They seemed to be working, slowly. She stood behind the door and slowly opened it. She carefully looked out; there was no drum and nobody about. She breathed in and out deeply and slowly. Sweat poured down her face, yet she was shivering. Gingerly, she held on to the handrail as she went down the steps, still looking around her… looking… breathing… shaking… sweating… breathing… looking. There was a hundred yards between her and the car. She saw the drum, laying on its side, motionless. With every step, she expected someone to jump out and physically throw her into that drum. If that happened, she would not have the strength to prevent it. She couldn't get the picture of Marlow out of her mind; talking gibberish and shaking his hands around. She knew that she would instantly die if she found herself in the same position.

She pressed her remote key fob and heard the familiar *beep, beep*. Still looking around her, she opened the door and looked behind the driver's seat, in case someone was hiding but there was nobody there. She jumped into the car, started the engine and locked the doors.

The restaurant was only a short drive away but it seemed like a hundred miles. She was slowly returning to normal but even that seemed to be a millennium away. Leanne recognised Kearney's car and parked behind it blocking in other cars. Getting out of the car was a mission in itself. Her co-ordination seemed to have deserted her but her determination was growing. As she got to the door of the restaurant, she saw Claire running toward her.

Sunday 10th July 17:55.
Queen's Private Nursing Home, Duns Town

Bernard Tell, pressed the remote control in his hand. The rusty, old gates, in front of him, creaked and groaned into submission. They opened slowly. He drove his van

straight into the private car park of the nursing home. He pressed the remote once more and the gates groaned. Finally closing. There were two cars already parked in, the weed covered, parking bays. One belonged to Julie Mortimer and the other one belonged to Nathaniel. The care home belonged to William Tell and it was earmarked for demolition in the coming months. Bernard had obtained all the paperwork and cancelled the pending works. He was using the building to keep his father and Leonard Gail, imprisoned and sedated, while he decided how he wanted them to die. It had not been his intention that they still lived but now he was glad that he hadn't killed them. Now he needed them. He never thought that he would ever say that he needed his father. He and Gail were the only ones that could give him and his brother what was due to them.
He walked into the ward where his two prisoners were kept. Julie, checked their stat's, every couple of hours, just as she would if they were in a real hospital. She would much rather kill them both, slowly and painfully for what they had done to her sister. Everything comes to those who wait. Nathanial was surfing on the computer, looking at various islands for sale. There were plenty of them and he was spoilt for choice. He constantly argued with Bernard about which one would be the most suitable.
"Hello Julie. How are the patients? Are they on their way back to join us as I asked?"

"Yes, they should be fully awake within the next thirty minutes or so. Are we ready to kill them yet? My patience is wearing very thin after all these years. We have waited long enough Bernard, much too long."

Julie had devoted her life to looking after her sister's child and her boyfriend, nothing else mattered. She treated Nathanial as her son and Bernard as her brother. The thought of leaving either of them for a life of her own had never entered her mind. She knew of the damage that had been done to Bernard and how much he had loved Mary, her sister. Julie was there for them in Mary's memory. She had been the glue that kept them all together. There were many arguments, as was normal between brothers but she always prevented them turning physical. Nathanial was always the instigator. He had a very bad temper when he couldn't get his way. But Julie always had the last word and she would make sure that she was there when William Tell and Leonard Gail took their last painful breaths.

"Just a short while now Julie. As soon as they have signed the papers, they will be ready to dispatch. I have the two drums all ready as you can see. The countdown is very near my friend."

"We have time to eat Bernard. I have prepared your favourite meal; braised steak and onions with buttered mash, and spring greens. Jam roly-poly and custard for dessert. I can see Nathaniel's mouth is already watering bless him. Come on you two, let us dine in peace, these pigs are going nowhere."

William Tell opened his eyes, the bright lights were very painful. He blinked fast, to try and get used to the pain. He had been in a strange place and wasn't sure if it had been a dream, or a nightmare? He had tried to speak and attract attention in this dream but he was ignored. It was as if he was in a permanent mist or fog.

But now he was awake. He tried to move his hands but he didn't have the strength. There was also something, around his wrists, preventing him from moving. He tried moving his head but he felt an ache in his neck. He took a deep breath and cried out. His mouth and throat were dry. He forced himself to make his mouth water by imagining his favourite food and he managed to lubricate his mouth. "Hello, is there anyone there? Hello help me… hello."

"William is that you my friend? This is Leonard, are you alright?"

"Leonard, my dear friend what has happened to me have I been in an accident or suffered a stroke or something? Where are you, I need to see you."

"I'm right beside you William but we are both chained to our beds. Your son has kidnapped us and I fear for our lives."

"William wouldn't do that. He knows nothing about us, Leonard. We have always made sure that until his thirtieth birthday he would know nothing about me."

"Forgive me Sir. His birthday has been and gone, like him. They killed him on his thirtieth birthday and in the most horrific way."

"Who then, if it weren't my son William, who else could it be?"

"I'm afraid that your first-born, Bernard, has surfaced with another man who claims that he too is your son. The son of Mary Mortimer. You raped her and left her with a child. I also have to tell you that Petra has also been murdered by Bernard."

"Petra, no not my Petra but why? Why now has he come and taken away all that I love? Is it money? If he came to you looking for money why didn't you pay him or get someone to get rid of him before he took my family? How long have I been here Leonard? Wherever *here* is."

"You have been gone for three weeks. I paid men to search for you and the bastard but he is a killing machine. Everyone around him dies. I fear that we will have to negotiate our release and pay him what he asks for."

"It is too late if he has done what you say Leonard. I really don't give a toss what he wants. He is getting fuck all from me. He has taken everything from me. My life is now empty. I thought at first that I was in a dream. I could see things but I could not speak or move. It appears now that it has turned into a nightmare that will soon end for me, of that I am sure. Where is this bastard so that I can tell him to kiss my rich arse and the other bastard to do likewise? Do you hear Leonard? I order you to tell them on my behalf that they will get fuck all"

"The bastards are here Father dearest, along with Mary Mortimer's sister. We have great things planned for you but first I will ask Miss Julie Mortimer to sit you both up, so that you can see what two fine specimens of manhood you spawned," Bernard said.
Julie sat both men up and took the opportunity to punch and dig at them whilst she had the chance.

Both men groaned at the sudden pain they felt. They looked around them and then saw the two men that stood before them. William didn't recognise either of them but Gail did.
"Who are you men? I have no idea who you are or who you pretend to be."

"I am Bernard and this is my half-brother Nathanial. You raped his mother and Gail, killed her on your orders. The police put her down as a druggie who had overdosed. Isn't that right Gail?"

"I have no idea what you are talking about. There is no Bernard Tell. There is nothing to say that he ever existed and that man with you could be anyone's bastard."

"Oh Mr Gail. That was indeed the worst thing that you could have said in front of Julie, Nathaniel's Aunt.

"Let's cut the shit Bernard," said William. "Why have you got us here, what do you want from us, or should I say what do you think you are going to get?"

"We want what is ours; what we are both entitled to, our share of your fortune, which is our birth-right. Even though you choose to deny me as your son."

"Oh Bernard…Bernard," he laughed. "You left your mothers body with your screaming mouth begging for food and from a very early age, started calling me Dada. I never learnt the truth until shortly before you left. Bernard, there is no way that I am your father. My God you could be anyone's bastard and they are your mother's words, not mine. Irrespective of whose bastard you are, I will state categorically that I will die before I give you a single penny. It was your mother who had convinced me that you were not a legal heir to our kingdom and I have blood tests, in a secure location, that will prove that. If we had never protected ourselves in that way, fuck knows who would have ended up with what I have worked hard, my whole life to earn. You are not even close enough to be a pretender."

"You seem to have forgotten Father dear, that I am well versed in law, as is my half-brother. We have both obtained DNA proof that you are indeed our Father and we have prepared all the paperwork necessary, for you to leave us both every penny of your vast fortune and all your estates. To be perfectly honest Pops we really don't need you at all. All I need is Gail's signature on the paperwork that I have prepared. Incidentally, I never killed Petra. Gail brainwashed your test tube son, William junior to kill her. It was all down to him that she died. He, like you, wanted her so badly that he decided to prevent anyone else from claiming the prize that had tempted you all."

"That's a preposterous lie William. He killed them both along with Hood and Dolan and fuck knows who else in his crackpot scheme to get to your money," interjected Gail.

"They will not get a penny from me Gail. Let them kill me. I fear nothing. I know that I have not long left to live in this world. Give my estate to a dog's home or whatever animal sanctuary that you choose my friend, with my blessing." He laughed out loud.

"Is that your last word on the subject Father. No last words of remorse, no apologies for the lives of your sons that you have ruined?"

"Fuck you both and that bitch with you. Her sister was a lousy fuck anyway. A typical virgin. Pity you never got there first to try her out but as I understand all you can do these days is talk about it! Do whatever it is that you have to do and make it bloody quick. I believe the Devil is expecting me."

"You are still a very rich man. It is a pity that you can't take it with you but very soon your company, your banks and your holding companies will be as empty as your heart. Some of it will be in the banks of South Africa where you stole it from. Sleep well Father dear and give my regards to anyone that you should meet on your journey."

Bernard removed the lid from one of the bright, yellow, steel drums and nodded to Julie.
"Do whatever you wish Julie but whatever that is, do not kill him. I want him to suffer a long, slow, painful death. But first, I think that it is only fair that you check his vitals, so we know that he will suffer and not die before his time."
Julie carried out the necessary health tests and said that he was remarkably fit for his age. She took a few blood samples then she injected him with a few ccs of morphine.

Nathaniel held him up and made sure that he could easily see what she was going to do to him. She picked up a rusty old bread knife and waved it under William's nose. "This used to belong to my father. He wanted to be the one to do this to you but unfortunately, he died before he could use it on you. I hope that he is looking down at me as I stand in for him and give my sister, her long-awaited justice."

"Do it then bitch. Why do all you twisted murderers have to make a speech? Just fucking do it I don't care."

She, very slowly, sawed off his withered, old, tattooed manhood and then his scrotum. She knew that he felt the pain because he screamed very loudly for an old man. She used medical tape and surgical gauze to slow up the bleeding, and then checked his pulse. She nodded to Bernard. He removed the chains from his father then Nathaniel lifted him up and dumped him into the drum. Julie threw the severed, tattooed, flesh into his lap in the bin. Nathaniel placed the lid on the drum and secured it in place with the clasp. They left the filler cap open for the moment.

Gail was hyperventilating. His eyes were almost popping. He couldn't believe the brutality that he had just witnessed. He watched, helpless, as the two men and the woman walked silently out of the room and turned off the light. Gail could hear William's moans coming from the drum and he heard the drum rocking. He knew that William was trying to escape. He wanted to cover his ears but couldn't get his hands near enough. He suddenly started shaking and then screamed out for Bernard to let him go but there was no answer. The room turned cold, he started shivering and the moans from the drum grew louder. Gail could no longer control his bodily functions, at the thought of ending up in the same place as William. He wasn't a fan of small places but had done well to hide that fact; all his life he had tried to control his environment. The thought of what might be in store for him caused him to void his bowels. He screamed out loudly and then started sobbing like a child. He knew then, that he would give Bernard everything that he asked for.

Monday 11th July 08:00
Duns Town Police Station

Claire and Leanne arrived at the office, feeling totally refreshed. They'd stayed at a hotel overnight and had two police officers sitting outside their room all night. Kearney was at her desk and they noticed that police Sergeant Janine Pratt was, in plain clothes, and sitting at Marlow's desk with a young woman, going through Marlow's papers. Janine waved to them. They were going to speak to her but they heard Kearney knocking on her window and calling them in.
"Hiya Frances, any news about Marlow? I see they are going through his papers. How is he?"

"I'm sorry to tell you that Detective Chris Marlow has been sent to a psychiatric ward. He has not responded to treatment. They hope that he will get the proper care that he deserves. I went to see him last night and… well all I will say is that he was bad. They will keep me informed of any change. I'm sorry.

Police Sergeant Janine Pratt is now Detective Constable Pratt and the young lady with her is Detective Constable Roisin Neeson. She has been sent from the Met' to assist us and put some fresh eyes on the case.
In spite of what Tell told you, Marlow was on to something and they are following up on everything that he dug up, including his internet searches. That is all they will be concentrating on and if you have anything that may be helpful to them please feel free to do so." She was interrupted by a knock on the door. The three women looked up and saw a young, handsome man standing there with a clipboard. Kearney invited him in.

"Good morning Detectives, my name is Patrick Finnerty. I am a forensic engineer, or 'cyberman' as they call us and I am looking for Detectives Callison, and Gavin; with regards to CCTV installation at their private quarters. I need to speak to them if that is at all possible."

"Well Mr Finnerty, look no further. They are standing in front of you. I apologise for their drooling. What is it that you wish to know young man."

"I'm hardly young Miss but I need as much personal information as I am allowed to be able to set up the said CCTV."

"Well surprisingly enough they can actually speak for themselves but I suggest that you use this office. I have to speak to those detectives outside who are also drooling. I do believe that there is a law against that? But I could be wrong." She laughed out loud and closed the door behind her. Claire and Leanne were visibly blushing.

Janine and Roisin had been in since six am searching through Marlow's papers. They used the whiteboard that was behind them and made notes of dates, names, and places. Kearney asked how they were getting on.
"I believe that you were in contact with South Africa, regarding Duncan Lee Winton Ma'am. Could you tell me what the result of that enquiry was Ma'am?" Roisin asked.

"Well first of all ladies, you can call me Frances, unless there are any bigwigs about. So, it's first names, it makes life a little less daunting and congratulations Janine on becoming a detective. To be honest they were not all that helpful. We believed that Chris… Detective Marlow had been mistaken about the whole idea. Have you found anything that makes sense?"

"Well M… Frances," Roisin said. "There appears to be a lot of question marks about South Africa. Mr Lee-Winton started working at the CPS in 2007, just under ten years ago. I believe that this Bernard Tell mentioned certain dates to DI Callison and we haven't got that information to cross-reference."

"Ok, as soon as she has finished with that chappie in my office, I will get her to talk to you. She has to make out a report about it and I'm sure that it will still be fresh in her mind. I don't need to tell you how important this is. He is personally attacking our colleagues. I want his arse."

Patrick Finnerty had left Kearney's office and Claire and Leanne went straight to see Janine and Roisin to help them out. Claire gave them as much as she could remember from her experience with Bernard Tell. She wrote out her

report about the incident the same time as she told them. Leanne was helping out by jotting names down on the whiteboard behind her, every time a name or a date was mentioned. Roisin looked at the new information, and said to Claire,
"I think that he changed his name to Mortimer, which was Nathaniel Tell's mother's maiden name. That is a pure guess but it is an educated guess. If that is so then we can try and get South Africa to share that information with us. He wouldn't have used his own name, because Tell senior was looking for him. We can scratch Tell and Lee-Winton from the search. I'm betting that they both have passports in the name of Mortimer. What do you think Claire?"

"Well, you've only been here five minutes Roisin and you've pulled the rug from under us. Well done because that is more than we have." Kearney joined them when she heard them cheering and high-fiving.

"So, Claire, he said to you that Lee-Winton was over here on his own and that he made regular trips backwards and forwards to his adopted country, which we all now believe to be South Africa. As you said Roisin, if his name is Mortimer there should be a record of his flights in and out of Africa."

"Thinking back to what he said, Frances," Claire said. "He gave the impression that he was some sort of enforcer. The rifle that he used was disposable and the gloves that he used had prints superimposed on them. What does that tell you or am I seeing something that isn't there? He may have had different travel documents every time he flew.

As for facial recognition, we haven't got anything apart from a corrupt image."

"But didn't he say that his brother, whatever his name is now, was no longer around. He was safe. Did he mean that he had gone back to South Africa? If so, that would make it easier to check. We have a rough idea of how far back to look and we have a part of his face for recognition. Claire and Leanne have both met him," Roisin said, excitedly.

"That's brilliant thinking Roisin. Even though it means sitting for hours looking at videos of travellers, it just might work. But we have the daunting task of having to work with the South African authorities."

"I will get on to that right away," Kearney said, already on her way back to her office. Claire called South African Airways. She spoke to the security director and explained what her problem was. They said that they would organise it ASAP and would call her back.

"What if this bastard is some sort of James Bond, working for the South African Government or maybe he is a professional hit-man Claire" Leanne asked.

"Well if that is the case, I dare say that we will never get him. But he is money orientated. He wanted a share of the sixty-five million pounds that Petra was going to get. His brother fucked that plan up, so he shot him. Now he is going after the father's fortune and he has to be here to do that."

"Unless he has already done it and flown the coop?" Leanne replied.

Kearney rejoined them and was not looking very happy. "Because we are not the Met', they are being hesitant about telling us anything. I have had to go cap in hand and ask the big boss upstairs to try and get it rolling. I'm not very confident that they are gonna be helpful. So, one step forward two steps back."

"Err… There may be another way Frances," said Janine, who was looking furtively around to see who was listening. "My Brother, Danny… err… He works for somebody who may be able to get answers. I can't say who it is but if it's alright with you I can ask him if he can get what we need. He will do it a lot quicker than upstairs will, if you forgive me for saying Ma'am… Frances."

"It sounds good to me. I won't ask who he works for as long as its legal and I'm not going to hazard a guess. So, before you ask him anything, we need to make a list of exactly what we need to know. I'm hoping that this is not going to come back and haunt us Janine?"

"I will talk to him first, tell him what we have and let him examine it. He will make an educated decision, and tell me whether it is viable. I will also tell him that you are getting facial recognition sorted out and then he will get the ball rolling. He is in a high position so it should be reasonably quick. He will make sure that we have the correct paperwork to take it further. So, let's have a look at what we have"

Janine had arranged to meet her brother, and pass over all the necessary documents. There was no guarantee that they would get the results they wanted but they had nothing else to go on. Whilst they were waiting, Claire and, surprisingly, Leanne started searching for the suppliers of the drums. The one outside her building was still there. It was dented but brand new, just like the other drums. It was examined for fingerprints but nothing was found.
Forensics found a manufacturer's code and traced the drums to a consignment of fifteen. They had been imported from Poland to a factory in Duns Town, two years previously but the factory no longer existed. It had been demolished by a local company who claimed that there were no drums on the site when they demolished it. The police asked, around the local industrial area, for information but nobody had seen or heard anything Cherise Day called Leanne and asked if she and Claire, could call in and see her. She had located a video of the pick-up truck at a commercial lock-up site and it would interest them very much because she had managed to follow that truck. Leanne grabbed Claire and told her what Cherise had said to her. She didn't need telling twice. They dropped everything and headed to see Cherise.

Cherise smiled, as she let her cousin Leanne and her partner into the Duns Town, CCTV main office. She was excited and couldn't wait to show off the video that she and her team had made. She knew that it would cheer Leanne up. She guided them into a private room and sat them down.
"Ok, Leanne, Claire. When I heard about what that narcissistic bastard had done to you, I had a look at your

address, through the CCTV and I caught him dropping the drum off outside your flat. Then he went and sat in a white van, waiting for the show to start.
I'm afraid that we have you on video freaking out Leanne. I decided to leave it in there as evidence. I thought what a big man he was or at least he thought he was. So, the team and I backtracked the van all over Duns Town. I will play it and you can see for yourself what happens, it's mostly all in reverse."

Claire let Leanne operate the remote control, so that she could stop it whenever she wanted and was there to comfort her if she needed it. It started off normal forward speed.
She saw Bernard place the bright yellow steel drum outside her flat and then sneak off back to his van, where it was plain to see that he was waiting for the action to start. Leanne saw her own reaction on the video and started shaking, not through fear but through temper. She saw the neighbours assisting her, and one of them picked the steel drum up and threw it over the balcony outside her flat. Still shaking, Leanne replayed her reaction to the drum and then started laughing at herself. Claire and Cherise looked at her but said nothing. Then she stopped the video.
"I really cannot say why I reacted like that but I know one thing for sure, my temper has overtaken my fear of suffocation. Forgive me, ladies. Let's watch the movie."
Bernard's van was followed through the outskirts of Duns Town until he stopped at a commercial lock-up yard. They saw him load the drum out of a garage. They followed him, in reverse again, and then stopped at Claire's house. The video showed him entering through the front door,

using a key at 05:00 on Sunday the tenth July. The van, that he was driving, appeared from out of nowhere. They had no video of him prior to arriving at Claire's house. It was beyond their camera's range.
"So, is that it, Cherise? Is there anything else on there?" pleaded Leanne.

"Press 'source' and click on video number two when you see it."

She pressed video number two and the white van had left her flat. Bernard went back to the lock-up garage, loaded two more bright, yellow drums and then he drove off. The video kept changing as the white van entered and left different areas. They they saw him drive into an old building, surrounded by a fence and an electric gate.
"I have seen that somewhere but I can't place it." said Claire.

"That's the old Queen's private nursing home, Duns Town. It was up for demolition the last I heard of it," said Cherise. "It looks as if it is ready to collapse any minute."

Claire was on the phone to Kearney, asking for a search warrant. She was told it would be an hour before she could get one and not to move until she told them to.
"There is another video if you want to see it, ladies?" Cherise said. Leanne pressed the remote for the third video. It showed Bernard loading a parked truck at the same lock-up. He was using a small, hand-operated crane to load two bright, yellow drums onto it. They looked heavy, as far as they could tell. They knew that it was the truck that they had found parked up outside the garage,

with the bodies inside. Claire got back onto the phone, relayed the information to Kearney and told her exactly where the lock-up garages were. The video lost the truck as it disappeared out of range, the rest was history.
"What's at the care home now Cherise. Can you see, is he still there?" asked Claire.

"I can show you, the answer to that Claire." Cherise showed a snowy screen to Claire. "We have no vision at all, from anywhere near that area," Cherise said. "But we know that power has been disrupted by a small fire in the main cable box. We have sent engineers out to repair it but it will not be ready for at least a couple of days."

Monday 11th July 17:25

Kearney called up Claire and told her that she had the warrant for the care home and one for the Bernard's lock-up. The searches would be run concurrently. The other team were standing by to hit it at the same time as they took the care home.
Claire and Leanne followed the patrol car in front. They were soon joined by Kearney, who closed up behind them. In front were a further two patrol cars with armed police. There were no blues and twos used because they wanted to surprise Bernard.
The gate to the care home was locked with a heavy-duty chain and padlock, to the front of the gate, which was bad news to them. It indicated that the target had already left. The uniformed police used bolt cutters to cut the chain and then forcibly pushed the gate open with the reinforced nose of a patrol car. The four cars drove up to the main entrance of the care home and armed police surrounded

the building. One armed officer pushed open the front door and shouted out,
"Armed police, show yourselves!" He then repeated his call. No-one answered. He made his way inside, his torch showing the way. Leanne saw a row of switches and flicked them to the 'on' position, all the lights flickered and came on.
The armed copper came up to her and let her have both verbal barrels; telling her that it could have been booby trapped and she could have blown them all to pieces. She acknowledged her mistake and apologised to him, fluttering her eyelashes, and smiling. He told her and everyone else to stay exactly where they were and then he stormed off with his other colleagues and continued checking the other rooms. The armed officer returned to where the three detectives were patiently waiting and reported to them.
"Forgive me Ma'am. My name is sergeant Wilson. I apologise for snapping at you earlier. I have lost colleagues in similar circumstances and it is not a nice sight. It gets engraved in your brain. What we found in the dining room is not nice either. I have called it in and a medical supervisor is on the way, as are crime scene investigators Ma'am."

"Does it involve two yellow, steel, forty-five-gallon drums officer?" Kearney asked.

"There is only the one drum. I should warn you what to expect Ma'am."

"Thank you for your consideration officer but there is no need. We are fast becoming used to this evil bastard's leftovers."
They followed Sergeant Wilson into the dining room and saw two fingers sticking up through the filler cap hole. Kearney felt the ice-cold fingers for life and stepped back as they moved back inside the drum. She then heard a weak voice from within.

"He's still alive Sergeant, help me to get him out," Kearney shouted. But Claire and Leanne had already stepped into action. They removed the clasp and the lid but the smell caught them unawares. They turned their heads away and took a few deep breaths. They gently laid the drum down and tried to pull out the man who was inside. He was wedged, his joints had frozen with inactivity and loss of blood. Sergeant Wilson took control and started talking to the man.

"Hello Sir, my name is Dennis. I am a police officer and I am trying to rescue you. Could you please try and relax your body so that I can get you out of there."

It sounded as if the man was laughing at the Sergeant's words and cursing him. Two female paramedics turned up and took over. They coaxed him into relaxing and, with the help of Sergeant Wilson, they pulled him out. One of the paramedics gagged as she saw the man's injuries but her professionalism took over and she assisted her colleague in administering medication.
"This man is barely alive. He has lost too much blood. We are taking him straight into A&E. They covered his frail

body in blankets and wheeled him and the cut off part of his body away to the waiting ambulance.

"Would you agree Frances," said Claire, "that the man, who they have just taken away, was Mr William Tell and that his own son put him in that drum?"

"I can only guess the same as you Claire. It looks that way and the tattooed regions point in that direction. But the bastard could still be playing with us and sending us red herrings"

"I think that we will find that he is Mr William Tell senior, what is left of him. I am going by what Bernard told me. Maybe that is why he never killed me. He knew that I would find out for sure. I know damn well that he is still playing with us but we have to put it behind us and find Gail before he transfers the money over. There is nothing here for us, let SOCO search the place. We can go and look at the lock-up, if that is ok Frances?"
The three detectives joined their colleagues at Bernard's lock-up. There was nothing there to find except a pair of registration plates, the stink of death and five bright yellow, steel, forty-five-gallon drums. They heard that William Tell senior had died within minutes of reaching the hospital. Kearney called it a day and sent her two detectives, home.
Claire drove Leanne home and kept looking over at her, worried that she may crack up any second.
"Would you like me to stay with you tonight Leanne, I don't mind."

“No thank you Claire. Do you know what? I have no thoughts or worries about that drum or any drum. I think that watching myself and laughing at my reactions have done me nothing but good. You and the station have me on your cameras now, thanks to Patrick Finnerty. So, I’m good, thank you.”
Claire left her friend, but was still worried about her. Especially now they knew that Bernard Tell was still about. She made sure that her flat was protected by her colleagues before she left.

Chapter Sixteen.

Tuesday 12th July 09:00
Duns Town, Police Station

Claire and Leanne walked into the detective's area and instantly saw Kearney in her office, standing face to face with two men and poking them both in the chest.
Claire walked over so that Kearney could see her but she waved her away. The detectives looked at each other searchingly and then went and sat down at their desks; with one eye on Kearney and the other eye pretending to look at the paperwork in front of them. They could hear her raised voice. It wasn't very often that she would shout. Usually, her look alone was loud enough. They then saw Copperstone come in. He steamed towards Kearney's office, knocked on the door and went in. Copperstone listened to Kearney and then he continued where she'd left off. The two men left her office red-faced but with a determined look that meant business.
"I wonder where the other ones are Claire?" asked Leanne.

"I'm sorry Leanne, where the other what are?"

"There are five drums missing. There were fifteen at first, five have been used… well four and the dented one with my name on. There were five at the lock-up so that means that there are five missing somewhere, maybe loaded with victims or ready for potential victims?"

"There is so much more to all this Leanne. We don't even know the half of what is going on. I think that we are missing shit that's staring us in the face."

"I get that impression too Claire. I think that it's because we haven't sat down with a bottle of wine and a writing pad each like we used to do; questioning each other about the shit that has happened. We know that it works."

"You're bloody right Leanne. Let's make it tonight so that we can get some answers."
Claire looked over at Kearney and Copperstone. They were looking through papers and then both of them picked up their phones. They were giving out to whoever was on the other end. After a while everything calmed down and they signalled for Claire and Leanne to join them.

Copperstone stood up as the detectives walked in and asked them to sit down. He checked, out of habit, that he was out of reach of Kearney's shin kicking zone.
"Ok, ladies I won't beat about the bush. The two people, that you saw in Frances' office earlier, were from MI6. They told us to stay away from Bernard Tell, his brother and also the woman, Julie Mortimer,"

"Who is this Mortimer woman? Is she related to Mary Mortimer?" Leanne asked.

"Apparently she is her sister and Nathaniel's aunty," Copperstone added.

"So, what does that mean exactly? Cos I'm fucked if I'm gonna walk away from this Sir, excuse the French."

"We have very little option. They are on the MI6 radar and we are treading on their toes so to speak."

"Hang on a minute. They are treading on our toes. He has murdered seven people, including his brother and his father. No Sir, they are the bastards who are sticking their noses into our investigation. They can kiss my arse… Sir," Claire said and sat down with her arms folded. She squeezed her lips together tightly as only an irate woman can do.

"I'm sorry, Claire. I have had it directly from the Chief Constable and the Commissioner, not to get involved in this mess. They will collect all the information and evidence and take it away to their James Bond hideaway in London."

"Have they taken away the evidence already Sir because we have a shitload of answers missing and if so when did they start doing it?" Leanne said.

"Unfortunately, Leanne, these spooks can get in anywhere and take what they want."

"So, Bernard Barton Tell, is working for MI6 and presumably has a licence to kill anyone who gets in his way?"

"No Claire. He doesn't work for them, he is working for another country and taking care of political asylum seekers apparently. That is all I know."

“Is this because Janine Pratt’s brother, Danny, got involved Sir?”

“I don’t believe so Leanne. They saw us raiding the care home and the lock-up yesterday and put two and two together. Whatever that means?”

“They must be looking for someone else then Sir, if they are letting him get away with murder. Out of all the people that he has killed, I think that Petra Tancred was the only innocent one to die. He also said that he didn’t kill her. He is far from being innocent himself, whether the victims were good or bad and his own father? I can’t get my head around that shit Sir.”

“I understand your pain and confusion Claire but the bastards have got us by the short and curlies,” Copperstone said, shaking his head.

“There are five drums missing Sir,” said Leanne, “so where are those drums? Would they be in the back garden of number 34, Cutenhoe Gardens containing asylum seekers? How well was it searched? That surely has nothing to do with MI6 Sir?”

“I’m afraid that they have pre-empted you Leanne. They are at the premises with machinery, as we speak and our orders are to stay away from them.”

“Ok Sir. If it is ok, may Claire and I go and see Marlow to see how he is getting on? We need a bit of fresh air as well Sir.”
“That’s a good idea, Leanne. Give his family my regards.”

Claire said nothing until she was in the car. Leanne was driving.
"What the fuck is going on and why are we going to see Marlow?"

"We are not going to see Marlow. We are going to have a nice cup of tea and a chat with someone, to see how her garden grows… Guv."

The two detectives arrived at the home of Mrs Janet Higgins in a taxi and saw all the machinery and commotion going on outside number 34, Cutenhoe Gardens. They knocked on the door of Mrs Janet Higgins. She looked through the living room window, recognised them and let them in.

"Forgive me Mrs Higgins. We are working undercover and we wanted to see what was going on next door without raising any alarms; it being a different department to ours."

"I see, ok, follow me upstairs but please remove your shoes. I have a place that I'm sure you will be comfortable in."
They followed her upstairs into a back bedroom with a side window that faced the rear garden of number 34. There was a small table underneath the window and an empty tea cup sat there. She pulled up two more chairs.
"It's better than the telly officers. Would you like some tea? I was just going to make a fresh pot. We may as well be comfortable," she giggled.

The three women were silent as they watched the large machine that had demolished the garden shed to allow it to gain access to the rear garden. They didn't have to wait long until the first, muddy, not so bright yellow, drum was found. It was placed into a dumper truck, taken to the front of the house and lifted onto a flatbed lorry. A second drum soon accompanied the first, along with a wooden crate that remained closed. They were covered with a tarpaulin, secured and then disappeared. The machines were taken away and then a road sweeping machine appeared. It cleaned up the muddy mess in the road, whilst three men cleaned up and repaired the ruined pavement.

Mrs Higgins' face was full of tears as she saw the front garden that she, her husband and Mrs Lee-Winton had spent many hours of love and devotion turning into a place of beauty. Now it was just a mud-filled bog. Claire and Leanne tried to pacify her. They made her a drink, tidied up and were about to call a taxi when they saw a car pull up in front of next door. The two detectives rushed up stairs so that they could get a better look at who the driver was but they were shocked when they saw who it was; "Copperstone!" they both said together,

"What the fuck is he doing here Claire? Unless he is checking up on us, to make sure that we never turned up here?" Claire shrugged her shoulders as they both watched Copperstone walking up and down the mud-filled garden talking, angrily it seemed, at someone on the other end of his phone. He then left as quickly as he had arrived.

"Good job he didn't see us Leanne. He would go straight to Kearney and drop us in it. Strange though, what do you reckon?"

"What do I reckon? I reckon that there are three drums missing Claire. We can now account for twelve. We know that he had two drums when he went to the care home but there was only one body. So, we have to find him and the last three drums before he gets to use them. Let's get a taxi back to the station, in case they have anything good for us."

Tuesday 12th July 11:00
Duns Town Police Station.

Kearney was in her office tapping away on her computer. There was a knock on the door. She looked up and saw D.S. Janine Pratt with an armful of papers. She called her in.

"Yes, Janine. What can I do for you?"

"I need some important papers signed Ma'am. Overtime sheets and suchlike Ma'am," she said looking all around her. Kearney looked at her strangely.
"Ok, let's have a look and see what we have."

Janine laid the papers on the desk and stepped back. Kearney read the top page and looked up at Janine who nodded and said nothing. She looked through the rest of the paperwork, signed where she had to and returned the papers to Janine, who thanked her and left the office.

Kearney made a self-note on her phone and carried on tapping away at her computer for the next two hours. She looked at the clock. It was 13:00. She decided to go for lunch and to do a bit of shopping. She jumped into her car and headed towards the supermarket. She bought a few necessities and then sat in the supermarket restaurant and ordered a meal. She finished the meal and then ordered a coffee.

A young man asked if he could sit in the seat opposite her, at her table. She nodded. He opened up a paper and started to read it, then he spoke.
"Detective Kearney, my name is Danny Pratt, Janine's brother. I apologise for the cloak and dagger dramatics but you see, your station is still bugged as is your home and your detective's homes."
His meal arrived and he put down the newspaper and waited till they were alone again.
"I know that you have been kneecapped as it were by MI6 and you are no longer supposed to be involved in these murders. To be honest, there is no way around it but you have insufficient information about who it is you are actually after."

"You are going to give me that information, are you, Mr Pratt?"

"You will have to start reading the newspaper Frances but not while you are at work. You need a quiet place to relax and keep up with the latest gossip. I'm afraid that is all the help that I can give you but your quarry is soon to leave the country; a darn sight richer than when he first came back into it. Trust noone Frances, except the two

detectives who are on the case. They are nearer than they think but it hasn't sunk in yet."
The young man finished his meal, smiled at her, excused himself and disappeared amongst the shoppers. She picked up his discarded newspaper and then she too disappeared.

Kearney arrived back at the station and saw Copperstone sitting outside her office, talking on his phone. He smiled at her and then put away the phone.
"I hope that I haven't kept you waiting Denver, is it anything important?"

"Nothing, really Frances. I was just, hoping that we had made some headway in our investigations. I have had the Chief Constable on the phone. He is constantly breathing down my neck and reminding me that each case had a limited life and a certain amount of money allocated to it. Now the case has been stolen from us, he wants to know if we have passed everything over to the spooks. So, that's why I'm here basically. But there is something else that I would like to run by you."
She invited him into her office closed the door after him.

"Ok, Denver. What is it? I can tell by your face that all is not well"

"Not exactly the phrase I would use Frances but… I was worried about Claire and Leanne, all of a sudden wanting to see young Marlow. It just didn't sound right, the suddenness of it. So, after pondering about it I went to the psychiatric hospital and spoke to Mr & Mrs Marlow. I enquired after his condition, which I'm sorry to say, there has only been a change for the worse for the poor man. He has been heavily sedated to prevent self-injury. Apparently, the poor man woke up and was totally confused. He ended up on the roof, stark naked, a couple of times. He was found screaming and flapping his hands about, as if he were trying to fly. The doctor I spoke to holds out very little hope that he will ever recover. Callison and Gavin had not been at the hospital. So, I thought then that it was just a ruse, to get themselves into trouble. I went to 34, Cutenhoe Gardens, in case they had gone there. The place was covered in mud and there was evidence of heavy machinery on the premises. I started to worry about them. I called the operative, that was there, to ask if they had been in touch but they hadn't been seen. Apparently, they found evidence which they couldn't discuss with me. I know those two are up to something that will come back and kick our butts Frances."

"I can't understand why you would want to follow them Denver. If they get themselves into trouble, we would soon hear about it. So, my friend what is it that's really bugging you?"

"In a word Frances, 'promotion.' Promotion for me, you and our two detectives. I am looking to take it a bit easier and you will have more power. All we have to do is keep our noses clean and that means the whole unit Frances. I promised that I would keep it quiet, and say nothing but now you have it."

"So, you are saying that everyone will be doing a shoe shuffle, if we do exactly what Denver? I am quite happy in the shoes that I have," she laughed out loud.

“We need a quick transition; making sure that we pass everything as requested over to MI6. The Chief Constable believes that we are sitting on information that no longer belongs to us.”

“What sort of information is he talking about Denver? Everything we had, including coffee stains has been handed over. They can search the place if they want. I have nothing to hide Denver. Do you?”

“What! Of course not, we are a team and have shared all of our knowledge. All I had was the information that I have just told you about. There is nothing else Frances.”

“Well, Denver you can go and tell the Chief Constable the same thing. We have nothing else and we are hiding nothing from him or from you come to that. Now, if you would excuse me Sir, I have some urgent paperwork to evaluate.”

“I’m sorry Frances… I… I’m sorry. Forgive me, I believe you, it isn’t me that’s....”
He looked at the blank face that was staring back at him. He knew that he had overstepped the mark and if he stayed any longer sore shins would be the least of his troubles. He turned and let himself silently out of her office.
Kearney was just about to leave her office to get a coffee when she saw Claire and Leanne walk in and avert their gaze away from her.

“Callison and Gavin, my office now,” she roared.

The two detectives entered her office and she pointed to the two seats. They sat down and didn't interrupt her whilst she was writing something on a piece of paper. Finally, she looked up.
"Very well Callison, where have you both been? The truth would of course be expected and accepted from you."

"We didn't go to see Marlow, we went to Cutenhoe Gardens, Frances. We saw them take out two drums, and a wooden crate. They loaded them onto a truck, covered up the drums and crate and drove off. Then all the machinery was loaded up and the pavement was repaired. We couldn't leave until everyone had gone. We were about to order a taxi and then… you will never guess who erm… turned up?"

"Copperstone turned up, Claire. He knew that you didn't go to the hospital. What were you doing waiting for a taxi?"
Claire filled her in on what and why they were there and the need for a taxi. She asked what Copperstone doing there and why was he following them.

"Apparently you sounded too eager too fast. He is a copper, a good one come to that and you were told not to get involved. I'm afraid that you will hear from the Chief Constable about this. He is not amused. While you are here, I have a query about your overtime expenses. I wish you to clarify this for me Claire. Can you have a look and justify them for me?"
She passed the expenses sheet over to Claire, who stared at it and then nodded.

“That’s correct Frances. That was when we went looking for snouts. I had to drop Leanne home and it is all time spent at work Ma’am. I forgot to put it in the next working day. It should be similar to Leanne’s time sheet and expenses Ma’am.”

“Ok, thank you. I will convey that back to accounts. Now I need to know if everything has been passed over to MI6. I want to see the back of everything to do with these Tell people. It is someone else’s headache now.”

“They have, everything Frances and as usual we have nothing.”

“Right, get an early night. We can go back to being proper coppers tomorrow, if they let us. We have a backlog of important work that needs to be sorted. Now get your arses out of here. I want you back in the morning completely refreshed and eagerly ready for all the desk work that will face you. Now go!”

Chapter Seventeen.

Tuesday 12th July 21:00
The Rainbow Bar, Duns Town

Kearney walked into the lounge area of the pub, went straight up to the bar and ordered three drinks. Whilst she waited for her order, she looked around at the clientele and recognised a few people that she had met before. They nodded and smiled to each other in recognition. The bar was reasonably quiet. Tuesday, in any pub, was much the same; regulars were either still suffering from a weekend hangover or were just short of money. The cost of drinks had risen dramatically over the years. This was particularly noticeable to Kearney because she very seldom frequented bars.

However, sometimes, when she was wrestling with a problem over an investigation she would chuck on a coat and mix with other people, just for the hell of it. The next morning, nursing a hangover, she would be in a better frame of mind to come up with an answer to her problem. If not, she would just suffer in silence.

The barman smiled at her and put her drinks on a tray. His attempt at small talk was rudely interrupted by one of those aggravating people, who just banged their empty glass on the bar demanding instant attention. The barman rolled his eyes and excused himself. Then he walked slowly over to the woman, who was dressed like some sort of Hell's Angel, without a bike. She had all sorts of piercings hanging from her face. They were all linked together by a large chain from ear to ear. The woman stood there with her fists clenched, showing off more jewellery than it appeared she had fingers.

She smiled at Kearney and her teeth matched her other metallic adornments. Kearney smiled back and took her drinks over to a corner table, where she could see the front door and everyone who came through it.
The Hell's Angel decided that she wanted company and started to walk towards Kearney but changed her mind when she saw Claire and Leanne walk in. She backstepped towards the bar and tried very hard to look nonchalant. She finished her pint of Guinness in two or three gulps, slammed the empty glass down on the bar and stormed out of the pub.
"Do you come here often Frances?" asked Leanne. I never put you down as …"

"Gay." Frances finished her sentence for her and laughed. "I'm not gay. I just like coming here for the peace and quiet. I either talk to people or I just sit here contemplating my navel. You should try it Leanne."

"Oh, I do Frances, frequently. Some of my best friends and colleagues come here. So, why are we here, exactly? It's not someone's birthday is it or coming out party? Your friend, who just left, wasn't too happy about you having company"

"I just have this knack of attracting people Leanne. I asked that you meet me here because I have information that I need to share with you and this is, I hope, the only place that isn't bugged. Your homes are still bugged. As a matter of fact, that Patrick Finnerty is working for the government, MI6, to be exact. All that he has actually done was to upgrade the bugs that were already in situ and

replace the ones that had been removed. That is why I asked you to leave your phones at home."
She reached into a bag. pulled out two mobile phones and gave them to Claire and Leanne.

"Don't use these unless it's absolutely essential and certainly not in the station. Text if you have to."

"This sounds like some real heavy shit going down Frances," said Claire. "So, what the hell is it that's going on with this spy stuff exactly?"

"I have all the information about Bernard Tell and his gang; or should I say Bernard Mortimer, Nathaniel Mortimer and Julie Mortimer. I know where they lived in South Africa, who they worked for and their address in Duns Town. MI6 knows that he killed those people, because he works with them and so does Nathaniel. They both worked for the South African Secret Service, now the South African Intelligence Agency, similar to our MI6. They share information.
William Tell senior supported dissidents, who were living in this country and successfully importing diamonds and gold through various routes out of South Africa. They were investing huge sums of money into offshore holding companies set up by William Tell senior, Walter Gail, and George Ashridge. Bernard worked for the secret service, getting rid of political troublemakers between the two countries, since he moved to South Africa. He had a licence to kill. This country presented a problem in getting rid of evidence, as in dead bodies. He came up with the idea of the drums, which were actually paid for by the South African's and incidentally that was the second order

of drums that he had received. So, there are a few drums in this country that are… well… buried. But there was a price to pay for that licence to kill and it concerned William Tell and his organisation. He had to arrange the return to the South African Government, the fortune that had been smuggled out of the country. That meant the best part of the Tell fortune needed to go back to South Africa."

"So, all their legal training was to find a way to transfer the money and Bernard could kill two birds with one stone and get away with it," Claire said.

"It looks that way Claire, I'm afraid."

"Well as good as it sounds, it gets a little better. Once the Tell fortune had been transferred to the arranged account, wherever in the world that would be, the South African Government would take it all and dissolve the partnership. Bernard probably knew this and wasn't really worried, because of Miss Tancred's sixty-five million pounds and her own substantial fortune, that she had accrued over the years. That he would be sharing that fortune with her and leaving the William Tell organisation without a penny was his prime target in life. But, as we now know, the shit well and truly hit the fan, thanks to William Tell junior killing the money mule. No disrespect to Miss Petra.
Bernard will now have to try and syphon enough out of Tell's fortune to keep him and his brother in financial luxury and provide their new home. I have been informed that their intention is to purchase an island somewhere, far from any interference from the British and South African Government. But… The Secret Police actually guessed his

intentions when they heard that Miss Tancred had been murdered. They are now aware of Bernard kidnapping his father and Gail and are expecting the double-cross to take place sooner rather than later. But in order for anything to happen they need Gail. He is the only one who can make all the arrangements. So, I am thinking that Gail is still alive."

"Isn't Gail a baddy as well Frances? He supposedly killed Mary Mortimer" Claire asked

"I don't think so Claire. I think that Gail wanted to make sure that Tell's fortune stayed where it belonged. It was his job to protect it but he never expected family to kill family."

"A truly fucked up family! So, where did you get all this information from and how true is it? More to the point, what can we do to stop the fortune from being taken out of the country? Can we catch Bernard and his brother?"

"Well Claire, that is indeed a good question and I haven't got a scooby but what I do know is that there is someone else, another person, who is involved in this fiasco somewhere. It's someone who has been sitting quietly in the background. Either a South African plant, waiting for Bernard to make his move or he is guiding him. It could be someone from this country trying to protect the fortune? I haven't got the faintest idea who this person is and I have no idea how to find him or her? So, we could just sit here a while, put on our thinking caps and think of a way that we can arrest Bernard and his mob before he leaves the country. I have his address, sitting temptingly before me but I have no chance of getting a warrant. The person who gave me all this information is helpless and has to be careful not to tread on anyone's toes. It could all blow up into a political, national and probably international shitstorm. I really don't know what to do for the best ladies. So, we should just drink and think."

"No, Frances," Claire said angrily. "Let's not drink anymore but we can think. We can go through all the what ifs, the where's and whys. We should write down, on a piece of paper, what we would really like to do and why. Bernard told me that someone else had taken the two Dolan women to the house and if it wasn't Nathanial or Duncan, whatever his name is, then who? I have had enough of this and I really am not bothered about the political shitstorm, as long as we get the baddies. We are coppers, and we are supposed to catch the baddies, that's our job. We can go and spend our time sitting on our arses, doing paper pushing for the rest of our lives but I, for one, have done that and got the tee-shirt. So, three bits of paper, three votes, simple as that."
Claire went to the bar and returned with three bits of paper and pencils. She gave a piece to Kearney and Leanne. "Ok, ladies. On these bits of paper, write what you would like to do this minute, and why. When you have done that, screw up the piece of paper and place it in the middle of the table. When all three are ready we will close our eyes and pick out a piece of paper, then read out what's written on it. Then we follow the majority decision."
The three detectives wrote on the paper and hid it from view like three schoolchildren protecting their work from the cheats.

They had all finished writing at the same time and looked at the three crumpled pieces of paper silently, trying to recognise which one was theirs. Claire shuffled them up and asked Kearney and Leanne to close their eyes and take their pick. She picked up the last piece of paper, looked at it and smiled. It wasn't her handwriting but she recognised Kearney's precise and neat hand. She had more or less said the same thing. She read out from the piece of paper. "Go to the address and watch them. Then make an educated decision" She looked at Leanne and asked her to read out her piece of paper.

"Go to the address and nick the bad guys."
Kearney smiled as she read out hers.

"Go to address, watch them, nick them. They are the baddies, not us. Well ladies it appears that we have reached a sober democratic conclusion to our question. My car is outside. I was going to leave it there overnight but as I have been democratically denied alcohol, I will drive. We can discuss how we are going to push this through on the way."

The three detectives parked a little way down the road from Bernard's house but could still see it clearly. They saw that there were three cars and a van in the driveway. The lights were on inside the detached house.
"Let's just go and kick the door down Frances, let him know how it feels."

"I really wish I could Leanne but I like my job at the moment. As it is, we are saying goodbye to being promoted apparently."

"Promoted Frances?"

"Yes Leanne. Copperstone came and told me that if we kept quiet and kissed arse, we would all get promoted. He said it came from upstairs but I really can't see that happening. I think that Copperstone has been pussyfooting around with the boss."

"I have never thought about promotion." Leanne replied. "I am quite happy the way things are. We all get on well with each other and there are no starchy, bossy boots, constantly on our backs. We don't need telling what to do, we know what to do. Yeah Frances, I am happy as things are," she giggled.
Claire smiled and said nothing. She wanted to kick Bernard's arse and prevent him from becoming a super-rich runaway. A jail cell was the only thing that she wanted for him. He was lucky that capital punishment no longer existed but he had to be caught first.
They sat quietly in the car and watched the house, until the windows misted up for the fifth time obscuring their view. They climbed out of the car and leant against it twiddling their thumbs. The silence was deafening.
"Fuck the shit out of this for a game of soldiers, ladies," Kearney said. "Leanne call in anonymously saying that you have heard gunshots and screaming coming from that address. Then throw the Sim card away. As soon as you have done that, we will make our move."
Leanne did as she was asked. She bent the Sim card and threw it away.
"C'mon ladies, it's time that we kicked arse." Kearney said, while rolling her eyes and crossing her fingers.

The three women walked silently towards the house. They were shielded by overgrown trees on one side. Slowly and silently they got closer and then they heard the Sirens in the far distance. Claire and Leanne went to the back door. Kearney went to the front and tried the door. It was unlocked. She opened it quietly and went inside the house. Claire and Leanne looked at the rusted, dust covered, back door and knew that it hadn't been opened in years. It had been screwed shut, probably to keep out the squatters and burglars.

Suddenly, they froze as they heard a gunshot coming from inside the house. They heard another gunshot and Kearney scream out. That was all that it took to unfreeze them. They both, foolishly, ran into the house, without thinking about their own safety.

Claire heard scuffling and grunting coming from the front room of the house. She popped her head around the doorway, just as the police cars turned up at the front of the house. She heard armed police running towards the front door. She saw Kearney sitting on the floor in a pool of blood with DCS Denver Copperstone, firmly grasped in a headlock. His face was turning blue. There was a man sitting on the armchair. He was handcuffed, gagged and trying to talk. Claire struggled to release Copperstone from Kearney's powerful grip. When she eventually succeeded, she noticed a handgun on the floor near the armchair. An armed police officer burst into the room and told everyone to get down onto the floor.

"We are police officers," shouted Claire, "there is a gun on the floor and my colleague has been shot. I'm not letting go of this man until you move the gun and help me put cuffs on him. I'm not actually sure what has happened here but this man is the only person who could have shot

DCI Kearney. So, your help would be appreciated officer."

Leanne had taken off her jacket to stem the flow of blood, from the bullet wound in Frances's thigh. Kearney was staring daggers at Copperstone, which distracted her from the pain of her injury. She then noticed the three, bright yellow, forty-five-gallon, steel drums standing against the wall near the windows and the small runs of blood that tarnished the brightness.

She couldn't get near them because the room was slowly filling with police and paramedics. She shouted out that this was a crime scene that was being seriously compromised but it was too late.

Kearney was taken outside to the ambulance. Copperstone was sitting on another armchair firmly handcuffed. He was silent, except for his heavy breathing. Leanne tapped the top of the drums with one of her fists and it wasn't an empty sound that she heard. The uniformed, armed police helped her and Claire open the clasps on the drums. They removed the lids and one by one they revealed three dead bodies; one female and two males. All three had been shot in the forehead and their open eyes stared lifelessly upwards.

The three bodies were; Bernard Tell, the man they knew as Lee-Winton and a woman who was probably Julie Mortimer.

A senior detective, DCI Clarke (Nobby), arrived from Duns Town police station and took charge of the investigation. He worked alongside Claire and Leanne. He was an old friend of them both and like Kearney he was a pretty laid-back guy. Claire asked Kearney to tell her what happened. Kearney took a gasp of gas.

I went into the room and found Copperstone pointing the gun at Gail. I asked him what he was doing. He then pointed the gun at me and called me a nosy interfering cow. I could see Mr Gail sitting on the armchair. He was gagged; he was terrified and looked in a very bad way. I told Copperstone to put the gun away and talk to me. To explain what he was doing there. It never actually registered with me that he was involved in all of this, until he raised the gun and pointed it at me. I saw the look in his eyes and recognised the evil that stared back at me.
I kept asking him to put the gun down but he refused to do so, then once again I saw that look and knew what his intentions were.
I charged towards him, which surprised both of us and managed to knock his arm down. He pulled the trigger and the shot went through the floor. I struggled with him and the bastard shot me in the leg while smiling through his gritted teeth. I was lucky that I had his arm forced downwards. I remember screaming but it wasn't through pain, it was temper and that gave me the extra strength to turn the tables on him. I managed to get a slight punch into his throat and he dropped the gun on the floor and held his throat. He realised what he had done and made a move to retrieve the gun but I punched him in the gonzos and grabbed his neck. That was when you came in Claire. That bastard had us well and truly conned. I want to question him Claire, so keep him nice and comfortable until I get there. That is my statement and I will write it out as soon as I can. So, it appears that we were too late to save Mr Bernard Tell and his brother. He received some of his own medicine but he died a quick death, which was more than he deserved.

I wanted so much for you two to arrest him and watch him and his brother serve their time in a prison cell but what's done is done. We will see what Copperstone has to say about the whole thing and maybe he will answer all our questions. More importantly, you have to question Gail and make sure that he hasn't transferred the money to the South Africans. Our own HRMC will want to know about it and may even take over the financial side of the investigation.
We have Copperstone and that is all we have apart from a shitload of paperwork. Because of the situation, I believe that we can take back control of this case but it isn't my shout ladies. We have to go with the flow."

"I'm sorry that I have nothing for the Dolan Family but I will try and answer their questions as best I can. There are always innocents involved in this job Frances. We do our best to catch the criminals, fighting against the system that breeds them but we are fighting a losing battle Frances," Claire said sadly.

Kearney was taken off to the hospital. She had decided, at the last minute, that she should stay and head the investigation. But, she didn't realise the seriousness of her injury and admitted defeat for the first time in her life.
Claire and Leanne helped Nobby with the paperwork, which seemed to be never-ending.
SOCO took over the crime scene.
They took Copperstone and Gail into custody.
Copperstone said very little, even when he was charged with the murders of Bernard, Nathaniel, and Julie. This was enough to hold him in custody, whilst further charges were being discussed with the CPS.

Leonard Gail was released into protective custody at an unknown address. He worked closely with Forensic Accountants and the HMRC. South Africa never received a penny of the William Tell fortune. The crime of the murder of Mary Mortimer, that Gail supposedly committed, was thrown out due to insufficient evidence.

The agents from MI6, after a fierce legal battle, took Copperstone away. But Detective Inspector Claire Callison and Detective Sergeant Leanne Gavin wouldn't let them take Gail, their star witness. They hid him, until they had answers from the 'big bosses' upstairs.
MI5 made their presence known and appeared in the shape of a certain Danny Pratt, followed closely by Internal Affairs. It was a long investigation resulting from the original murder but it was a good investigation. Frances Kearney spent just a week in hospital and went straight back to work. She got stuck in where she had left off.

Detective Constable Chris Marlow opened his eyes. He could hardly move. He was restricted. He looked through the hole above him and could smell the air, the oxygen that he was so short of. He struggled to move his arm upwards inside the tight restrictive enclosure and managed to reach up to the hole. He managed to get three fingers out through the hole and started wiggling those fingers trying to attract someone's attention but only the birds came. They started pecking at his fingers. He pulled them back in and screamed out but to no avail. There was no one but the birds. They came nearer and peaked inside the hole. They could smell something but they weren't sure

what it was. They flew away as soon as whatever was inside screamed out painfully loud.
Marlow cried himself to sleep. He dreamt of Copperstone and Bernard Tell who had both beaten him with a gun and forced him inside this prison of which there was no escape. He opened his eyes and tried to dig his way through the metal roof of his prison until the pain stopped him. He pushed the painful fingers through the hole and kept forgetting that the birds would peck at him stealing bits of his flesh from his bloody fingers but he no longer felt the pain. He opened his eyes again and saw the birds flying above free and unhindered, soaring high and low. He tried to move both of his hands, flapping them in their tight restriction and squawking for the birds to keep him company, to talk to him, to bring him water, to bring him help. But there was no help. There were only the birds looking for more of his disappearing flesh. He heard his bones screeching like chalk on a blackboard as he scratched at the steel and kept trying to dig through. He cried, he slept, he called to the birds but they would only come when he put his fingers through the hole. He slept. He opened his eyes and wished that he could fly out through the hole to join the birds, who were flying freely high above him he called out to them, but they never heard him. He knew that he must fly up and join them but his wings were not working. He tried harder but they would not work. He slept. Marlow opened his eyes and flapped his wings. Yes, they worked. He soared through the hole, that had kept him away from his friends. He soared high and low, this way and that, he was happy, he was free. But he kept sleeping, he didn't want to sleep he wanted freedom.

He opened his eyes and flew through the hole playing tag with all the other birds, it was hard work. He stopped and landed on a flat surface to get his breath back. He saw his friends waving and calling to him.
He started running, faster and faster urging his wings to give him the lift that would help him to join his friends and then he would be free forever. Finally, he managed to take off and felt the cool air blowing in his face and over his body. He smiled and squawked but then his closed eyes one last time.

After the DNA testing of William Tell senior, Bernard Tell and Nathaniel Tell; it was proved that the two sons were not related to Tell Senior and that Bernard was the father of Nathaniel. Bernard Tell had tattoos of underwear on his lower body as did Nathanial.
Inside Copperstone's car, forensics found a wig and gown with Cara and Maria Dolan's DNA on it. Copperstone's whereabouts has not been disclosed. Rumours circulated that he was a Governor in a prison in Pretoria, South Africa.

Detectives Kearney, Callison, and Gavin, remained together with their colleagues as a strong team with a very high detection rate.
There was another rumour circulating that they had all turned down promotion. But one rumour, that they never denied, was that they constantly searched their homes looking for spy cameras.

The End

Acknowledgements

The publishers and authors would like to thank Russell Spencer, Matt Vidler, Susan Woodard, Janelle Hope Leonard West, Lianne Bailey-Woodward, Laura Jayne Humphrey and Heidi Hollowbread for their work, without which this book would not have been possible.

About the Publisher

L.R. Price Publications is dedicated to publishing books by undiscovered, talented authors.

We use a mixture of traditional and modern publishing methods to bring our authors' words to the wider world.

We print, publish, distribute and market books in a variety of formats including paper and hard back, electronic books e- books, digital audio books and online.

If you are an author interested in getting your book published; or a book retailer interested in selling our books, please contact us.

www.lrpricepublications.com

L.R. Price Publications Ltd, 27 Old Gloucester Street, London, WC1N 3AX. (0203) 051 9572 publishing@lrprice.com

Lightning Source UK Ltd.
Milton Keynes UK
UKHW022018090822
407073UK00010B/2517

9 781915 330161